D0680760

SAVAGE SIEGE!

Scott, firing from behind a boulder at hostiles on the other side of the gap, saw the whole ridgetop lighting up with gun flashes through the blooming powder smoke, the din continuous. As if on signal, it suddenly broke off to sporadic shots. Upon that, Scott could hear a rumbling and crashing and bounding. The Apaches were pushing boulders down the steep slopes of the gap. Troopers yelled and ran dodging. The firing from above commenced again, as heavy as before. . . .

A FAR TRUMPET

Fred Grove

BALLANTINE BOOKS • NEW YORK

Copyright © 1985 by Fred Grove

All rights reserved under International and Pan-American Copyright Con-
ventions. Published in the United States by Ballantine Books, a division
of Random House, Inc., New York, and simultaneously in Canada by
Random House of Canada Limited, Toronto.

Library of Congress Catalog Card Number: 83-40131

ISBN 0-345-33281-4

This edition published by arrangement with Doubleday & Company, Inc.

Manufactured in the United States of America

First Ballantine Books Edition: June 1986

For Mary Bowlin, whose bookstore in Mesilla, New Mexico, not far from the old Butterfield stage station, is always a welcome stop for Western writers needing a particular research book—and finding it there.

CHAPTER 1

IT was over. Finally, it was over, on this day, March 17, 1886. After twelve years of service, First Lieutenant Scott William Dunham, 6th Cavalry, was now dishonorably dismissed from the United States Army.

He entered his quarters, softly closed the door, and became still, staring at the floor, feeling the old, helpless anger, and yet a kind of relief at the final decision, even adverse, transmitted minutes ago by telegraph to post headquarters. The realization drummed through his mind again: It was over, after weeks of waiting, himself virtually in limbo, restricted to the post.

All along the line of review, from the commanding officer of the Department of the Missouri to the Commanding General of the Army and the Secretary of War, the recommendations had been the same: guilty. Now, President Cleveland, as a formality, Scott supposed, had merely approved the recommendations of his generals and the secretary as to the fate of an obscure first lieutenant at Fort Sill, Indian Territory, who had come up through the ranks as an enlisted man and had no political influence.

He changed to civilian clothes and resumed packing, begun some days ago when the Army grapevine had leaked what was coming down. A surge of impatience struck across his bitterness. There was still time, if he hurried, to catch the stage to Sherman, Texas. Presently, he was finished, and the wry observation came to him as he looked about of how little there was to gather up after all these years, the past two as a bachelor officer.

Hearing a rap-rap on the door, he opened it and was not surprised to find Major George Martin and his wife, Genevieve, her dark eyes distressed in a face whose freshness always reminded Scott of a schoolgirl's.

Martin held out his hand, all the while shaking his head, overcome with indignation. When he stood back, his wife impulsively gave Scott a loyal kiss on his bearded cheek and embraced him.

"The court-martial was a farce from the beginning," the major exploded, his ruddy face flaming. "Nothing but vicious Army politics from this post to the top. All they wanted was a scapegoat."

"They had to blame some officer for the only son of a politically powerful U.S. senator being killed by a war party of bronco Comanches," Scott said.

"There's always the chance for reinstatement."

"I wish I could agree with you, sir. It would help if I had connections back East, but I know no one of higher status than a few Indiana farmers," Scott said dryly.

The Martins fell awkwardly silent. *It's like a funeral,* Scott thought, embarrassed for these good friends of years, *with none of us knowing quite what to say.*

Genevieve Martin's unhappy eyes, close to tears, took in the packed bags. "May I ask where you will go, Scott? And when?"

"For New Mexico on the afternoon stage. Maybe Arizona later." He had decided where long ago, if he lost. "I rather liked duty out there, harsh as the campaigning was. Emeline and I preferred Fort Bayard to Bowie."

"Didn't we all," she agreed, forcing a smile.

"It's in the wind that we may be posted out that way again before long," her husband said. "General Miles is expected to replace General Crook in the Department of Arizona, and will have no more success, if not less, in my opinion, than Nantan Lupan at running down Apaches on both sides of the border. I should not be surprised to see one fourth of the Regular Army out there by summer, chasing fewer than fifty Chiricahua Apaches led by Geronimo.'' Martin broke off, as if ill at ease to be discussing military matters that no longer concerned Scott. ''What do you think you might do out there, Scott?''

Scott managed a faint smile. ''Maybe some prospecting. Some hunting, of course. I'd like to live in the mountains for a while.''

''Just where?''

''Oh, east of the Mimbres Valley, up in the Black Range.''

''You're talking about extremely dangerous country for a white man. A lone white man. Keep that in mind.''

''I remember. It's also the most rugged and beautiful country I've ever seen.''

''And hell on horses and troopers.''

''I notice you put horses first.''

They both laughed. The small talk ran out, and another painful pause followed, until the major said, ''Let us know where you are, Scott. I mean that. We want to keep in touch.''

''Yes,'' his wife said, and held out her hand to Scott, who raised it to his lips and then said to Martin, ''Sir, if there were more women like your Genevieve, there'd be better men.''

''You must write us,'' she said, wearing a tight, bright smile that said all would go well for him. ''We love you and believe in you.''

For the first time he was close to losing his poise, aware of a tide of memories. Forcing calm into his tone, he said, ''I'll write, and I won't indulge in self-pity, I assure you. . . . I thank you both with all my heart.''

She smiled up at him in that appealing way she had, brushing at her eyes, yet maintaining her own careful composure. The men shook hands, and after another pause the Martins were gone. On the way to their quarters, she said sadly, "I only wish that Emeline were alive. Still, I'm thankful she doesn't have to go through this and bear the cut of the wives' malicious tongues. She would be destroyed. She was so frail." Her voice broke. "It's so unfair, Martin. Can't something be done?"

"Not now. But I'm not giving up on reinstatement down the line, pending a review, when the smoke has cleared."

Scott went over his quarters once more, looking for anything forgotten. There was nothing. The place was bare except for memories. In the distance, he caught the oncoming racket of the southbound stage slamming up the hill past the chapel.

On that reminder he picked up the bags and moved outside to the porch, estimating he had some twenty minutes to catch the stage. He glanced about. Captain T. E. Harrigan, who had served on the general court-martial, and Second Lieutenant Thomas Slocum stood chatting in front of headquarters. Scott seethed. *Harrigan—that pompous ass, who carefully shielded his career from any connection with failure or association with any officer who had fallen into disfavor. Slocum—that fawning sycophant, who followed in the captain's politic wake like the tail of a kite.*

Seeing Scott, they turned their backs on him and stepped briskly inside.

Scott stiffened, his blood pounding. He had the sudden impulse to shout at them, but he willed himself to let it pass. Instead, then, he set his jaw, fighting his anger, and said nothing. Why give them the satisfaction of seeing him lose his control? But goddamn their self-seeking!

He started across the parade ground, erect, looking straight before him, heading for the Fort Sill Hotel beyond, where the stage would stop this late Sunday afternoon.

A trooper hurried toward him from the barracks. "Lieutenant, sir," the man called.

Scott turned. It was First Sergeant Hugh Ryan of C Troop, a stocky man with a thick brush of a mustache.

"Yes, Sergeant."

"We just heard, sir. I want to say how damned mad the men are." His brogue grew stronger as he talked. "We aim to get up another petition."

"Thank you, Sergeant. But it would be ignored same as the first one. Thank everyone for me." Scott put out his hand and Ryan shook it vigorously.

"I will, sir. I hope your luck changes."

"Good luck to you, Ryan. And take care of yourself."

At the hotel he purchased a ticket for Sherman, and while his baggage was being loaded and the teams changed, he found himself gazing back at the post with mixed feelings: the stone buildings arranged around a common square, whitewashed fences enclosing each set of officers' quarters, in the blue distance the low summits of the Wichita Mountains rising humplike above the undulating sea of prairie. Associations surged: Emeline, his Emeline. Despite a delicate constitution, she had maintained her sweet disposition and endured the rigors of Army life with a minimum of complaint and tears. . . . Officers and troopers. . . . Noncoms like Sergeant Ryan, the backbone of the Army. . . . Bright times and dark times. . . . Vexations over the slowness of promotions. Some officers playing politics. . . . Yet not a bad life. He had come off an Indiana farm to this without regret.

His anger had subsided somewhat, leaving an aftermath of bitterness and stunned unreality. Accustomed for years to routine and regulations, he was now completely orderless. Although he had thought himself prepared for today's disaster, he discovered that he was not. He was shaken and adrift, his only anchor the sense out of the past that was drawing him away from the scene of his disgrace, deeper into the Southwest, into Apache country, toward a possible catharsis and a second beginning, where once life, though harsh, also had been good.

There were two other passengers, a wide-hatted cattleman and a paunchy, salesman-looking individual wearing a derby. Scott took a seat by a window. As the stage rolled out, he heard a bugle at the fort sounding Stables, which told him it was four o'clock. For a stabbing moment he had the reminder that he belonged back there, and then he cleared his mind to regard his fellow travelers. The cattleman struck Scott as a taciturn sort, further indicated when he merely grunted an answer to the drummer's question about talk in the states of opening the Comanche-Kiowa reservation to settlement.

"Interesting country," the drummer persisted. "Very interesting. Good prospects for farming."

"That's where you're wrong, mister," the cattleman bristled. "This is grass country—cow country. Wasn't meant for anything else. But the guv'mint'll ruin it, open it to sodbusters from here to Red River. Just give 'em time." He folded his arms and stared out the window, ending the conversation.

Rebuffed, the drummer turned to Scott. "Sir, could you possibly be associated with the post sutler?"

When Scott shook his head in negation and added no more, the man shrugged and was silent. Before long, however, he took a flask from an inner pocket of his coat and said, "Would you gentlemen care to join me in a drink of aged Kentucky bourbon?"

The cattleman continued to stare out the window as if he hadn't heard, and Scott declined with a shake of his head. Shrugging again, the would-be host had his solitary nip, returned the flask to his pocket, and the three passengers settled down for the boredom of a long and dusty ride.

Over and over, Scott played out the tableau of the general court-martial, seeing again the set faces of the nine-member board, no member of lower rank than himself, each officer sitting at the table in the order of his rank, each in full dress from spurs to silk sashes, Scott hearing again the judge advocate reading the charges and specifications:

"Charge first. Failure to provide adequate escort for

three guests of the United States Army hunting in hostile Indian country.

"Specification first. In this, that he, First Lieutenant Scott W. Dunham, 6th Cavalry, on or about the twenty-fifth of November, 1885, while in command of C Troop, approximately forty miles west of Fort Sill, Indian Territory, failed to warn said guests, to wit: Sylvester C. Hastings, Jr., son of U.S. Senator Sylvester Hastings, and two companions, Chester Billings and Darwin Reed, of the presence of nearby hostile Comanches and did fail to take proper measures for the repulse of said hostile Comanches. Result, to wit: Sylvester C. Hastings, Jr., was killed by said hostile Comanches and his two companions wounded, one seriously.

"Charge second. Disobedience of orders.

"Specification first. In this, that he, First Lieutenant Scott W. Dunham, 6th Cavalry, did proceed a considerable distance beyond the restricted limits as set by the commanding officer of Fort Sill for the said hunting party, thereby exposing the three guests of the United States Army to unwarranted danger, in addition to endangering the safety of C Troop; that, further, First Lieutenant Dunham violated his orders by making camp the first night out instead of returning to Fort Sill, thereby causing the hunting party to stay out the second and fatal day of the attack; that, further, First Lieutenant Dunham did neglect to take proper measures to pursue and attack said hostile Comanches."

Scott had pleaded not guilty to all charges and specifications, seeing as he did that he was up against an unfriendly court. Bits of his testimony and the questioning tolled through his mind again: "Now, Mr. Dunham, Second Lieutenant Slocum has testified that you did not warn young Hastings and his friends that hostile Comanches were in the vicinity. Did you or did you not?"

"I did not."

"State why you did not warn them."

"Because, to my knowledge, there were no hostiles out there."

"Prior to the hunt, hadn't hostiles been reported west of Fort Sill?"

"There were reports that bronco Comanches were raiding ranches across Red River in Texas, but not Indian Territory west of the post. The main Comanches and Kiowas have been peaceful since the late 1870s."

"Yet, hostile bands, or broncos as you refer to them, generally return to their reservations, do they not?"

"I should think so, in time, but I had no knowledge that any had. Nor had any other officers to my knowledge."

There was a short delay, and then the judge advocate said, "The court must ask you to confine your replies to the question asked, without your expanding on said question. Do you understand, Mr. Dunham?"

"I do, sir. I was only trying to clarify."

"I must warn you again, Mr. Dunham. You are still expanding the question. Now, Lieutenant Slocum has also testified that you carelessly allowed young Hastings and his friends to ride off without an escort. What is your reply to that?"

"That is incorrect, sir. They cut loose on their own. Said the troop was spooking the game. They were after antelope."

"Yet, you allowed them to go on their own?"

"I did not forcibly detain them."

"Yet, you did not ride after them either?"

"Not then. There was no sign of trouble. I wasn't going to nursemaid them."

"Yet, it was your duty to provide close escort for the young men as guests of the United States Army?"

"It was, and we were always within sight of them. I reasoned that was close enough on a hunt in peaceful country."

"When did you go to their rescue, so to speak?"

"When we saw horsemen suddenly come over a brushy ridge and charge them and heard heavy gunfire."

"State what you found at the site of the hostiles' attack."

"Young Hastings was dead—scalped. The other two young men were on the ground, wounded. The hostiles fled at our approach."

"How many hostiles did you estimate were in the war party?"

"Ten or more."

"Which a troop of cavalry should have handled—if you had escorted the hunters when, as you say, they cut loose?"

Scott hesitated. He was boxed in and knew it.

"Answer the question, Mr. Dunham, which I shall be glad to repeat for your convenience."

"Isn't necessary, sir. A troop of cavalry should have handled that number of hostiles."

"Very well. State how far you pursued the hostiles."

"Approximately a mile."

"Why no farther?"

"The hostiles were outdistancing us on their ponies, and I was concerned for the wounded."

"State to the court what you then did."

"We gave the wounded what aid we could, then constructed horse litters and transported them back to the post."

"Did one of the wounded youths curse you and the troop?"

"Yes, sir. It was young Billings."

"State what he said."

"He was in great pain and he accused us of not protecting him and his companions."

"What was your reply?"

"I reminded him that they had cut loose from the escort without permission."

"Was that all you said to him?"

Again, Scott held back. He had told the truth and the truth was devastating to his case.

"Did you curse him, Mr. Dunham?"

"Yes, sir, I did for running off."

"What did you call him?"

"I called him a spoiled rich man's son."

"Didn't you call him something else?"

"I did. I called him a damned fool."

"Now, Mr. Dunham, examine this paper which I hand to you and state if you recognize its contents."

"Yes, sir. It's a true copy of the written orders given me before escorting the hunters from the post."

"Read its contents to the court."

Scott read, "First Lieutenant Scott W. Dunham, 6th Cavalry, will march on the twenty-fifth instant with C Troop as escort to Mr. Sylvester C. Hastings, Jr., and his two companions, with one day's rations, for the purpose of hunting. Lieutenant Dunham will proceed no farther west than Wagon Spring. He is further directed to provide extreme protection for these guests of the Army. By command of Brevet Brigadier General Grayson."

The judge advocate turned to the court and said, "I now offer this order in evidence," and, facing Scott, said, "Did you exceed the limitations of the order, Mr. Dunham?"

"There are always imponderables in the field, sir, which prevent following orders to the letter."

"You are flanking the question, Mr. Dunham. I direct you to answer it. Did you exceed the limitations of General Grayson's order or not?"

"Well, sir, we'd seen no antelope—all the buffalo are gone—and I wanted to please the young men."

The judge advocate glared. His voice tore at Scott. "You persist in flanking the question, Mr. Dunham. But for your benefit I shall rephrase the question. Why was Wagon Spring set as the farthest limit of the hunt?"

"Because we patrol that far."

"But no farther?"

"That is correct, sir."

''Now, tell the court how far you took the hunters beyond Wagon Spring.''

''Some fifteen miles, sir.''

There was a relishing gleam in the judge advocate's eyes as he said, ''That is all, Mr. Dunham. You are excused.''

CHAPTER 2

STEPPING down from the train, Scott Dunham responded immediately to his reception of golden New Mexico sunshine and crisp, high-country air, and he stood awhile, viewing the growing outscatter of Silver City, sprung from little more than a sprawling mining camp during the bloody Victorio campaigns of '79 and '80.

When a hack drove up, Scott hailed it for the Timmer House. Riding down Bullard Street, which he remembered was named after young John Bullard, killed by Apaches in '72, he noticed here and there brick homes among the adobes and, farther on, two-story brick business buildings with Victorian cast-iron facades. In his absence, Silver City had become a lively little frontier town.

A crowd was milling outside the red-brick Timmer House at the corner of Hudson and Broadway. Not a jovial one, judging by the grim faces and the fist shaking. He paid the Mexican driver, made his way through the crowd to the desk, registered, and inquired of the clerk, "What's going on?"

"Two prospectors found ambushed other side of the Mountain Home stage station in Thompson Canyon. Public meeting's been called for three o'clock."

"Sounds about where the McComas family was murdered. Didn't Fort Bayard send out a detachment?"

The man's mouth curled. "As usual, the tin soldiers

marched out and marched back again, without sightin' one Apache.''

One thing hadn't changed, Scott could see, and that was the open civilian contempt for the Army, unable to punish every Apache war party that waylaid travelers on the roads and trails and raided the remote ranches and homesteads and mining camps. He said in a reasonable voice, "By that time, of course, the Apaches were long gone.''

"Even so, the cavalry could've followed their trail. Maybe caught up with the murderin' red devils before they got into Mexico.''

"*If* they left a trail.'' Scott's defense was sudden, surprising him. "It's only fair to remember that besides the trooper, a mount carries one hundred pounds of saddle, bridles, blanket, weapons, ammunition, the trooper's personal gear, picket pins, extra horseshoes, and saddlebags, whereas a mounted Apache has only himself and breechclout, headband, moccasins, rifle, knife, or bow and arrows, a few rounds of ammunition, and a little bag of mesquite meal. Or maybe he's afoot. If so, he can cover fifty to seventy miles a day at a swinging dogtrot, and every bush or rock furnishes a convenient hiding place if pursuit is close.''

The clerk, taken aback, but obviously not wishing to disagree with a guest, sighed and said, "You sound like one of the officers at the fort,'' and motioned to a Mexican boy to take Scott's bags.

In his second-floor room, a bowl-and-pitcher accommodation, Scott peeled back the blankets and felt of the mattress, which had the crinkle of straw ticking, and inspected for bedbugs. He found none. Relieved, he poured water into the earthenware bowl, took a bar of soap from his belongings, and treated himself to a cavalryman's bath.

The face he saw in the oval mirror could have been a stranger's: angular and drawn, framed by a close-cropped, pepper-and-salt beard and mustache. The brown eyes set deep, patient and hollow-looking, the mouth thoughtful, the nose almost Roman. He was prematurely gray, thirty-three years of age, and thought that he looked forty. He had dallied after leaving Fort Sill, stayed drunk two days in Sherman, which only worsened his state of mind; then aimless days in San Antonio, more in El Paso, yet needing the passage of time and anonymity, virtually feeling his way while he took stock of himself, alternately bitter and self-reproachful for allowing himself to dwell on the past.

He broke off. He was brooding again, and that would get him nowhere. He dried himself, shrugged into shirt and coat, pulled on his hat, and went downstairs. The clock behind the clerk's desk showed two o'clock. He eased through the loud, vengeful crowd, strolled across Main Street to Bullard and down it to the Centennial Saloon.

As he started inside, his eyes caught something displayed on a wooden box behind the dingy window. He looked again and pulled back in momentary disbelief and shock. The object was a severed head—yes, it was—an Apache's head, the hair blue-black, its soiled headband still in place, a streak of yellow ocher slanting across the harsh features, over the high-bridged nose and under the eyes, the black eyes like pieces of obsidian. Below the head on the box ran the laboriously scrawled letters:

> *A Public Service*
> *Generously Contributed*
> *By Mr. Jake Fenton,*
> *Poet-Scout of the Black Range*

Scott grinned with recognition of the name. Jake Fenton was another thing that hadn't changed out here.

He went inside, the smell of the packed place coming against him like a damp breath. Over by the bar rough-garbed miners and a sprinkling of townsmen crowded around a long-haired figure wearing a fringed buckskin jacket and broad-brimmed hat. Scott moved to the edge of the crowd.

"What kind of rifle did you use, Jake?" a miner asked.

Jake Fenton—a calm, impressive man, as Scott remembered, apparently unchanged by time. A small, nimble man, packed with aggressive energy. Raffish, but capable. A no-nonsense man on a scout, seldom reckless, who took all necessary precautions, but did not hesitate when bold action was required. Tough, canny, with a sense of humor. A fascinating, alterable face—behind the piercing blue eyes a hint of playful roguery, which went with the toothy grin and the beaked nose.

Fenton brushed at his pale, drooping mustache, the ends curled to a fine point, his leathery features warped in thought. "It happened so fast," he said, "I can't remember if it was Old Ginger, my Sharps, or Bad Medicine, my light .40-65 Winchester."

The questioner nudged a neighbor and, grinning, asked, "Would a little drink help jog your memory?"

"A drink?" Fenton echoed, cocking his head. "Might." Everybody laughed.

"Serve Jake a drink, bartender."

"After you pay," the aproned man behind the bar replied.

A spinning silver dollar bounced and danced on the mahogany, the barkeep set out a bottle, Fenton poured his own with a steady hand, to the brim, not one drop over, downed it without the faintest change of expression, and said, "Guess I'll have to start at the beginning." A sly grin spread across his face. "That is, if you want to hear the whole story. If you don't . . ."

"Go on, Jake!"

"Well, you see, my old pack mule, Silas, can smell 'Paches, an' one morning on the trail, when the sun was just up good, I noticed he seemed nervous. Not hisself. You know how a mule is? If something's not quite right, he senses it.'' Fenton paused, deliberately, Scott knew, to draw them on.

"How, Jake? How'd he act?"

"Kept flickin' his ears an' turnin' his head." There was another pause.

"What did you do, Jake?"

"Well, I knew it was either 'Paches or a mountain lion. A mountain lion will trail a man, you know, whether he's horseback or afoot—if the lion's hungry enough. Guess I oughta know, long as I've been in the mountains. . . . Well, I kept on the move. Been seein' Indian sign for days. I wanted to put that part of the Burros behind me. Been makin' cold camps—no fires—an' was down to a handful of jerky. . . . Well, finally Silas got so nervous I thought his ears would twitch off. That's when I spotted 'em. Two 'Paches behind me, comin' in that swingin' dogtrot. They can run a horse down, you know." He paused reflectively.

"What then, Jake? You tear outa there?"

A scornful look. "I can see you boys need to go back to school when it comes to 'Paches. I didn't ride any faster, like I knew they's back there. Idea was to make 'em think I was easy pickin's. Let 'em get a mite too careless." He inclined his head, his air confidential. "But when I topped a little rise, thick with juniper an' oak, I tied my mountain horse an' Si down below, ran back to the timber, an' waited." He folded his arms and hunched one shoulder. "Pretty soon here they come. A big buck in the lead. . . . Remember this, boys. The first shot is the most important in a runnin' Indian fight. . . . Well, I fired just as they started upslope. That big buck went backward like he'd been kicked by a mule. The other 'Pache took off for the tules. My second shot must've caught him right between the shoulder blades, 'cause he fell flat on his face." Fenton paused once more.

"Now tell us what kind of rifle you used, Jake."

Fenton's wordless answer was a squinting pondering.

"Think a drink would help you remember?"

"Might."

"Another round for Jake Fenton, bartender."

Not one, but three dollars rang on the bar.

As Fenton slowly savored his whiskey, a sort of light seemed to fall across his face. "Kinda comes to me now. The distance was about a quarter of a mile or a little more, I calculate. I set up my rest sticks, same as I used on the plains, you know, when I hunted the big shaggies. I called on Old Ginger, which is a Big Fifty. Too far away for my .40-65."

"Why didn't you bring in both heads?"

Fenton straightened, a statuary of injured pride. "Think I'm a heathen, do you?"

Guffawing, they crowded up to the bar, and after a round of drinks, a man asked, "Composed any poems lately, Jake?"

"Come to think of it, I have put one together . . . if I can just recollect how it goes." Fenton gazed upward with calculated modesty and pulled on his beard, as if trying to remember.

"Would another little drink help?"

"Not necessary . . . but if you fellows insist."

They did, and afterward Fenton cleared his throat, struck a reared-back pose, and said, somewhat thickly, "I've dedicated this to Silas, an' the title is 'Old Ginger Does Christian Work.' Here goes:

> "Once upon a daylight dreary, while
> I pondered weak an' weary,
> Over many a quaint an' curious map
> Of lost Spanish gold—
> While I nodded, nearly swaying
> Suddenly there came a braying
> A braying at my cabin door.
> It was Si, my pack mule, faithful an' dear,
> Warnin' me that 'Paches were near.

I fetched up Old Ginger an'
Stepped to the door.
Just then out of the brush slipped
One 'Pache, follered by two more.
Well, boys, Old Ginger took the
First heathen right between the eyes—
The second critter by the same surprise.
The third one lit out like a startled elk,
But I figured Old Ginger had his ilk.''

Fenton checked himself. "Now would you boys believe me if I told you that Ginger dropped that third varmint in his tracks? Would you, now?" He waited, his mercurial face unreadable.

"We would!" came the eager chorus.

Fenton raised a lopsided grin. "Sure wish it had happened that way. Sure do." He let them ponder what that possibly meant.

"Tell us, Jake!"

"Well . . . durned if that 'Pache didn't wheel an' fire an arrer straight through my honest heart."

They guffawed explosively at the surprise ending, slapped him on the back, and bought him another drink.

When Scott saw an opening around Fenton, he edged in, held out his hand, and said, "Jake, remember me?"

Fenton stared at him a moment. "Lieutenant! Sure, sure!" He shook hands eagerly. His quick eyes widened. "But where's the soldier getup? You on leave?"

"I'm out of the Army. If you think you can stand another drink, I'll tell you about it."

"If you insist."

Laughing, Scott said, "Yes, I insist. By the way, I enjoyed your poetry reading, even if it did sound just a little bit like Edgar Allan Poe's 'The Raven.' "

"Edgar Allan Poe? Who's that?"

"Don't tell me you've never read 'The Raven'?"

"Oh, maybe I did a long time ago," Fenton drawled,

doing a great deadpan, "when I was a schoolboy back in Ohio."

They moved to the end of the bar. Scott bought drinks and began telling him what had happened. At the start he intended to make it brief, but as he went along, warmed by the audience of an old friend, he expanded into details, neither denying his responsibility as the escort officer nor pitying himself. And when he had finished, he realized that, for the first time, he had related the entire story.

"That's just like the Army," Fenton sympathized, "lookin' for somebody to blame. I'm glad Major Martin did what he could for you. Always liked him when he was at Fort Bayard. He didn't look down his nose at civilians. Didn't think the Army knew it all. I still scout some for the Army now and then, though right now I'm on the loose. Rumor is the 6th may be headed out this way again soon to help round up ol' Geronimo. Maybe you've heard?"

"So Major Martin said."

"What you aim to do, Lieutenant?"

"Better call me Scott. First, I'm going out on the Mimbres. Want to see that river again and the valley. Used to think I'd like to settle out there if the Apache wars ever get over. From there, up into the mountains. Up the Mimbres Canyon into the Black Range."

Fenton took Scott's arm. "Now don't be a damn fool. They's little bunches of hostiles rangin' all through the mountains, from the Blacks an' the forks of the Gila down into the Floridas, over in Arizona from the Peloncillos down through the Chiricahua range."

An arm-waving miner called, "Time for the meeting," and Fenton turned to Scott. "Better come along, Lieutenant. I hear tell the citizens aim to fire off a telegram to President Cleveland for relief from the Indian trouble. Also, the boys aim to ask the county commissioners to put up two hundred fifty dollars for every 'Pache scalp brought in. The Lyons-Campbell Ranch has already offered a five hundred reward for ol' Geronimo's hair."

"Now that would be something for you to do in your idle time," Scott said, with a grin. "Bring in Geronimo's head."

"I'm not that crazy. You're the crazy one, goin' off into the mountains. Come on. You might change your mind after you attend the meeting an' listen to what's said. If you won't believe me, maybe you will somebody else. Come on, Lieutenant."

"Guess not, Jake. I want to see about a camping outfit, a good mountain horse, and a pack mule."

Fenton, feigning a last farewell, held out his hand and said mournfully, "It sure was nice knowin' you, Scott Dunham. You were a good man." Shaking his head, he joined the outflowing crowd.

By midmorning Scott was on the Fort Bayard road, astride a sturdy sorrel mountain horse, leading a loaded brown pack mule. A .56-50 Spencer carbine, used but in good condition, hung in a saddle scabbard.

Passing between the fort and Central City, south of the post, he heard a bugle blowing Guard Mount and, for a moment, he was somber and remembering as he visualized the formation. Still, he could feel amusement at Central's claim of "city." A collection of adobes and shacks, it lived off the entertainment-starved troopers and infantrymen and was notorious for its bawdy women, crooked gambling games, and cheap whiskey and mescal. An enlisted man anticipating a lively evening there would don his "drinkin' jewelry"—rings made from horseshoe nails with the rough heads of the nails worn on top of both fists—then sally forth for the usual free-for-all.

Continuing eastward, deeper into the rolling foothills of the Pinos Altos range, he rode by the sprawling mining camp of Santa Rita, which recalled for him the story he'd heard at Fort Bayard. Copper once so rich it stuck out of the ground, and Apaches tipped their arrows with the red metal. First mined by the Spaniards in the early 1800s with convict labor. Ore transported by pack mules and wagons to Chihuahua City, some 400 miles south. The mines constantly harassed by Apaches.

And so today, he thought.

From there he turned northeast into the rising mass of the hills and presently rode into the silver mining camp of Georgetown, built in the V of a broad gulch. He watered at the spring and took the well-traveled road leading to the stamp mill on the Mimbres River.

That evening he camped farther up the Mimbres under a giant cottonwood, the gelding and mule on picket in belly-high grama grass. He built a fire and cooked supper; afterward, his back to the cottonwood, wrapped in a heavy coat against the night's chill, he watched the fire burn down to cherry-red coals. Wind husked down the valley, singing through the treetops, an accompaniment for the solo of the river murmuring over its graveled bed. He had no particular thoughts, only a vague contentment for hav-ing come this far to this favored valley. Rising, he laid more wood on the fire and settled down again to muse.

The meshing sounds lulled his senses and he dozed. Jerking awake, he was aware of a subtle but unseen pres-ence. As he carefully reached for his rifle and searched the darkness, a browsing doe materialized in the gloom on the other side of the low-burning fire, then another and an-other. With a little smile for his alarm, he watched, enter-tained, until, feature by feature, his gentle visitors vanished as unobtrusively as they had come.

He slept past daybreak, awakened by the *cr-r-ruck, cr-r-ruck* of a flapping raven; smiling to himself, he could not help recalling Jake Fenton's barroom appropriation of the poet's work. After watering his stock, he bathed at the stream, shivering, made a small fire for breakfast, and then, saddled and packed, he followed a trail upriver for the destination that he knew awaited him somewhere in higher country.

Afternoon sun rode the valley when he sighted the

huddled settlement rooting for life not far from the river: an adobe house, a high, stone corral, a loopholed block- house of pine logs, and an apple orchard in bloom. Riding nearer, he saw a hitching rack in front of the adobe and a sign over the porch that read: MIMBRES VALLEY STORE. Glancing about, he noticed another adobe house and a pole corral about a hundred yards upstream. All this was new since he had led a scouting detail through here, and he could only wonder at the proprietor's boldness.

Just as he was about to dismount, a big, wolfish dog came tearing around the store, barking furiously, teeth bared.

Scott settled back in the saddle and spoke reassuringly to the dog, which, unappeased, and barring the way to the door of the store, continued to bark savagely, warningly.

"Hello, the store," Scott called. "Hello, the store." He now noticed that narrow slits, wide enough for a rifle barrel, flanked both sides of the stout wooden door.

"Hush, Rondo!" a woman's voice called sharply from the righthand slit, whereupon the dog retreated to the porch and, still growling, stood guard in front of the door.

"Who are you and what do you want?" the woman asked, her voice guarded. Scott had expected a man's.

"I'm riding through," he said, "and should like to inquire about the upper Mimbres."

"You mean upvalley from here or the Mimbres Canyon, where the river comes down out of the Black Range, and which some folks call the North Fork of the Mimbres?"

"The canyon."

"What about it?"

"I'm thinking of camping up there. Maybe building a cabin."

"You'd better stay on the river. It's safer."

"Has there been Indian trouble up that way?"

"Ranchers have spotted a few bucks. Some horses taken. No war parties yet. They will come when the weather warms up."

"I just came from Silver City and was told that Apaches had killed two prospectors on the Lordsburg road."

"That road through the Burros is the most dangerous in the territory."

Her voice had lost its edge, but not all its guardedness. A voice pleasant to his ear, raising his curiosity as to what she looked like. He said, "I see you have a store, which reminds me that I forgot to buy cornmeal in town. Do you have any?"

She didn't reply at once, as if she might be debating whether to open the door. Then he heard her drawing the wooden bar from the door and as it swung outward and she stood on the threshold, he blinked at the rifle in her hands.

"I can spare you a few pounds," she said. "No more. My stock is low." All the while her eyes were busy sizing him up and taking in the horse and mule.

"That would be fine," he said, smiling, and removed his hat. "I'm not an Army deserter, if that's what you might be thinking, and I wouldn't blame you, living this close to Fort Bayard. If I were, I'd hardly be riding a good saddle horse and leading a pack mule."

"Might—if you'd taken them."

"Or wearing civilian clothes," he said.

"Might—if you had 'em cached somewhere."

Her hard logic amused him. His smile broadened, and he thought, *My, she's a wary one and with good reason, living out here.* "Guess you'll have to take my word for it, ma'am."

"A deserter," she said matter-of-factly, "wouldn't be packing into the mountains. You'd be traveling light or headed south for the towns. Deming, Mesilla, or El Paso. Furthermore, I don't see a McClellan saddle or a U.S. brand on your horse. . . . I'll get your cornmeal."

Giving him another quick search with her eyes, she went abruptly inside and closed the door behind her. The dog maintained his vigil before the door. Scott dismounted and stood by his horse.

His impression of her, though brief, stayed with him. A slim woman with fine features and direct black eyes and chestnut-brown hair pulled back over her ears and knotted on the back of her neck. Brown skin tight over prominent cheekbones. Sun wrinkles at the corners of her rather large eyes. Her throat was smooth. Her mouth, firm as she spoke, would be full when relaxed or laughing. Although her face struck him as plain at first glance, her even, regular features suggested a hidden prettiness, now suppressed. The same self-suppression, as evidenced by the drab gray, high-necked dress and the heavy, square-toed work shoes, made her look older than she was. He guessed her to be a true twenty-eight or less. She wore a gold wedding band.

She soon returned and held out a sack to him. "There are three pounds there," she told him, "at eight cents a pound. I don't like to charge that much, but when I restock I go to Silver City and travel only at night." She offered a tight little smile. "Freight rates are high in Apache country."

"You travel at night?"

"Have to, to avoid Apaches—even deserters."

"You go alone?"

"If I didn't there'd be no supplies."

He paid for the purchase, thanked her, and as he mounted, she said, "It's none of my business, but you're taking big chances going up there alone the way things are."

"I was told the same in Silver City."

"But you're going anyway?"

He nodded.

"Well, a year and a half ago my husband went up the Mimbres Canyon and far into the Black Range, looking for gold. He didn't come back alive. A cavalry patrol packed his body out on a mule. Apaches got him." She waited for his reaction. When he didn't speak, she said, "I thought I should tell you that."

He nodded his thanks and said, "I'm not looking for

gold,'' and saw a question rise to the black eyes: Then what are you looking for? It remained unspoken.

Riding off, he glanced back and saw her shake her head and go inside and close the door. The dog posted himself before the door.

CHAPTER 3

Late that afternoon, up the Mimbres Canyon, he stretched a rope between two ponderosa pines, hung a tarp over it, and had his shelter for the night. He watered the horse and mule at the plunging stream, drank there as well, picketed his stock nearby, and gathered up armfuls of dead juniper and oak for his supper fire.

When the sun dropped behind the canyon wall at his back, it was as if a cloak had been thrown over the great dome of the sky. He built up the fire, set the coffeepot thereon, and contentedly watched the last tint of coppery light dissolve to purple darkness, thinking that he had almost forgotten how blue the sky could be out here, and how keenly pleasant the scent of ponderosas and piñons. Long afterward, as he drifted off to sleep, he could hear the chanting wind and his four-footed friends cropping lush grama grass.

Next morning he rode upcanyon, searching for a cabin site. Patches of snow still lingered in the shady places. Deer tracks dappled the pine-needled floor of the forest. Before long he found a location he liked, where the canyon broadened and a cliff rose at his back, and there was plenty of grass for pasture.

Come morning, he moved camp and started felling and peeling young pines for a one-room cabin. While resting, he was reminded that during his last days at Fort Sill, viewing his future out here, he had fancied himself doing considerable prospecting, though he had never attempted such, perhaps even finding a lode of silver or gold, or panning for gold in the river. But he had neglected to bring a miner's pan and he realized he wouldn't know a likely outcrop if he stumbled on one. So much for prospecting. He had a cabin to build.

In the days that followed, he chinked the logs with mud, laid saplings across the top for a roof, on them layers of brush and chunks of grassy sod, hung a crude door on leather hinges, built a fireplace of flat rocks, and mixed mud with fine gravel for mortar. He also made a window, which he overhung with a flour sack. Although the chimney smoked when the wind blew, because he hadn't built it high enough, he felt proud of his rough accomplishment. Furthermore, at night the fireplace was a cheerful companion. Meantime, he had constructed a pole corral; the crafty mule promptly loosened a gate bar and escaped, its freedom brief.

In his high spirits, he penned the Martins a letter:

Dear Major and Genevieve,

I am living in the Mimbres Canyon in the Black Range, with the joyous river but a few feet from my door. I've built a one-room cabin. I ride a stout mountain horse and have a good pack mule.

So far, there is no threat of Apaches, yet I stay alert. The frontier citizens out here are unhappy with General Crook because Fort Bayard's troopers haven't stopped every Apache raid within three hundred miles. General Miles is being hailed as the coming savior of the frontier. In turn, they will probably blame him as they have Crook.

I have bought supplies in Silver City and observed its lusty growth and metropolitan air. Genevieve, you would be delighted to see Bullard Street's new stores with their fancy iron facades. Very modern. The town is on the boom.

Sir, you remember Jake Fenton, the civilian scout? I saw him in town and he is in fine fettle, still going where and when he pleases in Apache country and entertaining the boys with exciting, if not quite believable, stories.

I think of you often. This is beautiful country. I am happy here.

Sincerely, with affection,
Scott Dunham

The days passed like shining coins, spent prodigally. To keep track of time, he tied a knot in a leather thong for each day. It was now April and there was still snow in the high places. He avoided the northern slopes, where footing was difficult. The sweet-water Mimbres, which he now thought of as "my river," was singing full voice, fed by melting snow. He rigged up a line and light pole and stalked wary trout in the deep pools. He continued to chop and split cords of juniper and oak, his physique hardening. He weighed less than he had in years. He was sleeping more soundly. His appreciations were keener, his senses purged. Up at dawn, he had time in the stillness to watch the subtle changes in the sky and to ponder deeper meanings in the order of things.

Farther up the river, he chanced upon a colony of beavers. He had brought no traps and had no desire to disturb them; rather, he observed them from a respectful distance, admiring their engineering, intrigued as they played and worked, fussing over their resourceful dams of mud and aspen logs, or diving, he supposed, to reach the sanctuary of their lodges in the pool formed by the dam. From time to time he would slip back to watch them.

Every evening he would sit in the doorway of his cabin untll darkness, then go inside to repose by a fire of crackling, sweet-smelling juniper and oak. Old concerns seemed far away, diminished by distance and time and the comfortable drowse of his fatigue. Tired muscles relaxed by the heat, he would go to his bed, a rough bunk built like a shelf against the wall. Sometimes he would wake up by the fireplace to find only the glow of coals and he knew the hour was past midnight.

Early one morning he saw a black bear and her cubs. After observing them for a while, he prudently gave them a wide berth, wanting no clash over territorial rights with an aggressive elder. Another morning he shot a white-tailed buck, cut the meat in thin strips, which he dried on a rope to make jerky, which would be his ration when prowling the mountains. Some of the meat he smoked over oak. Why not dress the skin? Drawing on what a Comanche serving as a government scout had told him at Fort Sill, he staked the hide out on the ground, fleshy side up, and scraped it with a hunting knife; next, switching to a sort of adz, made from oak, he scraped off the hair. Next, the Comanche had said, take a mixture of cooked brains and liver and grease and work it into the hide. The thought was repugnant; instead, Scott substituted meat broth, which he thoroughly applied with a wad of cloth tied on a stick. Frequently, he added salt. After soaking the skin overnight in the broth, he squeezed out the surplus moisture and stretched the skin over a framework of poles to dry, now and then rubbing it with the back side of the hunting knife to force out more of the moisture. To hasten the drying process, he handrubbed in cornmeal, and to soften the skin he drew it back and forth over the stout tent rope, tied between the forks of an evergreen oak.

Remember, the Comanche had cautioned, this is women's work, and Scott agreed when finished, judging his handiwork. Not bad, not good, either. The skin was too stiff for top-grade buckskin; for finishing touches, a Comanche woman would have cleaned it with a wash of white chalk clay, put on thick with a root fiber or dried grass, and brushed off when dry. Still, he had dressed the skin, and he was pleased with himself.

He had developed a prodigious appetite from his labors

these weeks and consequently his supplies were low. So he lined out for the store on the Mimbres, less than half a day's journey.

He could see the woman storekeeper and a Mexican man working on the heavy wooden gate at the stone corral as he approached. At the same time the watchful Rondo ran out barking. She called the dog back and Scott tied up at the store and walked around behind to the corral, noting the two rifles close at hand against the corral.

"Well," she said, turning to Scott, "I'm glad to see that you're still alive and hearty. There's been no news of you because none of my neighbors will risk going up the Mimbres that far. Oh, you could have a visit from the Army at Fort Bayard, looking for deserters, or the Grant County sheriff, looking for outlaws." She looked directly at him, a questioning look. "Sometimes travelers come through here seeking relatives who haven't been heard from since they left Texas in a hurry maybe years ago. Sometimes they leave hopeful letters at the store, which tells me someday this will be a post office. Now, would you want me to say where you are if somebody asks? But, then, I don't know your name."

"Scott Dunham is my name and it's quite all right to give my whereabouts if anyone asks," he said, eyes crinkling, "since I'm not on the dodge and you've already cleared me as a deserter."

"My name is Mrs. Holly Warren and I didn't mean to imply you are hiding out, if I did."

"If I were, would you tell?"

He was teasing her and she knew it. She shrugged and raised a half smile that was at once enigmatic, which also, for an instant, released a hidden liveliness in the even, brown features, and which she quickly controlled.

"I'm pleased to know you, Mrs. Warren," he said. "I've come down for supplies and to mail a letter."

"As a rule," she said, striking an overpurposeful businesslike manner, "I don't give credit to strangers, but if you're hungry I might stretch that a mite this once."

"That's generous of you, though I think I can scrape up enough for a few beans and a smidgen of flour," he deadpanned.

Showing amusement, she picked up her rifle, which he recognized as a lever-action Henry repeater, its broken stock bound with rawhide; calling Rondo to her side, she led the way through the rear door of the store. He followed her through a cluttered storeroom, one half of which served as a kitchen, off it a door which opened on a bedroom, and on to the front part of the store and its counter of rough pine and sparsely lined shelves. The dog positioned himself on the floor by the counter, between her and Scott, his yellowish dark eyes never leaving Scott.

"I like your dog," Scott said. "He looks part wolf."

"He is half wolf and half shepherd. A member of the family. A prospector gave him to me as a pup. I never worry about anybody sneaking up on me."

"Would he let me pet him?"

"Maybe—if you want to risk some fingers."

Scott grinned. "Believe I'll wait till we get better acquainted."

While she filled his order for flour and cornmeal, dried apples, salt, sugar, soap, coal oil, bacon, coffee beans, potatoes, and baking powder, she asked, "Ever make sourdough biscuits?"

"I haven't. Understand you need a starter?"

"You do. Do you know how to start a batch?"

"I confess I do not."

"It's a wonder you haven't starved. A prospector wouldn't be without it. It's simple. You boil two potatoes until they fall apart. Remove the skins and mash the potatoes in the water to make two cups of puree. When that's cool, add two tablespoons of sugar and two cups of flour. Beat it into a creamy batter. Cover and put in a warm place to start fermentation."

"I'll try that. Thank you."

"Also good for pancakes."

"I'll try that, too."

"You'll need a jug of lick."

When the transaction had been tallied and completed, he felt no urgency to leave and he asked, "Is there any news?"

She tilted her head. "A rancher killed on Mule Creek. A teamster ambushed at Indian Point on the road to the mines at Mogollon. Been quiet along the valley." She made a sudden turn, her face firming. "It's too quiet. Makes me uneasy. I worry about the Mexican family, and during the day I find myself watching more than working."

"You are well prepared here, I'd say."

"There's a covered trench three feet wide and five feet deep that leads from the storeroom to the blockhouse. Another joins the stone corral. In case you hadn't noticed, it has loopholes like the blockhouse. An old stage driver who stayed with us awhile suggested we build ten-foot-square pits, roofed with stone supported by logs, such as used at the stage stations on the Smoky Hill Trail in western Kansas after the war. But a blockhouse like this one, two stories high, is much better. Makes a good lookout, too." She checked herself suddenly, embarrassed. "I'm talking too much."

"Please go on. I'm interested. Have you ever been under attack here?"

"We forted up twice last summer."

"You were under siege?"

"For two days in June. Mostly, they sniped at us from across the river. One morning at daybreak they made a rush for the horses, but we drove them off. We ran short of water, had to ration it. So now I keep a full barrel in the storeroom and the blockhouse."

"That's wise. May I ask why you live here?"

"It's lovely here in the valley. The danger is the price we pay for living here."

"I agree. That's why I came back."

Her eyes widened, surprised and interested, but all she said was, "That's reason enough." She was not a prying woman. He could see that. He said, "I served at Fort Bayard during the Victorio campaigns in '79 and '80."

"I see," she said, and he guessed that ended their conversation as she tidied up behind the counter. When he moved to pick up his purchases, she looked up in that way which even by this short time he knew was so characteristic of her, her dark head held high, an open, thoughtful expression fulling the dark eyes, her strong, brown hands still, and said, "We came out here in '82 from Texas. Before that it was Kansas. Before that Missouri. Always looking for the promised land that was just over the hill. Trouble was the hill was always in the next state. My husband wanted to go on to Arizona . . . over around Tucson . . . but when I saw the Mimbres Valley, I knew I wasn't going one step more. I wanted a home. I was tired of drifting." At once she began arranging things under the counter, her face, at ease while she was talking, now back within its even frame.

"I'm sorry about your husband," he said.

"Things happen. You either give up or make do and go on living."

Now it was time to go. He packed his supplies on the mule and was riding off when she appeared on the porch and called, "I forgot to tell you something about the starter. You cover it in a bowl and put it in a warm place so it'll ferment. Better let it work for a week before you use it, and put back what you take out."

"Thank you, Mrs. Warren. I'll set it by the fireplace. I've built a little cabin and a corral."

"What kind of roof did you put on?"

"Poles, then brush and sod."

She gave him the half smile. "That'll do till the summer rains start. Good luck."

"Good luck to you here."

Somehow the ride back seemed longer and Scott did not hurry, letting the gelding plod along. The sun was dipping behind the jagged face of the canyon when he drew up at the cabin. He unsaddled and watered the stock and placed them on night picket for grazing and started taking in sacks.

The moment he stepped inside the emptiness got to him without warning, and as he stopped short, the past, shut out for so long, caught up with him. Stung by a sharp annoyance, he put down the sacks and went out for the rest. Coming back, he understood why. It was his brief return to civilization that had broken through the insulation of his new solitary existence and planted a seed of discontent. *Civilization—and the woman*, he admitted ruefully. *Yes, the woman.*

In the prior weeks he had learned the antidote for such brooding: labor so unremitting there wasn't time to look back. Therefore, he made a roaring fire and cooked and ate supper; feeling a welcome diversion, he set a pot boiling with two potatoes for the sourdough starter. Later, he found a weeks-old Silver City newspaper which Mrs. Warren had obligingly included among his supplies.

Reading the weekly *Enterprise* by candlelight, he learned that small detachments from Fort Bayard were escorting government freight wagons. . . . Indians had killed a rancher in Graham County, Arizona. . . . A Mr. and Mrs. Yeater murdered at their ranch in the Florida Mountains southeast of Deming. . . . Three Silver City mining men reported missing in the Alma area. . . . Another meeting at the Timmer House of leading citizens. A delegate chosen to present to the President and Secretaries of War and the Interior and Congress "the true state of our Indian troubles . . . and ask that they take immediate action in ridding our sorely afflicted people from the hostile Apache Indians." . . . Some citizens were urging the formation of a ranger company to raid the San Carlos Reservation in Arizona, "the fountainhead of Apache murder and rapine." . . .

Indian raiders took twenty-five head of horses from the San Simon Cattle Company in Arizona and killed two Mexican herdsmen. . . . Geronimo was reported raiding between Tucson and Nogales, Arizona. . . . In Tombstone citizens were asked to pledge $250 for the scalp of any hostile Indian. . . . Recently the citizens of Pinos Altos met for the purpose of taking subscriptions toward the erection of a suitable monument to the memory of New Mexico citizens murdered by Apaches. . . . General Miles had not yet replaced General Crook, but the "prayed-for change" was expected any day, "with the blessings of all harassed citizens in New Mexico and Arizona."

The vitriolic editor of the *Enterprise* castigated Crook as an "Indian lover of the first degree" and the renegade Apaches the Army was chasing as "Crook's pets." Under the headline MURDERING REDSKINS! the editor wrote, "I do not believe I am overstating the number when I say that in less than eight years, more than eight hundred people have been murdered by Apaches within a radius of one hundred and fifty miles of Silver City. A terrible exemplar of their methods was furnished by the massacre within five miles of Silver City of the Marques family—father, mother, and three children. The youngest child, only six weeks old, was hung up alive on a meat hook. All this within a half hour's ride of Fort Bayard, with a garrison of six companies.

"General Crook's great hobby is his Indian scouts, with which he expects to run down the renegades. Who are these scouts? Why, they are mostly Apache Indians, friends and relatives of Geronimo's band. Time and again it has been charged that when the troops were getting too close to the hostiles, these scouts would lead the troops away from the pursued, or signal them with fire, smoke, and looking glasses, allowing them to escape. Welcome, General Miles! Godspeed you to our suffering citizenry! And Godspeed to you, General Crook, out of our sight and sound!"

Scott disagreed, based on his own experience and general knowledge. Crook's strategy was correct. Troops alone, heavily outfitted and therefore slow-moving, unfamiliar with the terrain and lacking the tracking skills of the Apaches, could never catch and subdue the hostiles. Only Apaches could run down Apaches. Getting troops into position to attack hostile camps was always a difficult operation. Apache scouts made that possible. A strung-out column of troops with a pack train, kicking up dust that could be seen for miles by keen savage eyes, made a big show but caught no Apaches. It took small, hard-hitting detachments, using Apache scouts, able to move rapidly, crossing broad valleys at night to avoid detection, to strike the *rancherías*. Jake Fenton could stay up with an Apache and think like an Apache, but there were few white scouts of his caliber, and even Jake had admitted that he couldn't "match a 'Pache's sense of smell," if that was a short-coming.

The government's removal policy of concentrating the diverse Apache tribes, often feuding among themselves, at San Carlos Reservation, a squalid hellhole, had led to the long and costly Apache wars, including the bloody Victorio campaigns, which had ended at Tres Castillos in Chihua-hua with Victorio's death when Mexican troops caught his Warm Springs band short of ammunition. Behind the San Carlos concentration was the so-called "Tucson ring," composed of contractors, merchants, and federal officials, who profited from Army contracts and opposed any with-drawal of Army garrisons. The operations of the "ring," Scott remembered, had been common knowledge when he was posted at Forts Bowie and Bayard. That left the Army and Apaches as pawns in a senseless policy motivated by greed and perpetuated by indifference. Over the years, Crook, both praised and blamed, twice assigned to the Department of Arizona to direct operations, had carried out the relentless groundwork for subjugating the wild tribes. Now Miles would receive credit for ending the wars when Geronimo, the last war leader, surrendered or was captured or killed.

Scott was glad to be out of the frenzy, which was what it would be with a new general coming in, driving and eager to look impressive in the eyes of the Secretary of War and the department.

Bright morning brought its never-failing renewal, the brisk air a redolent mix of pine and juniper, the past like a bad dream, fading as he went about his chores. His mule was out again and he spent half the day finding it. His patience short, he laid on a good hiding with a leather strap. Feeling repentant back at the cabin, he gave it and the gelding a little treat of salt and bran and rubbed and petted the two and talked to them. His discontent, though not forgotten, he attributed mostly to isolation, no more. Almost any woman would look extra appealing to a man coming out of the mountains. And yet, as the day lengthened, he thought of Holly Warren now and then.

Thereafter, he took exploring rides up the Mimbres and its side canyons, a hank of jerky and biscuits for rations. One noon, stopping to water his horse at a sunlit spring, he happened to notice the mouth of a smoke-blackened cave beneath the brow of a low cliff. Several stunted piñons clung stubbornly there for survival. He dropped the reins and crossed over. Above the blackened entrance he saw sticklike figures incised on the reddish stone, figures apparently in pursuit of a sticklike animal. Neither time nor weather seemed to have dimmed them much. Spellbound, he stepped in closer to observe the savage artistry, until his nose was inches away.

Then, stooping, he entered the cave, expecting to find it slanting deeper into the vitals of the cliff. Instead, he faced a wall. The cave ended abruptly, a shallow shelter, the walls, protected from the elements, more blackened than the outside face and without its symbols. On the floor lay a stone slab, of lava he guessed, a round depression in its center. The identifying word came to him gradually: a *metate,* or corn-grinding stone, sometimes found at ancient campsites, and collected by Fort Bayard officers as curios. He lifted it, surprised at its weight, and over there was a *mano* or pestle, which he placed with the *metate.*

With his hunting knife, he dug tentatively into the earthen floor. Something surfaced. Just a piece of stone? No, a flint arrowhead, he saw, as delighted as a small boy. More followed as he dug greedily, among them some smaller, obsidian arrowheads, and pottery shards, the designs geometric, black-on-white, red-on-white.

Touching the possessions of these long-ago people, Scott felt somewhat like an intruder, and an obligation to treasure and protect them. As he examined his findings further, he imagined black-haired figures, clothed in skins, crouched around a leaping, crackling fire, juniper-scented smoke curling against the walls, while a winter storm raged and roared futilely against their rocky shelter. The men chipping stone, their wide-boned faces intent, the women cooking strips of meat or caring for tiny brown babies. Momentarily, the family tableau was as vivid in his mind as if cast in bronze. A strange feeling took possession of him: that these people had left the cave for just a little while and would return at any moment, protesting to find their hard-earned property taken.

He filled a saddlebag with the arrowheads and shards and fetched the stone and pestle to the spring, and he sat and chewed on luncheon jerky, warmed by the sun, idly looking again at his treasures. He had heard plains-reared troopers speak almost fearfully of the silence of the great forest. *Silence,* he mused, *with the wind in the treetops and spring birdsong all about,* seeing at this moment, in particular, above the entrance of the cave, a rusty canyon wren, busily harvesting the crevices for insects, now and then its clear, sweet voice going *tew tew tew. Silence with all this?* When presently he bent down to drink from the spring, cold and bright, something took his eye. Not mere gravel. Reaching in he came up with a handful of marble-size turquoise beads, blue and green, each rounded and smoothed. He sat back, conjecturing. *A votive spring, the beads offerings? Why else would they be here? For frugal water meant life in this arid land of mountains and desert.* An odd sensation moved through him, a kinship for these Ancient Ones. They had dwelled here for water, wood, game, and refuge, just as he had come here and found sanctuary, immune to the bitter past.

The feeling clung to his mind as he rode downcanyon to the cabin. Beside the doorstep he placed the *metate* and *mano,* and spreading the arrowheads and beads and shards out on his crude table, he asked himself, *What is my offering?* He could think only of silent gratitude for having found himself again.

CHAPTER 4

By the time the knots on the leather thong told him that June had come, he could feel the remembered change of season: afternoon heat building up, the sun a great copper-plate, the forest floor a tinderbox, the voice of the wind dry and querulous. This parching a teasing preliminary to the rainy season, when midsummer would turn to spring. Of late he had taken to scouting farther into the high country north and east, beyond the Powder Horn Canyon, to forests of lofty spruce and fir, to mountain meadows and aspen glades. Twice, from rocky peaks, he spotted the coiling smoke of distant forest fires. Far to the southeast, he knew, unseen, lay the busy mining towns of Kingston and Hillsboro. So far he had discovered no Indian sign.

On this day, returning earlier than usual from another ride, Scott came upon tracks entering the Mimbres off a side canyon from the east. Boot tracks and shod horse tracks. He dismounted for a closer inspection. Only one man walking. Here, evidently, they had stopped and the horseman had dismounted; in the circling clutter of tracks, Scott read the indecision of men lost in the mountains. The tracks led downcanyon. Going that way they could not miss his cabin. A kind of premonition hastened him.

When he rode into the clearing, his eyes sought first the corral. It was empty, his mule gone. He had expected that. And the cabin door, which he had left closed, blocked with a large chunk of juniper, mindful of prowling bears—

not that a mere door would stop a determined grizzly or black bear—was flung open, hanging on its leather hinges.

He rushed inside to ransacked chaos, his anger rising as he looked. His few cooking utensils scattered. Table overturned. Blankets and all his spare clothing taken. Yesterday's bread gone. Likewise his supply of precious jerky, which he had sacked and hung on a peg. Everything edible gone, down to his last few pounds of flour and a dribbling of coffee beans.

As he wheeled to go out, a heap of light blue cloth by the door caught his attention. He snatched up the cloth. It was a pair of ragged cavalry trousers, a yellow stripe running down the tattered seam of the leg. He knew then: deserters. His thoughts were racing. Since the deserters had come from the east, that meant from a post on the Rio Grande. Fort Bayard deserters, as Holly Warren had pointed out, would have gone down the Mimbres Valley toward the lower settlements, not into the mountains, then back down to the valley. These two could be heading for the mining camps around Pinos Altos, north of Silver City, or for Silver City. Once deserters reached the settlements, there was always a ready market for tough cavalry mounts that had cost the government $125 a head, and for Springfield carbines and other equipment, no questions asked.

He rode fast down the canyon, the fresh tracks easy to follow, feeling that he wasn't far behind. He could thank his mule for that, a dependable pack animal on the trail, but no fast traveler.

When he reached the Mimbres Valley, the tracks turned left instead of right as he had expected. Not taking the trail along the west fork of the river, which led to Sapillo Creek, and along it to the rough trail that rose south through high country to Pinos Altos. This puzzled him. But, on second thought, why should they take that devious route when the broad valley of the Mimbres beckoned with easy traveling, and when a detachment from their post was likely in hot pursuit? Another awareness crowded in upon him—the store. They would come to the store as certainly as they had to his cabin. He heeled the gelding into a hard gallop, his concern growing as the afternoon wore on, but he failed to sight movement on the trail curving ahead. He was farther behind them than he had thought.

A long time seemed to have passed when he heard the shot down the valley. A carbine's single crack. He tensed, expecting more gunfire. None came. In a little while the adobe of the Mexican family took shape and then the store and its out buildings, the blockhouse looming above all. Everything seemed so still. A gray horse and Scott's mule stood tied at the store. Scott had his mount going at a dead run now. He pulled up at the store and, carbine in hand, dropped from the saddle and ran up the steps.

That was when he saw Rondo lying on the porch by the door in a pool of blood. Rondo whined piteously and moved his head. He was dying. As Scott stared down at the dog, a young man stepped from the doorway and covered him with a carbine.

"Put down your gun, mister."

Scott lowered the Spencer.

"Lay it on the porch, mister."

Scott obeyed, damning himself for rushing in heedlessly.

"Raise your hands and come inside. One wrong move you're a dead Injun." He came farther out on the porch and gestured Scott in.

This man, Scott saw, wore a cavalry blouse and what looked like Scott's extra pair of gray trousers. He was short and burly, a shock of unruly yellow hair giving him a wild look. The sun had burned his pale features, inflamed his eyes.

The instant Scott went in he felt a gun barrel jabbed against his ribs by a man beside the door. "Get over there," he ordered, waving a carbine.

Scott stepped aside, seeing a wide-eyed Holly Warren standing behind the counter and her Mexican helper braced against the rear door, hands high.

"Hey, Grat," the yellow-haired man called, coming in. "Y'see that smooth gelding this feller rode in? We can sure use that. Get shed of that jugheaded mule."

"Shut up, Becker. Get a move on. Start sackin' up some supplies."

Becker grabbed a gunnysack and tossed in cans stacked on the end of the counter.

The trooper called Grat moved to the center of the room, nervously playing his Army Springfield about. A slim man, intense, in full uniform, his spade beard the color of rust, older than the other trooper. His skin was dry and his eyes, though revealing the strain of running, were quick and gauging. The sleeves of his faded blue blouse showed darker stripes where once he had worn a corporal's chevrons. There was an arrogance about him, a know-it-all, a swagger.

Scott knew his tag. A "latrine lawyer." Every post had one or more. Fast-talking troublemakers among the enlisted men, constantly complaining and dodging their duties, and whose glib tongues influenced impressionable troopers, especially young recruits, already discouraged by sparse field rations, low pay, hardships, manual labor, lack of amusement at remote posts, and monotony.

"You spitfire!" the older trooper snarled at Holly Warren, fingering a long scratch down the side of his face. "I'm not through with you yet. I want your money. All of it. Then you're goin' with us."

"You picked a poor place to rob," she said, looking him in the eye. "I barter mostly."

"Expect me to believe that? Where is it?" He advanced toward her.

Scott broke in, "Why don't you men just take my mount and vamoose down the river? There's probably a post detail not far behind you right now, closer than you think, under orders to shoot you on sight."

Grat jerked around. Into his cool eyes gleamed a knowing perception. "Ain't you the smart one? Sound like some Shoulder Straps wonder orderin' everybody around.'' Suddenly his strain broke through and his eyes turned gritty. ''Becker—if he makes a move, shoot him!'' And facing back to her, ''I said where is it?''

She flashed him a look of utter contempt. ''Here,'' she said, and pulled out a small box from under the counter and set it down hard upon the counter. ''Take it,'' she said. ''Take it and get out!''

He scooped up a dribble of silver coins, then slammed them back into the box, snarling, ''Chicken feed! Where's the real money?''

She faced him without answering.

''Where is it?'' He grabbed her arm, swinging her against the counter. Scott surged forward, but Becker motioned him back with the carbine. Just then she broke free, her black eyes blazing.

''Where is it?'' Grat demanded. ''Or would you like to get your friends shot?''

She glared at him. ''I guess you give me no choice,'' she said after a moment. Sighing, she turned slowly, submissively. ''There,'' she said, pointing to a framed bucolic print of shepherds and flocks on the wall at the end of the counter. ''Behind that picture.''

It happened swiftly, as he followed the line of her eyes. She snatched a long-barreled revolver from under the counter and clutched it hard with both hands, her brown face tautly determined. Scott glimpsed her closing her eyes as she pulled the trigger and flame burst from the muzale. The roar of the shot overran the room, powder smoke bloomed, and Grat crumpled with a cry, an astonished expression on his face. His body made a loose thumping. His carbine clattered.

Becker seemed frozen, drawn that way. In that fraction of time, Scott dived for Becker's weapon, grabbing. Becker swung toward him. For a split second Scott was looking into the carbine's barrel. He shoved desperately. The carbine went off, but Scott felt no pain, only the deafening blast in his right ear. He and Becker hit the floor, struggling, the carbine now between them. They rolled toward the counter. The next thing Scott knew was a crashing blow to his head from behind that brought showers of splintered light. He heard a series of rapid thuds nearby and felt Becker go limp in his grasp, and then his own whirling world turned black.

When Scott regained consciousness, he was lying on the floor by the counter and an apologetic Holly Warren was bathing his face with a wet cloth. He tried to sit up, but fell back groaning, his head spinning and throbbing.

"I hit you," she said. "I'm very sorry. I was trying to pistol-whip that deserter when he rolled over and I got you instead. I'm so very sorry."

"Did you get him?"

"He's in the storeroom, tied up, with Juan on guard. The other man will live. I feel sorry for him, though I shouldn't. Now I have a wounded deserter to care for and one to watch."

"I'll ride in to Fort Bayard. The adjutant will be glad to send out a detail to pick up two deserters."

"Not now you won't. You're not able and it's getting late." While she bathed his face again, he became aware of an enormous knot on the right side of his head. Just touching it brought shivers of pain.

"What did you shoot the man with?"

"An old Colt Army .44."

"It looked like a cannon." A bit of that action returned to puzzle him. "I didn't see you ear back the hammer."

"I keep it cocked under the counter."

He tried to smile and it came out all askew. "I see, where it's handy."

"I'm so sorry," she said again. "You've been out for some time."

"You did what you had to do and it's a good thing you did."

In the dusky light of the store, her face took on an added

softness. Her brown skin, he thought, was quite smooth and lovely, and her lips, at times so firm because she had to be, were now full and giving behind small, white teeth. There was also a very pleasant scent about her.

"I hate those men," she said, her voice hardening. "They shot Rondo." He could see the hurt in her face, embedded in the dark eyes.

He shook his head in sympathy. "How did they get in here?"

"I made a mistake. You're not allowed many out here and survive. I had said good-bye to a neighbor a little earlier and left the front door unbarred. I was in the bedroom when they rode up. Rondo tried to stop them at the door. They shot him and rushed in here before I could do anything. That man—that foul man—Grat—grabbed me—then you rode up."

"I should have been more alert coming in."

"If you hadn't come . . . that foul man . . ."

He sat up and when his head had cleared enough, he pushed up and held on to the counter. Little by little, the room ceased spinning. While steadying himself, he saw the print on the wall.

"Is there really a safe behind that picture?"

"No," she said.

"You fooled me as well. You took a big chance. He'd have shot you if he'd seen you go for the gun."

"I still shake when I think about it."

He said, "I believe my carbine is still on the porch."

"I brought it in. Over there."

He went to the storeroom and looked in, seeing Juan on guard, the Henry repeater across his lap. Becker sat sullenly on the floor, hands tied behind him. Grat, likewise tied, lay on a bed of gunnysacks. He kept up a steady moaning and regarded Scott with pleading eyes, all his bluster gone. Apparently he'd taken a bullet high up on his right side. Holly had even bandaged it.

Scott turned back as Holly called sharply, "Come here!"

She was standing in the open doorway. "I don't think you'll have to go to Fort Bayard after all," she said. "Look."

A body of cavalry, some ten troopers and a civilian scout, were pressing downriver at a fast trot. They drew up at the store and a young second lieutenant halted the detachment and waved. "We're from Fort Selden over on the Rio Grande," he said courteously, touching the rim of his hat. "Looking for two deserters."

"I believe we have them here," she said. "Come in, please."

"You're lucky," the lieutenant said afterward. "These men are killers. To get horses, they shot a stable sergeant and a trooper after they broke out of the guardhouse. We've been close behind them for four days. We lost their trail coming out of Kingston, then picked it up in the Black Range. If it's all right with you, ma'am, we'll bivouac here tonight on the river and head back tomorrow?"

"You don't know how welcome you are, sir. And I have grain for your horses and supplies. Whatever you need."

He bowed. "Thank you, ma'am. Our mounts are worn down. We could use some grain and we're short on coffee. I'll send a trooper over."

As the lieutenant and the detachment rode away with the prisoners, she turned to Scott. "You can't go home this late. You must stay the night. From the looks of you, you may not be able to leave tomorrow. You'll find feed in the corral for your horse and mule. Then I'll fix you some supper. I owe you that."

"Thanks, Mrs. Warren. I accept your kind invitation."

"I believe by now it is time you called me Holly." She was smiling as she spoke, and Scott thought it was the first time he had seen her fully smile. The effect was transforming, as if a light had touched her face. "I still feel very guilty about hitting you," she said.

"I prefer to look at it this way," he said, quirking his

mouth a little. "I'm glad you didn't close your eyes and fire."

"I'm glad I didn't either."

After caring for his horse and mule, he closed the heavy wooden gate and slid the bar in place, started to the house and slowly came still. Streamers of light were playing along the crest of the western wall of the valley like jeweled fingers. Still watching, he saw the light change and darkness clot the base of the wall and he could feel a coolness rising against his face. *A moment,* he thought, *a moment to remember*.

Entering the kitchen, he saw the woodbox was low. He walked out to the woodpile and was stacking pieces of firewood in the crook of his left arm when she came out of the house and said, "You don't have to do that."

"I'm perfectly able. I feel all right."

"Well, you don't look all right. You look peaked, and there's another reason."

He studied her at length. "I don't understand."

She said thoughtfully, "When I was left with this place, I made up my mind I'd never let anybody do anything for me that I could do for myself. A woman alone can't be weak or dependent and survive on the frontier. She can't be a leaner."

She had lightly taken his arm as if to stop him, and now he took her hand and said gently, "I can see that, yet no woman should pack in wood when there's an able-bodied man around."

She considered that in silence. "Since I hurt you, you may have your way this once," she said, pursing her lips, and withdrew her hand and walked with him to the house.

After supper, they sat in the kitchen talking. "I haven't had food like this in a long, long time," he said, nodding to her.

"You're just hungry."

"Hungry and appreciative." He leaned back and folded

his arms. "I've wondered how you managed to get started here. You didn't just hang out a sign that said store."

"Hardly," she said, with a looking back in her eyes. "I couldn't farm or ranch. I got on a horse and called on every rancher and farmer up and down the Mimbres for miles, Anglos and Mexicans. They were all for the convenience of a store and the company. Especially the women—they get lonely."

"You had funds to start on?"

"Barely enough to put in a stock of groceries, some tobacco, some dry goods and leather goods, some rifle and revolver shells, lamps, coal oil, a few hardware items. I've added things since then." She seemed to enjoy the telling. Her face had become animated as she talked, her eyes lively and warm, her lips expressive and sensitive. Her fine-boned features looked almost delicate, but were not with the clear, brown skin. Her small, slim body looked almost slight, but was not. She was strong and supple.

"Things?" he asked.

"Oh, things like Butterick patterns, ribbons, and buttons. Curling irons, toilet water, and complexion soaps. Women out here appreciate so very little because they have so little."

"I know." In tune with her, he had spoken out of the unforgettable past.

She gave him a sudden look, only that. She wouldn't ask. *Someday I'll tell her*, he thought.

"Has it paid you?" he asked.

"It's a close living. More a way of life. But I soon realized that if I managed to exist here, I should say survive, I needed protection. With the help of my neighbors, I built the blockhouse and the stone corral, which serve two purposes: protection from the Apaches, where families can fort up, and in peaceful times can get together. We celebrated the Fourth of July here. You know, picnics, patriotic speeches. The cool cottonwoods along the river are wonderful for picnics. And we had horse

races and sack races and the cowboys put on a rodeo. Last
year we had a Christmas dance.''

He gazed around, questioning the cramped quarters.

''I can see,'' she said, ''you wonder how we managed
that. Well, the orchestra—we had two violins and a
guitar—we put in the front part of the store, in the center,
so to speak, and the couples danced in the storeroom and
on the porch. Some even danced in the yard. It worked out
just fine. We had a beautiful Christmas tree—a fir packed
down from the Black Range. There were candles on it, and
every child had a little gift—no child was forgotten—and
we sang carols.''

He found himself nodding again and again as she
enumerated.

''There was plenty to eat,'' she continued. ''Everybody
brought something. Everybody had a good time.''

''I'll bet they did.'' He considered her for a moment.
''You get lonely sometimes?''

''Yes,'' she said, in that straightforward way she had,
''and sometimes I'm afraid. I'll miss Rondo so much.''

''I'm going to make a prediction: You will marry again.''

''I'd be afraid of that as well,'' she said, looking carefully at her hands. ''No, I'm not looking for marriage
again. Above all, not for a man who drifts from pillar to
post. Forever on the move. Sleeping in wagons. Cooking
out in the open. Fighting the weather. Hoping the water
will be good at the next settlement. Never stopping in one
place long enough to have neighbors. . . . A child dies of
whooping cough. You bury the child and go on, your eyes
trailing back, and you wonder how long the simple wooden
marker will stand; knowing it won't be long, and when it's
gone, no one but you will know the child ever lived.''
Pain, like a knife, cut across her face.

A great rush of sympathy for her welled up in him—
sympathy, not pity, because she was too strong for that—
and he nodded his understanding.

She had broken off. Unexpectedly, her voice reached a

higher, mocking key. "It'll be better in the next place, Holly. Sure it will. Why, a fella told me it's the finest climate in the world—beats California. The winters are short and never severe. There's gold and silver. Springs gush from every hill. The grass is green the year round. Stock gets rollin' fat. You can raise anything. . . . You'll see, Holly. You'll see. I promise you." Her lips firmed, her voice flattened. "No, I won't have that again. I won't marry."

He said gently, "I once heard a young girl make that declaration and a month later she was happily married."

"I'm no longer a young girl."

"You're still a young woman and a mighty fine choice for a good man."

She smiled, a dry little smile. "You seem to know a great deal about women, Mr. Dunham."

"I believe Scott is the first name," he said, amused in turn, "and I make no claims about women. A man who does is a fool and a liar. But don't shut life out, Holly. Don't be afraid of it. It can be good to you, too."

"Life is cruel," she persisted.

"Not always," he said.

Her expression changed, darkening, as if to exclude any more intimate talk. "When will the raiding and killing stop, when can people drive their wagons to town in daylight and not carry rifles?"

"When and if Geronimo comes in. I don't think the Army will ever capture him. I say that despite an agreement reached with the governors of Sonora and Chihuahua that when an American force is in hot pursuit of Apaches, it may continue chasing them across the border and operate inside Mexico for a considerable period without interference from the Mexicans. So far it hasn't caught any Apaches."

"Why can't the Mexicans catch him?"

"They've tried many times. But they don't want to pay the price of rooting the Chiricahuas out of the Sierra

Madre. It would cost many lives, and the Apaches would probably slip away if the Mexicans got close. It's a crazy game that's been going on long before the white man came to the Southwest. For instance, the Apaches will reach an armistice with a Mexican town, come in and do some trading, and get drunk. A few weeks later they might be at war with that town. Fact is, Mexico is an economic resource for the Apaches. A convenient place where they can raid and bring back horses and mules and captives and other booty. It's a game.''

She shook her dark head tiredly.

Scott went on, hungry for conversation and company. ''In fairness to Geronimo, he's not responsible for all the trouble. He couldn't possibly be in all the places the frontier press claims. There are other war parties. Some of no more than three or four men and a woman or two. Neither do all the Chiricahuas support Geronimo. His following is limited. Fifty at the most and likely just thirty or so. When I was in the Army, I found that a majority of the Indians on the San Carlos Reservation in Arizona feared and disliked him. He is neither a chief nor a subchief. He's a war leader, a skillful one. A man of tremendous physical courage and strength.''

At his mention of the Army, he saw her eyes acquire a deeper look, a deepening interest, and again she asked no delving question about his past.

They talked on and on, about the sweet-water river and its moods throughout the season: prospects for the valley, irrigation, great orchards, ranching, the effect of its remoteness, and then the evening was spent. She gave him blankets and a pillow, which he spread out on the earthen floor by the counter in the sallow light of a coal-oil lamp.

His attention stayed upon her as she turned at the door. ''Holly,'' he said, walking over to her, ''I've been wanting to tell you this all evening.''

She stiffened, almost suspiciously. Her large eyes widened even further.

"You are quite a woman," he said. "A mighty courageous and generous lady. You are indeed."

She looked confused. "I could never be a lady," she said, hesitating, a faint scoffing underlying her voice.

"Not by pretentious parlor definitions, perhaps. But as a true person you are much, much more." Almost before he knew it, he touched the point of her shoulder.

Their eyes met and held. Something rose to her face and remained there. Little by little it faded until gone. She moved away from his hand. "Don't do that," she said.

"I meant no offense, I assure you. It just happened, as life sometimes happens. Don't be afraid of life, Holly. Don't be."

Her lips formed the now-familiar suppression, and which, he discerned, was so foreign to her real self.

"Good night," he said.

"Good night," she said, and closed the door.

His fresh outlay of supplies packed on the mule next morning, he stepped to the saddle.

"About when do you think you'll be coming back?" she asked.

"When these supplies are gone," he said, looking at her. "I've developed an enormous appetite, as you well know, so it won't be long."

"Watch the river and creek banks for tracks," she said, as if she might be warning a passing rider. "Never leave your cabin without a gun, if it's but to the river for a bucket of water. Be on guard at dawn, when the shooting light is bad. That's when Apaches come jumping, when they think a white man's just getting up or sleeping. Some old-timers say sundown is also bad, when a man's tired and not watchful coming back to his cabin or camp."

He nodded to that and reined to go.

Her voice changed, losing its matter-of-factness, following after him. "There's plenty of good land along the river and in the foothills for homesteading."

"I might keep that in mind," he said, and rode off with a wave.

CHAPTER 5

THE restlessness took hold of him again. To counter it, he began to drive himself. First, enlarging and strengthening the pole corral, planting larger posts and building a stouter gate. Using flat stones, he laid a broad walk from the cabin to the river. Adding more brush to the cabin's roof and more sod on top of that. Rechinking gaps in the cabin and the rock chimney. He had bought a saw and nails at the store; thus aided, he made a rather nice chair and a cabinet of sorts, which he stood in a corner by the fireplace to store his few kitchen utensils and flour and meal. With precise care, he cut and sewed moccasins of buckskin, not realizing until he walked in them over rocks and gravel at the river that he needed stiff rawhide soles; thereafter, he wore them only in the cabin. The horse and mule now being without shoes, he trimmed their feet with his hunting knife. As a precaution against having his stock stolen a second time, he would tether them in a brushy box canyon upriver from the cabin when he left for a tramp in the forest. There was little he could do about protecting his cabin other than closing the door and blocking it.

Before starting a day's work outside, he would take the Spencer and scout up and down the stream for Indian sign, the absence of which had begun to puzzle him. While working, he kept the carbine within reach. So busy, he was, sometimes he forgot to tie a knot on his leather calendar.

Late one night a noise disturbed him, so gradual and faint it hardly registered, a change in the tone of the wind mewling through the pines, a faint rustling that brought him upright in his bunk bed. The rustling became a sighing, growing by the moment, and that a sweeping of the wind, and that a pattering upon the cabin's roof, then a swift drumming. At last the rainy season had arrived. He lay back and slept at ease.

The awaited change in the cycle set in: mornings of pristine freshness, and in the meadows a rebirth of wild flowers, bewitching blankets of mingling purples, yellows, blues, reds, whites, their bright faces turned in greeting to the sun, graceful and swaying; in the afternoon, with a fanfare of thunder, the cooling showers. During the thunderstorms, he wisely avoided the ridges where lightning often struck.

His watchfulness continued without letup as the days moved into late August and yet no sign of Indians. About now, before he needed to replenish his supplies, he decided to ride to the trail that led over Emory Pass and on to Kingston and Hillsboro, which lay to the southeast. Perhaps boredom drew him that way, or the desire to traverse again the country he had passed over fleetingly during the hard-fought Victorio campaigns. He was, he sensed, approaching the end of his exile in the mountains and the dread of leaving was already oppressively upon him. He was close to the brooding again.

He packed the mule and saddled the gelding and headed for higher country, following the Mimbres northeasterly in its plunge from the Black Range. Coming to the forks of the Mimbres, he took the middle branch, following the crest of a dim, rock-strewn trail up and down, his progress slow. He rode to where the south branch came in and followed it to its source, a sweet-water spring, and lingered awhile. After that his confusion began. He was lost, yet not lost, because the sun guided him, knowing he would reach his general destination by continuing south and southwest. At times he dismounted to lead the steady gelding and the surefooted mule around deadfalls of huge ponderosas, and also where the trail narrowed and one stumbling step could end hundreds of feet below on either side. The mountains stretched as far as his eyes could see, and he thought, *I'm leaving this. Soon I'll be leaving. But where?* And there his musing would halt.

That evening, making a dry camp, he considered his miscalculation. What he had figured roughly as about twenty miles to the Emory Pass Trail as the crow flies had lengthened considerably with the ups and downs and his wanderings. But time was no matter. He was rich in time and meanderings.

He woke to a misty morning, his blankets clammy and moist. He breakfasted on jerky and cold biscuits, continued on and found springwater. Around nine o'clock he reached the Emory Pass Trail, which, rising to his left, told him that he was on the west side of the pass. Another miscalculation, but not a grievous one. He would ride to the head of the pass before starting home and camp out again that night.

The drifting scent of sweet woodsmoke threw him alert, grabbing for the Spencer. Watching uptrail, seeing no movement, he rode carefully on. Not far along he spied a two-wheeled cart beside the brushy trail, two mules tied to the cart. Beyond, a low fire was smoking. Scott called. "Hello—hello."

A Mexican man stepped out upon the trail, rifle ready.

"Good morning," Scott said, sheathing the Spencer.

The man, smiling his relief, replied, "Good morning, señor," and waved and a woman and two children came out of the bush near the fire, followed by a gaunt female dog and five fat puppies.

"Sorry if I alarmed you," Scott said, nodding to the man and his family. The woman and children smiled.

"We heard you coming," the man said, and shrugged.

"*Indios* we would not. We are going to Kingston. There, God willing, I can find work in the mines."

"Good luck," Scott said, and was riding on when the dogs attracted his eye. The pups, a woolly-looking mix of brown and black, were romping and rolling and playfully snarling and nipping, while their depleted mother stood by, her thin teats hanging low. One pup took Scott's interest more than the others. He eyed it closely. He started to ride on, but took another and longer look. Suddenly he knew. "Señor," he said, "will you sell me one of the pups? I need a good dog."

"Ai, señor. I will give you not one pup, but two. Take them! They are too many for our old mother dog to nurse. She is worn out trying to wean them."

Scott dismounted and went over to the scrambling pups. "I just want one," he said, and picked up the one he had particularly noticed. A stout male, sturdy through the shoulders and hindquarters. "He'll be a big dog when he grows up to his big feet. May I have this one?"

"Ai. Take him. He is brave like *los toros*. We call him *El Toro Bravo*."

Over the donor's protests, Scott paid a silver dollar for the pup, and as he did he realized that his plans had suddenly undergone a change. He would not ride to Emory Pass; instead, he would go down the trail a way, cut across the foothills to the river, and hope to reach the store before dark. That way would mean much easier traveling than backtracking through all that rugged country to his cabin and then down the canyon to the valley and the store, which meant tomorrow.

In the beginning, Scott carried the pup between him and the pommel of the saddle. When the pup tired and wanted down, Scott let him trail behind the pack mule, an order of march that continued until Bravo sat down in the trail, spent, his quivering red tongue drooling. In sympathy, Scott cupped a hand and gave him water and petted him. Mounting, he folded a blanket and laid it across his lap for a bed and brought one end of the blanket over the pup and wrapped it around the saddle horn so Bravo wouldn't fall out. At noon, Scott halted and fed the pup a biscuit and a piece of jerky and watched him play awhile with a pinecone. He whimpered a good deal and seemed lost, for he would stand and gaze off with sad, hopeful eyes, as if searching, which told Scott that he missed his mother and his romping littermates, and Scott petted him again and talked nonsense to him before going on.

They drank at the singing river and struck off up the Mimbres, by now Bravo almost too worn out to whimper. Far to Scott's right, north and northeast, rising beyond the massive folds of the foothills, he could see the bold shapes of the Black Range, and was glad that he hadn't gone that way.

Dusk was a purple mantle cloaking the valley when he rode up to the store. No light shone in front; briefly, Scott wondered whether she had gone or something had happened. Riding around to the rear, and seeing the narrow swath of light from the one high window in the storeroom-kitchen, he called Holly's name once and again.

"Who is it?" she answered.

"Scott Dunham. I've got something for you."

He heard the bar being freed from the door. "What in the world?" she asked curiously, coming out, the light streaming across Scott and the gelding.

"You'll have to take him," Scott said. "He's worn out—asleep."

"*Him? A him?* What is it?"

As he handed the pup down to her, it began whimpering, and she exclaimed, "It's a puppy!"

"His name is *El Toro Bravo.*"

She took the pup as she might a child, tenderly, her eyes softly maternal. "Poor little thing. Did you steal him from his poor mother?"

"She was already trying to wean him and four others. I

bought him off a Mexican family camped in Emory Pass. I hope you like him.''

"Oh, I do. I'll just call him Bravo." Without another word, she took Bravo inside.

When Scott came in after corraling and feeding, Bravo was finishing a large bowl of milk.

"What did you feed the poor little fellow, if anything?" she asked, concerned. "He's starved."

"Same as I got—biscuit and jerky. I believe he'll make you a good dog. Has the frame to go with those big paws."

"I like him very much," she said, picking up the pup and cuddling him. "If you'd come a day later I'd have missed you. I'm going to Silver City tomorrow night for supplies."

"Alone?"

"I have to. Juan has to stay with his family and keep an eye on the store."

"Why not restock in Georgetown?"

"My banker is in Silver and I can get wholesale prices there."

"I see. I don't have to tell you it's risky for a woman going alone."

"Or a man, for that matter," she said with equal emphasis. "They say Apaches won't attack at night. Something to do with their religion. If killed at night, their souls won't go to their heaven."

"They prefer to attack at dawn—that's true. But I wouldn't rule out a possible night attack."

"There's no other way, and I have to take my own risks."

"There is another way. I'll go with you."

She seemed not to understand.

"I said I'll go with you."

She stood a little straighter. Her eyes blinked several times. And then she smiled broadly. "You will?"

"Will. If you don't mind my company?"

She sobered. "It's not that, of course not. I'd welcome company. But I don't want you taking chances on my account just because I'm a woman."

"Then it's settled. I'm going with you."

She fixed him a big supper; afterward, they devoted the evening to Bravo and commenting on his antics after Holly gave him a piece of rawhide to chew on. His bed was a thick quilt next to the door of her bedroom. When he went back to his bowl, she gave him more milk. Twice she let him outside. "He's learning," she said, smiling.

Little else was said and soon Scott arranged his own bed again on the floor by the counter. Waking later to Bravo's whimpering in the storeroom, he got up and found Holly already at the back door, looking out at the pup.

"I'm afraid he'll run off and coyotes will get him," she said.

"He won't. This is home. And before long he'll be big enough to make any coyote take to the hills."

She seemed so much smaller there in the dimness of the moon, her hair falling to the shoulders of her blue robe. He caught the clean scent of her hair.

She called Bravo and when he waddled back, she picked him up and hugged him and put him down on his bed while Scott barred the storeroom door.

"It strikes me," she said, turning about, her face a pale outline in the gauze of light from the high window, "that you need a dog as much as I do."

"It didn't occur to me. Besides, I couldn't handle two on horseback."

"I say that because a footloose man is as lonely as a solitary woman." She was moving across the room toward him as she spoke.

"You think I'm footloose?"

"Aren't you? Riding in one day, drifting in here? Living alone in the mountains? Taking long rides? Here today, maybe gone tomorrow?"

He stared at her, startled at her frankness, which stopped

just short of accusation, not knowing how to answer her for a moment. "I haven't gone yet," he said. "But someday I will. Probably soon. I'm not a hermit."

"Oh, no," she said, suddenly apologetic, "you're not a hermit. I didn't mean that. I'm sorry for speaking out like that. I just want you to have a dog. That's all."

"Why, thank you, Holly," he said, and saw something undefinably warm and appealing come into her eyes; gradually, but surely, it faded until gone.

Before he could say more, she murmured an abrupt "Good night" and left the storeroom and entered her bedroom and closed the door. It occurred to him then that she had not yet spoken his given name in all the time that he had known her, and that she would not allow that familiarity so long as she thought him a drifter like her late husband, and perhaps that was what he was about to become, because he didn't know where he was bound next. Yet, at her suggestion, he called her Holly, which brought a wry grin to his face at the contradiction.

After breakfast, Scott inspected the Warren wagon, a decrepit-looking Shuttler, its red sideboards faded down to the wood. He checked the linchpins and rolled a log under the wagon, using it in place of a jack, and greased the axles and wheels, pounded on one loose iron tire and rolled the wheel to the river to soak the felly. The wagon cover was patched but serviceable. He opened the tool box ironed to the left side of the wagon and found the usual gear for hard travel: an ax, a kingbolt, some nails, some rope, and a few extra linchpins. He filled the water barrel lashed on the wagon's right side.

She was watching from the storeroom door at noon while he rolled the wheel in from the river and set it on the axle and slipped in the linchpin.

He swept off his hat and bowed. "Your carriage is now ready to roll, madame."

She smiled and the insight rose to his mind that she

smiled more now than when he had first met her. "One night," she said, "coming back, a linchpin broke and the wheel came off."

He frowned. "What did you do?"

"Believe me, I didn't try to lift the wagon. I waited there with a rifle across my knees until daylight, when two prospectors came along and rescued me. Rondo was with me."

"I see you don't have a wagon jack."

"No, but there's a stout pole inside the wagon for leverage."

"I'll remember that," he said, grimacing.

"I've learned it's a good idea to take an afternoon nap. We'll be driving all night. I like to reach Silver City before daybreak, when the trail is the most dangerous." The ubiquitous Bravo was nipping on the square toe of one of her heavy work shoes. She shooed him away. "I'll leave him with Juan's family."

They pulled away when the sky still held an hour's soft light, Holly driving a pair of fast-stepping mules, Scott on the gelding, in the wagon a picnic basket of food, water jug, blankets, and lantern. "You never know what to expect," she said. "I've been caught in blizzards and thunderstorms."

Their departure, so prepared for all day, was an anticlimax, he judged, after her virtual transformation. When Holly came out of the house, carrying the Henry rifle and a box of shells, Scott had swept her a second look. Gone her drab gray dress and her work shoes, which he detested on a woman of her quality, on any woman for that matter. She wore a navy blue waist shirt that modestly displayed her pretty throat and the suggestion of her bosom, enhanced by a simple necklace of blue-green beads; and a long dark skirt and button shoes of brown leather with pointed toes, and a tiny straw hat trimmed with scarlet ribbon loops.

"You look mighty nice," he told her, and could tell that

she wasn't used to masculine compliments because she didn't know how to take it, other than to show no expression.

"I'll be a country girl talking to my banker," she said, going to the wagon. When he moved to give her a hand to the wagon seat, she appeared not to see it and pulled herself upward. He grinned at her independence.

"I don't like the feel of this weather," she said, taking up the reins. "It's muggy. We may run into something before we get back."

She drove steadily, Scott flanking the mules.

The Mimbres twisted and turned, a sheen of ribbon in the dingy light. Now and again they crossed running water. Miles on, they passed an abandoned adobe by the trail. Scott, who was riding ahead, dropped back in question about the house and she reined up and said, "Apaches kept taking their stock. When the husband was wounded and crippled, the family gave up and went back to Texas. They were nice folks. Most of the settlers live on the lower Mimbres, where it's safer."

Later, seeing the stamp mill bulking out of the night, she halted the team. "I always rest the mules here before we take the grade up to Georgetown. It's just a few miles, but it's a hard pull and the road is rocky."

They rested and journeyed on. As they topped the crest of the high road and dropped down into Georgetown, the saloons lining the gulch were still alight. Raucous voices and racehorse piano music rode the night wind. A woman screamed, a scream that thinned off into skittering laughter, and then choking sobs, and laughter again, higher this time. Glass crashed. The laughter stilled. A gunshot followed and boots pounded a wooden boardwalk. Suddenly the piano quit, leaving a humming wake, and, as suddenly, the piano player resumed and the pulse of the camp, with the coarse voices and the woman's off-and-on laughter, picked up as if nothing had happened.

"Guess somebody hit a big strike today and they're

celebrating," Scott remarked while they watered the team and the gelding at the spring in the center of the camp.

"Miners are all drifters," she said. "They'll sweat for months at day wages, and when they've saved several hundred dollars, off they go prospecting into the mountains. If they get a strike, they sell to the first moneyed easterner that comes along, then throw the money to the winds and start all over again."

"However, some of them invest their money and open local businesses. There are opportunities in trade out here."

"A few do," she admitted. "Very few. Failing here, most will drift over into Arizona, or go up into Nevada or Colorado. All their lives they will be drifters."

"I'm thinking of men like Meredith and Ailman in Silver City."

"You're talking about my bankers. They're exceptions."

"A man is always looking at the stars. You can't blame him for that. He has to go seeking. He has to believe there is something for him out there, if he takes a chance and strives. He has to search. He has to find out."

"The stars can also blind a man to what's around him."

"Sometimes, instead of riches, he's just groping to find himself, and, finding it, that is fortune itself."

He saw her turn fixedly toward him, but she had no reply and he, likewise, was silent. After a short while, she said, "It's about twenty-five miles to Silver. We'd better get on if we make it before daylight." She picked up the reins, clucked to the restless mules, gave them a slap of the leather, and struck out on the winding road down to Santa Rita.

Up and down, they angled through the hills past Central City and Fort Bayard. The night air had a clammy feel. Now they were as voyagers breasting the long ridges fingering out from the foothills as waves on a great, heaving sea. No word was spoken. They had not spoken since leaving Georgetown.

They entered Silver City an hour or more before dawn.

Holly drove to the Legal Tender Corral on Main Street, where they watered and bought feed from a sleepy hostler.

"Would you like to go to the Timmer House and rest before I take you to breakfast?" Scott suggested.

"An elderly friend will be expecting me. I always rest there and have breakfast and lunch with her. There are sandwiches for you in the basket. I could meet you back here after lunch. That will give me time to go to the bank and the store. Then we'll load up at the store."

"I'll be glad to rent a hack from the man here and drive you to the lady's house."

"Thank you. That's too much trouble and a needless expense. I'll walk. It's just a little way from here up Market Street."

"It's more than a little way since you have to go down Bullard to Market past some saloons," he said disapprovingly. "I'll walk you there."

She patted a large cloth handbag. "I carry the Colt Army .44 in here, with the clasp of my handbag unfastened."

That, and she strode away.

He watched her reach Bullard Street and turn down it, watched until the gloom enveloped her, and was left thoughtful. He sensed more behind her refusal than the prearrangement. Whenever there was any hint of consideration between them, particularly as man and woman, even a mere courtesy, such as just now, everything seemed to swing back to her withholding of herself, to her independence and asserted self-reliance. There was always that guardedness, a fear almost, it seemed, that she might be caught up in another burdensome relationship. There'd been far too little fun in her life, far too little laughter; he saw that, too. It made him wish to break through to her, though he was at loss how.

He slept in the wagon until broad daylight, when the feeding in the corral woke him. He washed at the water trough and ambled down Main to the Timmer House for a late breakfast.

With time on his hands, he wandered into the Centennial, hoping to sight Jake Fenton. Not seeing him, he inquired of the bartender, who said, ''Jake's not been in much lately. He's back scouting for the soldier boys at Fort Bayard.''

Strolling back to the Timmer House, Scott took note of the overcast sky and the darkening hedge of clouds far to the west. In the lobby he gleaned a copy of the weekly *Enterprise*. . . . General Miles was now on the scene over in southeastern Arizona, headquartered at Fort Bowie, pushing worn-out detachments after Geronimo and his band of Chiricahuas, believed to be in the Sierra Madre Mountains of Chihuahua. . . . There was further unrest on the San Carlos Reservation, caused by hostiles slipping out of Mexico. . . . General Crook all but had Geronimo ready to surrender back in April when an American bootlegger, camped on the border, sold the Apaches mescal and the band bolted into the mountains. . . . Crook, blamed by General Sheridan for the failure, had asked to be relieved of command of the Department of Arizona and was now in command of the Department of the Platte.

''Southern New Mexico and Arizona are more than relieved to be rid at last of Chief Crook and his pet Indian scouts, who join the hostiles as soon as their enlistments are up,'' concluded the volatile editor of the *Enterprise*. ''No doubt General Miles will soon round up Geronimo and his murdering renegades and bring them into Fort Bowie for long overdue justice. At those glad tidings the *Enterprise*, echoing the wishes of its many God-fearing readers, recommends a general redskin lynching bee for the common good of all suffering humanity in these parts.''

Reflectively laying the paper aside, Scott recalled Major Martin's words. Could Miles do any better than Crook? Whatever, time was on the side of the Army. Scott, knowing the rigors of campaign, was glad to be out of it.

He left the hotel and idled up Broadway, just looking, and back down to Main and there turned north, feeling the contradictions of this growing frontier town. Here was the hum of commerce. A few blocks away up Broadway the gentility of imposing Victorian homes of brick and the new Methodist Church. Yet a mile out of town in any direction a family traveling in daylight took the chance of being murdered from ambush. Back in the seventies, he recalled, Apaches had murdered an entire show troupe just beyond the outskirts of town. The ambush of Judge McComas and his wife on the Lordsburg road several years ago and the unknown fate of their small son had sent a ripple of shock across the nation.

He went strolling up the street. A musical tinkle caught his ear. He walked on; it continued to tinkle. A sweet sound, an arresting sound. He turned and glanced back and a thought began to take hold. He studied a moment more. A sudden impulse sent him into the store. By then the music had stopped.

A young man was dusting merchandise on a long wooden counter.

"That music," Scott said, gazing about. "Was that a music box?"

The clerk grinned. "It was. Came from this little box here."

"How does it work?"

"You wind it up with a key. It runs automatically by spring movement. Plays two popular airs."

"Mind playing it for me?"

Sensing a possible sale, the young man wound the box and out issued tinkling music, light and airy, which continued for about a minute. As that number ended, another followed, in the same lilting manner.

"Know the name of the tunes?" Scott asked as the music finished.

"Afraid I don't. They sound like waltzes, though."

Scott nodded.

"This is a genuine rosewood music box, sir, made in Switzerland. There's a glass cover inside to protect the mechanism. The lid is hinged. The picture on top is a chromolithograph. Would you care to look at it?"

Scott picked up the box. The reddish wood was pretty and smooth and thereon the somewhat overdone but charming face of a little girl with long curls. "I'll take it," he said without hesitation. "How much?"

"Seven ninety-five, sir."

At the wagonyard Scott wrapped the music box in an extra shirt he carried and stuffed it inside a saddlebag, delved into the picnic basket for lunch, and waited for Holly.

She arrived a little out of breath. "Some Army freight wagons will be leaving the depot around three o'clock under escort for Fort Bayard," she said. "The lieutenant in charge, who happened to be at the store while I was going over my list, said we could tag along with them. We can start loading now at the store."

"That will save us some time," Scott agreed, casting an eye at the changing sky. "Get us out of Central City by dark." He held a look on her. "Hope you came out all right at the bank?"

"We're going to the store, aren't we?" Her voice sounded a bit strained, higher than usual.

"Look, Holly. I've saved some money. You're more than welcome . . ."

"Thanks—but I'm still in business," she cut him off and set about harnessing the mules.

The boxes and sacks struck Scott as much too few for the long and hazardous trip into town as he and a clerk loaded the wagon while Holly stood by checking off her list of supplies. Scott said nothing. Holly drove to the depot. After a long wait, the Army freight wagons lined out slowly under escort. Holly pulled in behind.

Light was failing before the column reached Central City and turned off toward the post. A rollbeat of thunder sounded in the west. Full darkness settled down as Holly drove the mules down the long slope and headed into the hills for Santa Rita.

Somewhere near Georgetown Scott felt the first spit of rain. Untying the slicker behind the cantle of his saddle, he held it out for her. "Better put this on."

She halted the team. "I have one back here." Carefully, she took off her little hat and pulled on a man's wide-brimmed one, dug out a yellow slicker behind the wagon seat and slipped into it.

They hurried on. By the time the mining camp's saloons shone ahead of them, the wind was whipping the rain like buckshot, accompanied by almost continuous salvos of thunder and crackles of lightning. Scott flinched at the near strikes.

"Want to hold up here awhile?" he called to her, shouting against the wind.

"Let's go on to the river!" She was yelling to be heard. "This won't let up for a long time."

He was not surprised. He had expected her to go on. By now he knew her that well, and perhaps not at all.

She slapped leather and the mules took off at a jingling trot, soon traveling downgrade. In a very short time by Scott's reckoning they dropped down to the stamp mill and were following the upvalley trail, the river's wall of trees weaving and shaking on their right. Although the bluffs on their left sheltered them from the wind to some extent, there was no letup from the downpour or the constant play of lightning. The night seemed endless. Scott's sense of time was blurred. Off and on he heard Holly shouting at the punished team.

At some vague point in time the abandoned adobe ranch house emerged out of the lightning-lit blackness, distorted, indistinct, its color changing as the light struck and dulled.

Scott didn't hesitate. They had gone far enough. The store was still miles away. He shouted at her, "Let's pull in here!'' At the same time lightning exposed a pole corral and sheds near the house.

She drove off the trail and stopped at the house, and he knew that if she hadn't he would have made her. ''Hand me the lantern,'' he called.

''I can light it,'' she told him. Taking the lantern, she stepped down and ran to the house, and he unhitched the mules and led them inside the corral and under a long shed, then went back for the gelding. Hurrying, he remembered to fetch the Spencer and the Henry from the wagon; in the house Holly had lit the lantern.

He looked around, smelling the closed-in mustiness, feeling the damp cold. There was a stone fireplace across one corner of the room, beyond it a kitchen and two smaller rooms. Seeing a pile of juniper wood in a box by the fireplace, he looked for pieces of kindling to start a fire. Finding none, he said, ''I need the ax,'' and started to go outside.

''Might as well bring in the blankets,'' she said. ''And the picnic basket and the water jug. We'll be here all night.''

In a little while he had a fire crackling. He found a table and a bench in the kitchen and brought them in. Holly was standing with her back to the fire, arms hugged to her. She had taken off the man's hat and the yellow slicker. A strand of chestnut-brown hair had fallen across her forehead and over her left eye which she kept brushing back, but it wouldn't stay. In that moment, he thought, she looked not like the resolute Mimbres Valley woman who drove a rickety wagon to the settlements at night to avoid Apaches, she looked like a very young girl. He wondered what her girlhood had been like. Likely, she'd grown up too fast.

He hurried out to see about the stock. The rain had set in to a steady drumming. For the time being tonight's lightning display was over. He unharnessed the team and unsaddled the gelding and fed them grain in nose bags and

carried the saddle farther under the shed. At the touch of
the saddlebags, he suddenly remembered the music box
and tucked it under his coat. In the house, while Holly was
taking food from the picnic basket, he hid the music box
under a blanket.

"Here's meat and bread and preserves," she said. "I
hope that will be enough for you."

"Couldn't be better."

They sat on the bench and ate supper and drank from the
water jug. Afterward, he built up the fire and they sat
there, soaking up the heat, Scott thinking that now was the
time to give her the music box. At that moment, without
preliminary, she said, "I guess you'll be leaving the canyon before long?"

He nodded vaguely.

"Where will you go?"

He shrugged. "I don't know. A footloose man seldom
knows, does he?" and smiled at her. "He's like the
wind."

"You're making fun of me for what I said."

"Not really."

And all at once the knowing, rising swiftly, established
itself in his mind. *I must tell her now. Now.* And he said,
"I'm going to tell you something about myself, Holly. I
know you've wondered. Been meaning to for a long time,
but the time never seemed right." He checked himself,
dreading, in a way, what had to be told, fearing it might
end their relationship.

She turned quite still, the wide eyes regarding him with
concern. "You mean you're a wanted man? Wanted men
come through the valley. Most are from Texas. Some from
Indian Territory."

"Just the opposite. An unwanted man. I was dishonorably dismissed from the United States Cavalry at Fort Sill,
Indian Territory, a few months ago." He waited for her
response, which came after a wait: "You didn't have to
tell me."

"I had to. It needs to be told. All of it." And he plunged into what had happened while escorting the young hunters, and the ensuing general court-martial, and the waiting for the foregone decision from higher up. He told it bluntly, as factually as he could, without self-pity, not sparing or defending himself. Now his words seemed to flow. He described his whole Army experience, from leaving an Indiana farm and enlisting, to the years of slow promotions, his marriage and service at Bowie and Bayard and Fort Sill, Emeline's death at childbirth with the loss of the baby, and why he had returned to the Mimbres Valley.

"I believe I told you once I didn't come here looking for gold," he said. "I was trying to find myself . . . what I used to be . . . and I have, I know."

"I'm glad," she said. Her face softened visibly.

He started to say more, because she was part of his rediscovery; but he sensed there was still distance between them, still that wary guardedness, and so he left it unsaid.

A hopefulness rose to her voice. "You said your friend, Major Martin, told you there is a chance for reinstatement."

"I don't put much stock in that. The Army moves at a snail's pace. If reinstatement comes at all, even a review, it will be years. Probably never." Standing, he made a sweeping gesture of dismissal. "Enough of this dreary history." Anticipation filled his voice. "I have something for you," he said, and went to the pile of blankets. Unwrapping the box, he held it against himself, away from her sight, while he wound the key, and turning quickly placed the box in her hands just as it began to tinkle.

She caught her breath. "What in the world?" Her pleased astonishment kept growing. She listened a short while, as a child might, looking down at the box, and then she carefully set it upon the table and clasped her hands together, her eyes never leaving it. She listened through the first tune, and the second tune, her rapt expression unchanged. When the tune ended, she said, "It's so very, very nice. Thank you. It's enough to spoil a woman."

"I think you need some spoiling," he said, emphatic about it, winding the key again, and as the music began, he executed an exaggerated bow and said, "May I have the honor of this dance, madame?"

She shrank back. "I've never waltzed in my life?"

"Not even at the Christmas dance?"

"I was too busy to try."

He became very frank. "As pretty a woman as you are, you had to have hidden out if you didn't dance. Well, there's not much to it. You just sort of glide along." He took her right hand in his left and placed his right arm lightly around her waist, aware, at once, of this first time to hold her in his arms. "Like this," he said. "On second thought, I think you are supposed to flounce a little . . . like this. . . . To move briskly . . . like this. . . . Also, if my memory is correct, I think you are supposed to turn round and round . . . like this."

She was light to hold and light on her feet, while he, in contrast, was determined but awkward. After the first initial steps and turns, she followed his strong lead smoothly.

"I thought you said you'd never danced?" he teased her.

"I haven't before."

"Just natural ability," he teased her again.

The music ended and he wound the key again and again they danced the tunes through, leaving both a trifle breathless. And he laid more wood on the fire and they sat on the bench, watching the flames until Holly yawned.

They spread the two blankets just beyond range of the popping juniper fire, Holly's to Scott's right.

"Good night," he said, and pulled off his boots and lay down.

"Good night. Thank you for the music box. It's lovely. I always wanted one when I was little."

"I can see you were never spoiled."

"I am now."

"I wouldn't say that. To my thinking, every little girl

and every woman should be spoiled a little. Makes them feel appreciated.''

''Did you spoil Emeline?'' Her voice sounded sleepy.

He reflected on that a moment. ''I couldn't very much. She was a good deal like you. Independent and brave and believed in giving more than she received. Yes, I tried within my limits. I loved her very much.''

''I'm glad you loved her and were good to her.''

''Did you love your husband?''

''I was sixteen when I married. I loved him then . . .'' Her sleepy voice trailed off.

Then, Scott thought. *People changed either for better or worse.*

He couldn't sleep. The floor was cold and he knew the one thin blanket wasn't comfort enough for her. He thought of his saddle blanket in the shed, thought of it and ruled it out as wet and too smelly. He got up and fed the fire and lay down, listening to the banshee wind and the slashing rain, and still feeling cold. He began to think about her again. Rising, he took off his coat and tiptoed over and spread it softly over her and tiptoed back and lay down.

Finally, he slept, a broken sleep.

''Scott.''

His name had been called. A long time seemed to have passed. Was he dreaming? He turned over and opened his eyes, not quite certain that he had heard it. The fire was low, no longer popping, down to a bed of glowing coals. The wind was still howling; however, the rain had slacked off.

''Scott.''

She *had* called him. It wasn't a dream. That roused him and he thought of her on the cold floor. He stepped over to her, feeling a stab of apprehension. Her face was a pale oval, framed by her dark hair.

''Holly, what is it?''

''I'm cold.''

He knelt down and took her hand lying outside the

blanket. She felt cold to his touch. He rubbed her hand. "This won't do," he said, and brought his blanket and spread it over her and took her hand again.

"I'm still cold," she said, her hand in his seeking his.

"You've caught a cold," he said, his tone blaming himself.

"No—I'm just cold."

Another gust of wind shook the house.

"Keep me warm, Scott."

His breath came short. He seemed frozen, unable to move. Then he drew back the blankets and slipped in beside her and took her in his arms, holding her, sheltering her. She was shivering and tense. A while, and she quit shaking and he could feel the wonderful heat of her body. Her arms slid around him now, her lips seeking his as he sought hers.

"Holly—"

Her mouth was tender and sweet. He kissed her again and again, and her cheeks, her eyes, her forehead, conscious of the sweetscented mass of her letdown hair.

"I'm warm now," she murmured.

A while longer they lay like that, not speaking, and then she freed her warm hands from him and he heard the soft rustlings of her garments. The room seemed to float in an unreal haze. He got up and undressed, and when he lay down beside her she was waiting for him and the shock of her nakedness coursed through him. He kissed her, feeling the length of her against him. Her body was slim and supple. Her breasts were small and firm.

"You must think me shameless," she said in that murmuring way.

"I think you're beautiful and I love you very much. I have for some time. But I couldn't tell you till I'd told you about myself."

"Scott," she murmured. "Scott."

"Tonight's the first time you've said my given name. Why?"

"I was afraid of you. Afraid you were a drifting man. I won't go through that again—never. I wanted us to be together that night after the deserters came. I wanted us to be together that night after you brought me Bravo—but I was afraid. Maybe I'm still afraid."

"You couldn't run me off." He turned her over very gently and lay upon her.

"At least we have tonight together," she said, as if uncertain. "Even if you drift on, I'll love you . . . but I won't go with you."

His lean body was strong and hard; moaning softly, she lifted her face to his and opened her arms to him.

CHAPTER 6

He followed the winding Mimbres up its rocky canyon, hardly aware of the pristine beauty all about him, his mind riveted back there with her.

"I'll be back tomorrow," he had promised her. "Then we'll go to Georgetown and be married."

"You don't have to go now, Scott."

"All my gear's up there. All my things."

"Things." She was almost bitter. "Things. You could get them later."

"Everything I own is up there except my horse and mule."

They were standing on the porch of the store. She moved to the door and faced him. "Juan saw moccasin tracks yesterday on the Sapillo."

He said nothing.

Her voice broke. "You'll go into those goddamned mountains and I'll never see you again!" Her face was taut, drained, pale. "I'm afraid for you, Scott. Afraid!"

"Holly!" He crossed to her and reached out to draw her to him. She pulled away from his touch.

A tearing moment went by. "I'll be back," he said, and strode out to his horse and mounted and rode off, leading the mule. Just before the trail made a bend into the river's timber, he held up for a final look.

Holly was still standing on the porch, watching. Scott waved. She did not move. In her rigidity, he could sense her unforgiving resistance to his leaving. Well . . . He was preparing to ride on when at last she waved. He waved back and rode out of her sight into the timber.

Because he had lingered at the store, reluctant to leave but feeling he must, the afternoon was in long shadow when he rode up to the cabin. He unsaddled, turned his stock into the corral, and fed them shelled corn in nose bags.

A gloomy solitariness crept over him while he built a supper fire. He ate a cheerless meal, and in the darkening purple of a mountain evening he strolled to the river, over to the corral and back to the cabin, the heavy depression of having left Holly and now leaving this heavily upon him. Holly was right. Things didn't matter much. He hadn't told her his main reason for coming back. Not things, though he had said so. He wanted one final communion with this virginal place where he had regained himself. His stronghold, his Elysium: the rough-hewn cabin built with his own awkward hands, the singing river, the sanctuary of the canyon, the forest, the challenging mountains, the great dome of the sky. He owed them something; together they had also given him time, which he had sorely needed.

He kept waking during the restless night. At dawn he was up and packing his bedding and clothing, eager to be off. No time this morning for a breakfast fire; therefore, he ate cold biscuits and drank cold coffee. Ready now, he walked out to the corral and suddenly stopped in his tracks.

The corral was empty, the top bar of the gate down. He damned the mule for a full minute before looking for tracks and seeing where it and the gelding had wandered downriver. Taking the Spencer and a rope and bridle, Scott followed the tracks. Here the two had grazed, here they had chosen the trail to the Mimbres Valley, here they had watered. About a mile on he saw where the escapees had parted company, the mule turning east up a side canyon in the direction of the Powder Horn Canyon, the gelding continuing down the Mimbres.

Scott followed the horse's tracks as of first importance. Along here the canyon narrowed and twisted. Again and again Scott waded the river. By this hour the sun was climbing, its bronze eye watching above the canyon to his left.

Sorrel color moved behind an oak thicket at the mouth of a short box canyon. At the same time Scott heard a stamping. His pulse jumped. As he eased forward, the horse threw up its head and trotted to the opposite side of the thicket. Scott cut him off. The horse darted to the other side. Again, Scott intercepted. The game had now reached a stalemate, but Scott had shortened the distance between them.

He was ready when the horse made another dash. Anticipating, Scott swung the looped rope and the sorrel wheeled back into the box canyon. Scott ran to the entrance and blocked it. When the horse turned and halted, blowing, wall-eyed, cut off by the rear walls of the canyon and blocked in front, Scott eased slowly toward him. "Hu—damn you—hu." He slipped the rope around the neck and quickly slid the bit between the teeth and bridled him.

"You sure picked up some bad manners running around with that escape artist," Scott gritted. "I'll halter-tie you and hobble you tonight, by God."

He sprang to the bare back and whipped the gelding into a grunting run, not slowing until they reached the side canyon. He halted, considering. He had promised Holly to return today. Unless he found the mule pretty soon, which was unlikely, the hunt would consume a day's time and cause her needless worry. But he had paid three hundred dollars for the culprit, which he must have to pack back all his belongings. He decided to go after the mule.

Well past noon he crossed the Powder Horn at a wide place and found running water where in June the stream bed was dry. The meandering tracks took Scott down the canyon. More stops to water, more whimsical grazing, a venturesome nosing into a side canyon and out. Now a capricious saunter to the other side of the stream. Now an aimless drifting, grazing here and there.

The sun hung just over the western brow of the canyon when the mule's trail suddenly changed, the tracks digging in, swerving, wider apart, running. About fifty yards on more tracks joined the mule's, bunching, cluttering, its evident race for freedom in vain. Moccasin tracks and unshod hooves converging, then turning down the Powder Horn toward the Mimbres Valley. Scott made a guess: two Apaches on foot, two horseback.

Suddenly the stillness became very tight and heavy. He heeled the sorrel clattering across the stream. Thereafter, he rode on guard, at a steady trot, eyes sweeping, the Spencer cocked.

Darkness veiled the Mimbres Canyon long before he reached the cabin. There would be scant moonlight tonight with these clouds. Moving through mealy gloom, he rode past the cabin to the corral and dismounted, feeling the wear of the long day, wondering whether he could risk a little supper fire.

"About time you got in here, Lieutenant. I'se afraid the 'Paches had got you."

Scott jerked that way, lowering the carbine as he recognized the drawling voice. "Jake—Jake Fenton! What the hell?"

Fenton bulged from alongside the corral. "That's just what it is—hell. War parties on Sapillo Creek, in the upper Mimbres Valley an' up in the Blacks. Emory Pass Trail closed. Folks in a hurry to fort up at Holly Warren's place. Also San Lorenzo."

"She sent you?"

"Her an' the colonel."

"The colonel?"

"Now Lieutenant Colonel Martin. None other. He's the new CO at Bayard. Like what was in the wind, remember?

He wants to talk to you. Didn't say what. Figure it has something to do with you an' the Army.''

"Not me.''

"He said it was important.''

"The Army? Not anymore.''

"It's important enough for me to risk my hide—ride some fifty miles from Bayard up here. Why didn't you just move to the end of the earth? For your information, I found plenty Indian sign farther down the canyon, but no Indians. I got in just before dark. My horse is over behind the cabin.''

"Maybe that was the bunch that took my runoff mule over on the Powder Horn. That's where I've been, looking for him. Four Apaches, I figure.''

"Well, don't count on that bein' all of 'em. First thing is to get out of this deep canyon. I don't fancy goin' back the way I came in.''

"We can go west, up on North Star Mesa and make a circle down to the Mimbres Valley.''

"North Star is just another passageway to the Black Range,'' Fenton said. "I don't like it.''

"It's fairly open country. You can see what's coming at you.''

"Same as they can see you.''

Scott's laugh was clipped. "That's fifty-fifty. Better than stumbling down the canyon in the dark. Unless you'd rather ride at night?''

"Not when I can't see where I'm headed. We'd make enough noise to wake up every war party from here to the Gila.''

"After I saddle up, let's make some coffee damned quick. Better sleep across the river.''

"Lieutenant, you're beginnin' to sound like that Shoulder Straps fella I used to know.''

While the coffee boiled, Scott made a light pack of his clothing and blankets and tied it behind the cantle of his saddle. After wolfing down biscuits and jerky with the bitter-strong coffee, they rode across the river, picketed their mounts close by, and bedded down under a giant cottonwood. Fenton took first watch.

Scott's thoughts kept turning to Holly and the people at the blockhouse. At least she wasn't alone. He must have slept several hours when something roused him. He sat up and reached for the carbine, sensing that Fenton was no longer on his left. Scott rose, peering into the canyon's blackness. Something scraped on rock. He spun to his right.

"It's me," Fenton whispered. "Thought I heard something down at the river."

"See anything?"

"Yup. Deer comin' in to drink."

"Better get some sleep. I'll watch."

The night was still sooty and formless, the pine-scented air heavy with the dank feel of the river as they led their mounts up the narrow trail that angled toward the top of the mesa. A pallid light was glowing through the cape of clouds over Scott's left shoulder. The dim trail bent and bent again, climbing sharply. When Scott glanced skyward again, the first stroke of light brushed the sky. Little by little the light broadened from gray to pink and the blurred ridge across the canyon took bold shape. Daylight caught the horsemen as they topped the mesa.

Mounting, they trotted off through stands of piñons and low-growing junipers. Fenton rode slightly ahead, which was his habit, Scott remembered, looking as fresh as if he'd enjoyed a good night's sleep and a big breakfast at the Timmer House. At intervals he would stand up in the stirrups to scan the country. A sweat-stained slouch hat was pulled down to his brows. He wore a durable cloth coat of blue, the pockets bulging with shells, a gray flannel shirt, gray pantaloons, and heavy black boots. He carried Old Ginger, his Sharps, across the pommel of his stock saddle. Bad Medicine, his Winchester, rode in a long boot under his left leg with the stock exposed, the butt slanted to the front, near for sudden grabbing. Heavy revolvers hung at both sides of his broad gun belt.

Fenton held out a plug of dark tobacco. "Breakfast, Lieutenant?"

Scott made a face. "Believe I'll wait for the ham and eggs, with biscuits, gravy, and coffee."

Within a short distance, they came to a trail. Fenton halted to frown over a passage of unshod hoof tracks going in the direction of the Mimbres Valley. He swung down for a closer study; stooping, he poked at a deep print with a forefinger.

"How many?" Scott asked.

"A bunch. Six or eight. These tracks are a day old." He spat a deliberate stream of amber, wiped his mustache with the back of his right hand, and displayed a toothy grin. "I have been known to be off one or two when countin' a trail." He stepped to the saddle, reined out a way, and riding parallel to the trail went ahead.

The red ball of the sun climbed higher, burning off the early coolness. A jay squawked from its juniper perch and sailed swooping away. Scott's horse kicked a loose rock, the clacking sound like a shot across the morning quiet. Fenton paused to look around before riding alertly on, his eyes constantly sweeping. For all his josh and palaver, he was a careful man on the trail.

The next minutes seemed to loiter. In the green distance the land broke away and the deep swath of a long valley stretched out before Scott, Sapillo Creek somewhere to his right, he recalled, the Mimbres River plunging down to its valley several miles to his left.

At almost the same time he saw smoke rising down there, a thin column of gray and black ascending the brass-bright sky.

Fenton looked and said, "Some poor homesteader got it." He reined and bit off a quid. "Now, Lieutenant, which way would a war party go after they'd hit that homesteader's place? Down the valley or up it? Or into the Black Range? I'm tryin' to think like a 'Pache.''

"I'd say into the Blacks, virtually safe from pursuit."

"Afraid that's my notion, too. Let's keep off the trail for cover. Not hurry too fast. Hurry's killed a heap of men in these mountains.''

Riding on, they had covered less than a mile when Scott spotted dust hanging over the trail where it narrowed and vanished into some scattered junipers. A bullet whined and Scott swerved, hearing the crack of a rifle, both horses jumping at the sound.

"Over here!" Fenton yelled and spurred right, Scott with him.

As they swept away, Scott glimpsed the blurred shapes of riders moving through the junipers. In an instant four Apaches burst out on the trail, behind them two more horseback Apaches jerking on laden mules.

Fenton's Big Fifty boomed and powder smoke bloomed. An Apache horse broke down, its rider springing free on catlike feet. "Goddamn it—too much hurry!" Fenton growled and switched rifles without reloading the Sharps. His horse going at a dead run, Scott cocked the Spencer's hammer and aimed at the nearest rider. The carbine banged and he tasted acrid powder smoke and saw the man jerk and slip sideways, clinging to his horse. The unhorsed Apache and the two remaining riders spread out.

"Turn 'em!" Scott shouted.

But Fenton, in advance, was suddenly yanking rein before a high outcrop of gray-colored rocks and stunted trees blocking his rush. "No can do!" he cried, swinging his rifle. "Go straight at 'em!"

They wheeled and charged toward the trail. The Apaches hesitated as if surprised, then veered away from the frontal attack, the riders exposing their sides. Fenton fired. A rider pitched and rolled. Scott snapped a shot, missed. Fenton fired again. The Apache reeled but hung on, slumped over the withers of his horse, desperately clapping heels as he rode out of the fight.

At once Scott found the dismounted Apache crouched before him, rifle raised. Scott ducked and swerved his horse. He heard the blast of the rifle and saw smoke puff, but felt nothing. Reining hard, he rode for the crouching shape and felt the jar and heard, simultaneously, the man's lifting cry and the meaty crunch of the mountain gelding's heavy front quarters smashing flesh and bone. Wrenching about in a tight turn, Scott then put a bullet into the thrashing, kicking shape.

"Two more downtrail!" he heard Fenton shout.

There was a strange lull in the firing where the two mounted Apaches leading the mules should be. And then Scott saw them riding at right angles from the trail, bent low, tugging on the mules' halter ropes.

Scott and Fenton charged with yells, angling across, closing the distance.

The Apaches were losing ground. Apparently seeing that, one rider let go his mule and whipped about, shooting. Scott flung up his carbine. Something tore at his hat brim, spoiling his aim. When he looked again, the Apaches were only flitting targets behind a screen of trees. By this time the second Apache had released his mule.

"Hold up!" Fenton barked and quickly changed rifles. The Apaches, now beyond carbine range, were circling back through patches of timber. Gauging the distance, he adjusted the rear sight, yanked down the loading lever and ejected the empty, and punched in a long shell and eared back the big side hammer.

He watched the circling Apaches for a moment. Bringing up the Sharps with his left arm, he leaned back in the saddle, left elbow braced against his hip, and drawing bead slowly followed the first rider, his slate-blue eyes narrowing.

Scott saw the Apache come to an opening and check and whirl his horse, saw him spring to the horse's back and shake his breechclout at the white men.

At that instant Fenton squeezed the trigger. There was a big puff of smoke with the roar and the taunting warrior flipped over backward as if performing an acrobatic feat. The second Apache ducked deeper into the junipers and disappeared.

Scott and Fenton rode off at a lope. Before long the trail, turning right, took them around a sharp bend; down its winding course, Scott sighted no movement. After a while, it led them down into the tree-studded valley.

"That particular .50-caliber shell carried ninety grains of powder and four hundred seventy-three grains of lead," Fenton said simply. "My .40-65 Winchester won't reach that far. Now we can hurry a little, Lieutenant, after you reload that Spencer."

"The homesteaders," Scott said with dread while reloading. Fenton nodded and they rode faster.

The burning cabin was now down to a smoldering fire. Two shapes sprawled in the yard. The horsemen rode closer and looked down, averted their eyes, and looked again: a bearded man and a boy hardly in his teens, neither scalped. Apaches generally didn't scalp, so Scott remembered.

"Looks like a father and his son," Fenton deplored. He glanced at the cabin and its brush *ramada*. "I just hope . . . not . . ." and didn't finish.

They left their horses and looked inside on a smoky wreckage of broken dishes and glassware and chairs, dumped flour, an overturned table with its legs torn off, slashed corn-shuck mattresses, the scattered contents of a round-topped trunk, and shreds of women's clothing.

"I guess," Scott said, "this man sent his womenfolk down to Holly's while he and the boy stayed to defend the place."

After some indecision, they placed the bodies in a shed behind the cabin, covered them as best they could with bedding, carried water from the spring, doused the slow fire, and rode off.

The valley seemed unusually quiet to Scott, or was it his uneasiness about what lay ahead at the store? The fairly broad trail presently revealed fresh, unshod tracks, but not enough to suspect a big war party, Fenton said, if that meant much.

When the store and its outer buildings jutted into sight, the two halted in river timber and observed everything warily, all around. There were wagons and buggies. Nothing moved.

While they watched, a man carrying a rifle left the blockhouse and walked to the stone corral.

On that clear signal, they rode out waving and the rifleman swung about at the hoof clatter, looking, and waved back and shouted. Another man appeared at the blockhouse, and another. Two men peered out from the corral. All at once the opening between the store and the corral and the blockhouse filled with grown-ups, and closely herded children, and, Scott saw, a romping Bravo among the children.

Rushing their horses up to the yard, Fenton called, "You folks all right?"

"We are," a man answered. "They fired on us early this morning and hung around in the timber—that's all. We had all the stock up. We figure they went on down the river. No Indian is fool enough to rush Holly Warren's blockhouse."

In another moment Holly was there and Scott dismounted. She ran up and, face flushing, openly embraced and kissed him. "Did you have any trouble?" she asked, short of breath.

"Just a little," Scott said, holding on to her.

Her quick black eyes swept over him. "Just a little and you with a bullet hole in your hat, Scott Dunham?"

"It's a little hole," he said, trying to shrug it off.

She turned to Fenton and to his vast embarrassment hugged him long and hard. "Thank you, Jake. Thank you for bringing him back. Of all times, he had to go up there, you know."

"He takes right good care of himself, ma'am, I can tell you that. We had a brush with a war party comin' down the North Star Mesa trail."

"Then you passed the Edwards' place above where the Mimbres comes in?" Holly asked and paused, sensing wrongness when Fenton clamped his jaws and looked away.

Still hesitating, Fenton looked painfully at Scott and a heavy quiet fell over the milling little crowd. Fenton waited and Scott began in a halting voice, "Folks, we have bad news. . . . I don't know how else to tell you. . . . The man and the boy . . . We found them . . . both dead. Mighty, mighty sorry." He hung his head, seeing again the bodies in the yard.

A tall, thin woman shrieked and covered her face with her hands, and after a moment clutched two little girls at her skirts. Holly hurried over and held her and started leading her inside the store. A wave of women followed. The shocked men removed their hats.

"Jim Edwards and his boy, John," a man said. "John just turned thirteen." Anger flashed into his face. "Now where the hell's the goddamned Army? I ask you, where the goddamned hell are they when you need 'em? I ask you." He made a chopping motion of furious disgust.

"Why, they're all cuddled up at Fort Bayard, restin' on their big fat butts, eatin' the rations we pay for—that's what," another said bitterly.

Inside the store an anguished wailing rose, piercing, paralyzing, heartrending. Scott wet his lips and muttered to Fenton, "I can see now a far more important reason for going to Bayard than whatever the colonel has to say to me."

"You mean gettin' some help out here?"

"We'll go as soon as I see Holly."

He went to the rear door of the store and entered the crowded storeroom. Through the open doorway of Holly's bedroom he could see Holly and others trying to comfort

Mrs. Edwards, who was lying limply on the bed. He waited, hat in hand; he could wait for that poor woman and the two little fatherless girls. He glanced around. The faces of the children got to him, the big-eyed little ones, so quiet and solemn and wondering, struck silent by this tragedy of their elders which they didn't understand, not knowing what to do, what was expected of them.

After a while, a sad-eyed Holly came out with a wash pan and dippered water into it. "Yes?" she said inquiringly, seeing Scott.

"I need to talk to you when you can," he said.

"Wait." She turned away into the bedroom and Scott saw her dampen a cloth and bathe the pallid face, murmuring, "Yes, Martha. . . . We know, dear, we know." Another woman was rubbing Mrs. Edwards's hands. Someone closed the door. From within continued the undertone of low, consoling voices and an unbroken weeping. Scott stood with head bowed.

When Holly opened the door a little later, Scott saw the frowning inquiry building across her eyes. She looked at him and he followed her into the front part of the store.

"What is it?" she asked.

"Jake and I are going to Fort Bayard to get some help out here."

"The Apaches will be long gone by the time any troopers trot out to the valley. I believe the regulation pace for cavalry is four miles an hour, is it not?" Her tone was not only as bitter about the Army as the man's outside, but also mocking.

"You can't stay cooped up here for days," he said. "The country has to be cleared out so the settlers can go home in safety."

"Safety?" she mocked.

"Holly, the Army can't be everywhere. I only wish it could."

"Is getting help out here your only reason for going?" Her lips were compressed.

"It's the main reason."

"Oh, I suppose I know," she said, her voice changing, a soft expression coming into her eyes. "Jake said he was looking for you on order of the new commanding officer at Bayard."

"That can wait, whatever it is. The people out here can't."

"Is this the way it's going to be for us, Scott, always leaving?"

"I have to go. You know that. I understand how you homesteaders feel after what's happened. It's human to lay blame. But you don't know Colonel Martin, the new CO. He'll be sending scouting details into the mountains and they'll flush out the game if it's still there, believe me. I know him, Holly. He's a tough campaigner."

"Of course that has to be done." Her voice sounded small and uneven. She looked down, then up at him, her face a mingling of emotions: hurt and disappointed, sad and sweet, resigned and penitent. "Although we are safe here for the present, I was being selfish, Scott. I was thinking only of us. I was thinking only of what you said about going to Georgetown." Her eyes grew moist. Her lips trembled. At once she left him to go to the kitchen; soon back, she handed him a small sack. "I doubt if you've eaten today." She started to leave.

"Holly." He took her arm. "Don't go off like that. I'll be back."

Her face suddenly clouding, she kissed him and held the kiss and hurried back into the bedroom.

He stood there for a very long moment, heavy of heart, then walked through the storeroom and out to his horse.

CHAPTER 7

TATTOO wasn't many minutes away. Scott and Fenton turned off the Central City road for the orderly cluster of Fort Bayard's buildings and presently rode across the parade ground to the adjutant's office. A yawning orderly was on duty. He said he would fetch the adjutant.

That worthy, as Scott expected, turned out to be a lowly second lieutenant new to the command who introduced himself as Lieutenant Mather Robinson.

He looked intently at Scott when Scott gave his name and said Colonel Martin had sent for him. "Why, yes . . . er-uh, Lieutenant—I mean, Mr. Dunham," he said hastily. "I believe the colonel will see you directly. Hello, Mr. Fenton," and he sent the orderly flying to the commanding officer's quarters.

The orderly returned, also on the fly, and there was a whispered conversation and the adjutant, smiling genially, said, "The colonel will see you gentlemen now at headquarters."

Lieutenant Colonel George Martin, looking somewhat leaner under the stress of his new duties, was standing when they entered. He broke into a broad smile, his ruddy face anticipating, and shook hands warmly with first Fenton, then Scott. He motioned them to be seated.

"Mr. Fenton," he said, "you brought him in remarkably soon. Just finding him was quite an undertaking, I know. I didn't expect you for several more days; in fact, I wasn't sure you'd even locate him." He eyed Scott with approval. "You look fit, Scott. Most fit."

"Thank you, sir. I feel fit. And I am pleased to see those two silver leaves, Colonel."

"Thank you, Scott. I had just about given up." His face took on a certain wryness. "A price goes with such fine foliage, I've learned. And too much may be expected of a very mortal new lieutenant colonel. I have been placed in charge of a post responsible for the security of an area larger than some states, where Apaches have virtually raided at will for years, and where frontier citizens regard us as parade-ground soldiers rather than fighting men. In addition, I've been given the strongest of instructions to carry out a certain objective which I shall explain shortly . . . . But, first, there is considerable good news to report. Geronimo and his band of Chiricahuas surrendered a few days ago, September 4 to be exact, to General Miles at Skeleton Canyon. All the prisoners are now en route by train to prison in Florida."

"Not all the Chiricahuas have surrendered, sir," Scott said. "Settlers on the upper Mimbres are forted up at Holly Warren's blockhouse and at San Lorenzo. Jake and I ran head-on into a war party on the North Star Mesa trail. The same bunch that had just killed a Mr. Jim Edwards and his young son in the valley."

Martin stared back in surprise. "We have not been aware of any raids. Perhaps I should say, as usual, we are the last to know." He set his teeth. "But they fit in with what I am about to tell you. This is something that probably even Mr. Fenton hasn't heard about," he said, and pacing behind his desk turned and faced them. "You're quite right, Scott, that not all the Chiricahuas came in with Geronimo. He is not a chief, he's a war leader, and because of his extreme ferocity, even for an Apache, not all tribesmen followed him. All he could promise them was extinction. Some are still in the Sierra Madre. Some are still in Victorio's old haunts up in the Black Range where his Warm Springs band used to range. Some are still on the San Carlos Reservation. Some live among the White Mountain Apaches. The disturbing thing is this. A new leader has risen among the Chiricahua remnants. A persuasive man who calls himself Medicine Shirt. Ever hear of him, Mr. Fenton?''

"No, Colonel, I have not."

"No doubt because he is only now emerging into prominence. My information comes from Chiricahua scouts I've just enlisted from San Carlos. These warriors wouldn't join Geronimo because they didn't like him or feared him or were weary of war. They now oppose Medicine Shirt because he's starting the same kind of war, one that will lead to the death of the Chiricahuas as a nation. They want peace. . . . Medicine Shirt is not a war leader in one respect. He's a shaman—a medicine man. Story is, he had this dream and a voice spoke to him four times. Four being the magic number to an Indian. The voice told him that no gun could ever kill him, that it would guide his bullets and arrows. . . . So he now claims to have the power to make Apaches invulnerable to the bullets of the Mexicans and the White Eyes. That's enough to make any diehard join him for one more chance to rub out the hated *pindahs*—the Americans.''

"What is his medicine?" Fenton asked.

"What else but a buckskin medicine shirt? On it painted symbols of the sun, moon, stars, clouds, lightning—to name a few—for power, for belief. Something tangible for a doubting Apache to see and feel.'' Martin split his gaze between the two men. "So we have a new Apache war on our hands. It hasn't become full-blown yet, but it's in the making sure as hell. General Miles is overseeing the entire operation from Fort Bowie. As senior officer in central and southwestern New Mexico, I've been given unrestricted authority over here."

Scott said, "If the Army knows all this, the Army must have an idea where Medicine Shirt is."

"You flatter us, Scott. Medicine Shirt stirred things up good at San Carlos, while the Apache telegraph spread word of the new Messiah and for everybody to join him, then vanished before General Miles could arrest him. He's a sly one. These raids are just rumbles of what's to come. Our scouts think he's in the southern Black Range or the Mimbres Mountains. My objective is to nip this war in the bud: to find him, destroy him, if need be, or make him prisoner before he can gather many warriors around him."

"Sir," Scott said, speaking very urgently, "the people on the Mimbres need help at once. I hope you can relieve them."

"I've already anticipated you, Scott, with Medicine Shirt in mind. Two troops with Army Indian scouts will proceed at daybreak for the Mimbres Valley. In that connection, there is an immediate and private matter that requires discussion with you." Martin glanced at Fenton, who got the cue and rose to go.

"Mr. Fenton," the colonel said cordially, "I trust I've made myself clear to you that you will be chief civilian scout, working closely with the lieutenant in charge of the Indian scouts, and advising the officer in charge?"

"Yes, sir, Colonel. And I'm obliged. You bet."

"He got us through the war party," Scott added when Fenton had gone. "The reason I'm here. It was close for a while."

Martin nodded with self-satisfaction. "Don't I know how to pick my scouts?" He sat down behind his desk, folded his arms, and seemed to reflect on how to frame his next words. It seemed like a long time to Scott before he spoke. "Now, Scott, I want you to hear me out . . . weighing carefully what I have to propose . . . looking at this in its entirety before you answer."

Scott looked at him and frowned, his puzzlement growing.

"Here it is: I want you to enlist as a civilian scout with Jake Fenton and help the Army bring Medicine Shirt in, dead or alive. I may want proof as strong as that shaman's head."

"Enlist . . . as a scout?" Scott sat upright, startled. "That's the last possibility I thought you might have in mind."

"What did you think Scott?"

"Wasn't much time to ponder it. I was curious. Maybe I thought you knew of a job somewhere, on a stage line or with a freight outfit?"

"A job, all right. Here in Apache country where you're needed."

Scott began to feel uncomfortable. "There are other civilian scouts you could get. Jake knows some."

"There are a few over in Arizona who scouted for General Crook. But I'm in a hurry and I'm also particular. I don't want some Wild West Show-looking character brought out of a Bullard Street saloon to sober up and play cowboy and Indian. I liked the way you and Fenton worked together during the Victorio campaigns. That's what I want. I need you both together."

"Before we go any further, sir, there is one aspect of this that bothers me."

"Speak up."

"Well, sir, you said Geronimo and his band are en route to Florida. Well, I don't give a damn about Geronimo and warriors like Nana and Naiche. They've murdered hundreds of innocent people, especially Mexicans. I can't forget the little Mexican kids I've found butchered. Nor the dead and wounded tossed onto burning wagons. Even so, I feel concern for the Chiricahua women and children and the warriors who didn't follow Geronimo. Shipping them off to Florida is equivalent to a death sentence. That damp seacoast climate will be deadly to these mountain and desert Indians. Combine that with homesickness and they'll die like flies. It's genocide, sir. That's all it is. I won't be a party to that." He was breathing fast. He had spoken in a rush, astonished at the depth of his feelings.

"You wouldn't be," the colonel said, speaking with assurance. "There's something you should know, Scott.

How this came about. General Miles had recommended that the Chiricahuas be sent to Indian Territory to live among the Comanches and Kiowas, but the President and General Sheridan said no. General Miles knew they could never be placed on a reservation in Arizona or New Mexico. Not only would that be political disaster for the administration in Washington, the citizens out here wouldn't stand for it after the loss of life and property they've suffered. If the hostiles were brought back, say, even after some years, we'd have another Camp Grant massacre, when the Tucson mob of whites and Mexicans, with a horde of vengeful Papagos, just about wiped out a ranchería of Arivaipa and Pinal Apaches in '71.''

''And the survivors taken to Sonora and sold as slaves,'' Scott joined in, ''the little girls to grow up as prostitutes.''

''True,'' Martin agreed gravely. ''Yet, the Chiricahuas can never come back to a reservation in Arizona. Not in our lifetimes, at least.''

''But why the rush to send them to Florida?''

''Because civil authorities in Arizona were demanding that the hostile men be tried in state civil court. You can well imagine the preordained outcome of the trial—a holiday community hanging. General Miles refused to give in to mob rule. Forbidden to send them to Indian Territory, he piled the Chiricahuas onto a train for Florida. Anywhere to get them out of Arizona. He had no other choice. By doing so, he saved their lives. It was the humanitarian thing to do.'' There was a grim expression to Colonel Martin's face, close to disgust, as he continued. ''Now I'm going to tell you something else that will never be in the history books or the newspapers or Sheridan's biography, if one is written. What General Miles did was contrary to what Sheridan and the Washington authorities approved.'' Martin's expression deepened. ''An order actually came down to turn Geronimo and the warriors over to the Arizona authorities. Imagine that! I could be busted for saying this, but I'm going to, nevertheless. General

Sheridan may be the General of the Army, but he knows next to nothing about Apaches—or any Indians, for that matter, and cares less. He would have condoned the mockery of a trial and the hangings.'' Martin's voice toughened. ''Well, by heavens, there are some humanitarians in this man's Army, and General Miles is one of them! I admire the man. He has guts and he has honor.''

Scott nodded in understanding.

''Fortunately for General Miles, he is a protégé of General Sheridan's. Otherwise, he would have faced severe reprimand or possible demotion. He got around the order by saying it was not received till the Chiricahuas were already well on their way. As it was, the train was stopped in San Antonio before it was allowed to proceed. By then Sheridan could hardly have sent Geronimo and the others back to be hanged. Think of the public outcry from the Society of Friends and other church groups.'' Martin sighed and sank back in his chair. ''Later, as passions cool and there are a few level heads in Washington, I hope the Chiricahuas can be moved to Indian Territory. I sincerely believe that will come about in time.''

''Where will Medicine Shirt and the remnants be sent if we bring them in?''

''I'm not in position to promise anything after what's happened. You can understand that, Scott. However, in Medicine Shirt's favor he is not another Geronimo, nor does he have Geronimo's bloody reputation—as yet. I feel confident that General Miles again would recommend that the hostiles be sent to Indian Territory. Certainly that would be my recommendation as well.'' He regarded Scott with warm approval. ''That isn't all, my friend. Whether Medicine Shirt is brought in dead or alive, I shall recommend that your case be reviewed on the basis of meritorious service as exemplified by your willingness to enlist as a civilian scout when needed at a crucial time, and that you be reinstated to your former rank with full back pay.'' A further encouragement rose to his eyes and voice. ''Now that some time has passed, the department is beginning to see your case in a more favorable light. I believe this is worth the undertaking for you, Scott, which is why I sent for you.''

Scott looked down, grateful and moved. "I appreciate your doing this, sir. I do very much. No one else would, I know.''

"It's a second chance, Scott. A slim one, true, but your only chance. I might add that I've dropped an opportune word in your behalf now and then when certain ears were listening.''

"I cannot fully express my gratitude, sir.''

"Not necessary. It's a matter of fairness. One man to another." His tone was not obligatory, instead was almost fatherly.

"What if we don't bring Medicine Shirt in dead or alive?'' Scott asked. "What if the campaign drags on and on without resolution?''

Martin's eyes seemed to spark. "Even Victorio was finally hemmed in, even Geronimo finally tired and surrendered. There will be no *without resolution*, Scott.''

Scott stood and moved to the window and looked out. A sickle moon laid light as pale as water across the parade ground. While he watched, a bugle sounded Tattoo, calling the men to quarters. Figures passed through the dimness. He caught the soft undertone of voices. He turned and asked, "How long would this be for, sir?'' thinking of Holly.

"For the duration of the campaign, whatever it takes. Pay, a hundred twenty-five dollars a month.''

"That's starting pay for a second lieutenant," Scott said, smiling.

"You would furnish your own mount. The Army still provides arms, ammunition, and rations. What weapon are you carrying?''

"A .56-50 Spencer carbine.''

"Wish we still had 'em. You'd be wise to take along a Springfield for the extra ammunition.''

Scott said nothing, still undecided.

"I'm trying to remember your length of service. Wasn't it ten years or more?"

"Twelve, sir."

"It's worth trying to salvage, Scott."

"At times I have missed the service," Scott said, an utter candor in his voice. "I must admit that." Speaking, he could feel both a longing and a pulling back, an uncertainty. His concern went first to Holly and all she meant to him, then his thinking journeyed backward over the years: to Emeline and what they had gone through together, the moving from post to post, the sacrifices; and still, it had been worth the doing. As a farm boy in Indiana, he had dreamed of serving in the cavalry. And, last, there leaped to his mind the smoldering cabin and the father and the son lying in the yard, and the heart-stricken woman and the two little girls. *Enough. Too much. It has to end.*

"Sir," he said, "I accept your offer and thank you for going out of your way to do me this favor."

"You understand it's a gamble, Scott? Even with Medicine Shirt rounded up and no longer a menace, nothing may come of this from higher up."

"Only too well, sir. But it's the only chance I have."

Colonel Martin came around the desk and shook hands. "I'm glad, Scott. Very glad. We may all rise or fall with this campaign, myself included."

"I understand, sir."

Martin stepped back to the desk and when he spoke he sounded more formal. "There will be a brief conference here of officers and civilian scouts before departure in the morning. I want no surprises to impair the success of this mission. I want the air cleared over any personalities before the column leaves. In addition to my written orders, there will be verbal instructions, which, as you know, although they allow more latitude for judgment in the field, equally bring on more make-or-break responsibility.

"You'll know everybody except Second Lieutenant Enoch

Lane, commanding the Indian scouts. You remember the old basis for picking an officer to lead scouts in Indian Territory? 'Must be young and vigorous, of undeniable courage and patience, judgment and disceretion.' Same holds true out here, even more so. Apaches won't follow an officer who's not physically strong, highly courageous, and willing to take the hardships they endure. Rank means nothing to an Apache—it's the man that counts. Lane fills the bill so far. Robust, enthusiastic—even brash at times— ambitious, and actually likes and respects Indians. He's even picking up some of their lingo. I won't say he's patient, but that will come.'' Martin broke off, in his eyes the understanding of an older man. ''As I said, you will know the others. Second Lieutenant Thomas Slocum will be in charge of C Troop, your old outfit. Lieutenant Brad English in charge of L Troop. Captain T. E. Harrigan will be in command of the column.''

Scott froze at the two names, Slocum and Harrigan.

Martin rambled on. ''As you can see, we're short of officers, according to the Tables of Organization for Cavalry, with a first lieutenant instead of a captain in charge of L Troop, and a second lieutenant commanding C Troop. Why? Retirement and illness. The rump-spring geniuses in Washington wouldn't approve if they knew.''

Scott clamped his lips tightly together in spite of himself. He couldn't help it. He felt let down, his peak of moments ago dulled. ''Slocum and Harrigan?'' he asked.

''The past is going to pop up now and then,'' Martin said reasonably. ''You can't avoid it, Scott. Cool down, face it, and go on and do your duty. It won't be easy, but you can handle it. You have to. . . . Now, I believe there's a certain lady who will disown me if she doesn't get to see you. Come on. We'll have a drink and a long overdue visit.''

CHAPTER 8

CROSSING the parade ground in the predawn darkness with Fenton, Scott arrived at a further realization. He had dreaded the meeting since Colonel Martin had named the two officers; in another way he welcomed facing his two old self-seeking adversaries. The scouts passed the guard and entered headquarters. Their arrival interrupted a hum of voices.

"Gentlemen," said Martin without delay, "I believe you all know Mr. Jake Fenton, our chief civilian scout and interpreter. With him is Mr. Scott Dunham, formerly of this regiment, and now enlisted as a civilian scout."

The amber lamplight struck across turning faces and Scott read the frozen surprise of Harrigan and Slocum in particular. He faced them and nodded, feeling his controlled tenseness, also his bitterness.

Harrigan, his austere face tightening, stared at Scott, glanced in surprise at the colonel, then, as if he must, nodded back, meticulously proper. Slocum just stared, slack-jawed, his expression likewise frozen, an angular man with a long face and deep-socketed eyes.

Lieutenant Brad English, gray-bearded and lean, now going on forty and still a file closer after seventeen years of service, amiably put out his hand and said, "Glad to see you again, Scott. You look fine. Brown as an Apache."

"Mighty glad to see you, Brad," Scott said, meaning it. "You look fine yourself."

"I'm Enoch Lane," said the remaining officer, a young man, stepping forth to shake Scott's hand. "Pleased to meet you, sir." He had a blocky build, a quick, positive manner of sizing up a person. He wore a close black beard and his coloring was a rich brown, which seemed to create an impression of strength, and which Scott thought the Chiricahua scouts would esteem. His wide mouth went with the square face and solid jaws and deep brown eyes under heavy dark brows. He smiled easily, at the same time giving Scott a somewhat curious but courteous look.

"Pleased to meet you, Lieutenant," Scott said.

There followed a stretch of silence, an uncomfortable one, Scott thought, which Colonel Martin broke tersely. "I cannot impress upon you too much the importance of your objective, which is to bring Medicine Shirt in alive or to leave him dead in the field. As added proof, if the latter is necessary, I want you to bring in his head, if positive identification is possible. This is not in my written orders to Captain Harrigan, but since it bears equal weight, it is desired. From what the scouts tell us, I'm hoping you will catch up with Medicine Shirt in the southern Black Range or in the lower Mimbres Mountains. . . . First, however, you will proceed to the store and the blockhouse in the Mimbres Valley and relieve the people forted up there, at the same time running a broad sweep up the valley.

"As you know, I am not a member of the Eastern Bleeding Heart Society so far as Apaches are concerned. You are to hunt Medicine Shirt down and destroy him and his followers to the last hostile warrior. As long as he's alive, diehards will flock to him and the war will go on and on. But avoid killing women and children. Take special precautions. I impress that upon you. Prisoners are not to be abused in any way. They will be fed the same as scouts and troopers. You have sufficient rations for three weeks."

He gave the appearance of fixing each man within his gaze. "The hot-pursuit policy agreed on with the governors of Chihuahua and Sonora, which has been off and on for years, apparently is on again. It all depends on the official mood down there, if the Mexican authorities feel they need our help or not. They are extremely sensitive about American troops on their soil, particularly enlisted Apache scouts. I guess you can't blame them, after all they've suffered. But there is a time also for logic and fair play, apart from Mexican politics. You will pursue regardless of national lines. Proceed where you think advisable and necessary." A little sliver of anger worked its way across Martin's face, heightening his ruddy color. "Take the windup of the Victorio campaign in October of '80. Colonel Grierson, up from Fort Davis, posted detachments at the waterholes and Victorio couldn't cross below El Paso, forcing him back into Mexico. Meanwhile, columns from here and Fort Bowie closed the New Mexico and Arizona borders. It was time for the kill. Other columns, including a party of Texas Rangers, crossed into Chihuahua. With pursuit closing in from all sides, Colonel Terrazas hurrying up with a thousand Mexican troopers, Victorio was forced to hole up at Tres Castillos, short of ammunition." Martin smiled thinly. "The great Terrazas then ordered all of us to go home, to leave the sovereign State of Chihuahua, claiming he didn't trust our Apache scouts. A massacre followed. Only a remnant of Victorio's people survived. Those sold into slavery. Our forces were just beaters for the honor of the politician Terrazas."

Martin slapped his right thigh for emphasis. "Well, gentlemen, this time there will be no going home, no turning back if ordered by the authorities there, and you may be. If Medicine Shirt runs to Mexico, you follow. If the Rurales stop you, you will have to use means which are beyond me at the moment to circumvent them and move on to your objective." His voice flattened. "No excuse will be accepted for abandoning Medicine Shirt's trail. If the horses play out, you go on afoot. If you run out of water and rations, you go on as long as your men can stand. Mule meat isn't too unpalatable in a pinch. I repeat: There will be no excuses. Good luck, gentlemen. You are dismissed.''

Grim-faced, the officers saluted and turned about. Harrigan, in the lead, glanced once at Scott and went out, followed by first Slocum, then English and Lane.

The command formed on the parade and Captain Harrigan set the order of march and the column moved out, with the two civilian scouts and Lieutenant Lane's scout company of some twenty Chiricahuas in advance and the pack train under guard in the rear. The scouts, carrying the .45-70-405 Springfield carbine and wearing issue cartridge belts around their bellies, wore red headbands, wool Army blouses, brass identification tags around their necks, breechclouts and moccasins that turned up at the toes, and buckskin uppers that reached almost to their knees.

The advance was going at a fast trot in crisp daylight through the shouldering hills before Santa Rita when a courier cantered up to the point, where Scott rode with Fenton and Lane, and asked for ''Mr. Dunham.''

Scott reined toward the trooper. ''I'm Dunham.''

''Captain Harrigan's respects, Mr. Dunham. He directs you to reconnoiter the left flank, keeping a sharp lookout for sign, maintaining an interval of one mile from the column until we reach Georgetown. Then report to the captain.'' The trooper wheeled away.

''What kind of damn-fool order is that?'' Fenton growled. ''We've already got scouts out.''

Lane's expression was just as curious.

''I think I know what it's all about,'' Scott said, his tone remembering. ''Well, I asked for it, I guess.''

He rode off the trail and began working his way up a steep, rocky slope, and soon passed the last Indian flanker, who paid him a wondering glance. It was a horse-grunting climb to the brow of the first towering hill. Turning, he rode along the top for a time, then dropped down to the other side. Once out of sight of the column, he followed the lower stretches on to Georgetown, thinking, *It's already started. But how was I to know Harrigan would be in command? I'm in for it.* He could almost suspect Colonel Martin of testing him to see whether he could take it or not.

At Georgetown he rode back along the line of march to Harrigan, who was riding with Slocum.

"Morning, Captain," Scott said, keeping his voice ordinary. "Understand I am to report to you."

Harrigan sat erect in the saddle, his large head held high, his profile patrician. That pompous gesture made him, a man of less than medium height, appear taller than he was. His small, stern mouth was set like a slit in a frame of graying side-whiskers that fringed lean cheeks. His gray eyes, harsh and ascetic, regarded Scott coldly, officially. "What did you find, Mr. Dunham?" he asked, his face wooden.

"No Indian sign. Plenty of timber and rocks."

A faint color touched the flesh below Harrigan's eyes. "Mr. Dunham, I trust, based on your experience, that you understand civilian scouts operate under the command of the officer in charge?"

"I understand that. Also that civilian scouts operate more in the role of advisors than as troopers carrying out orders."

"I consider that a quaint interpretation, sir."

"My point is, Captain, that Lieutenant Lane already had Indian scouts working the flanks."

The captain jerked his mount still. "So? Mr. Dunham, I warn you that you are very close to insubordination."

"It was my understanding, Captain, when I signed on that I was under Mr. Fenton's direct command."

"And, may I point out to you, Mr. Dunham, that Mr. Fenton is directly under my command. You will continue to keep the one-mile interval to the left until the command reaches the Mimbres Valley. That is an order. You will follow it or return to the post and be discharged. Is that clear?''

Scott stared at him, his face hardening, his eyes locked on Harrigan's. His anger near tearing loose, Scott had the impulse to tell Harrigan to go to hell. The feeling surged, higher and higher, then slowly subsided, and Scott knew that was what Harrigan wanted: for him to go, to leave the command, that Harrigan was riding him so intolerantly that he would.

''It is,'' Scott managed to say, with effort, with control. ''That is all, Mr. Dunham.''

Scott rode off, his mind opening and closing on when and where this had begun. Harrigan's dislike, Scott knew, had stemmed from their first meeting at Fort Sill when the newly posted captain, from a prominent Pennsylvania family, a West Point graduate and a brevet colonel in the Civil War, had tried to impress Scott. Scott was not impressed and although he had said nothing, but had skirted joining Harrigan's clique, the captain had taken his avoidance as a personal slight not to be forgotten. As time passed, Scott, further, saw Harrigan as an intolerable egotist with high ambition, adept at the tricky game of Army politics.

So much, he mused, for vanity and pettiness, and which the confinement of Army posts aggravated to the point of childishness, swollen far beyond their trivial importance. Not one to forgive, Harrigan had shown no sympathy when Emeline had died in childbirth, and Scott had neither expected nor wished any condolences.

At the Mimbres, the pack train was left under guard and the main column swung up the river. Scott did not rejoin the point until the Chiricahua scouts fanned out on both flanks.

Seeing Fenton's questioning look, Scott said, ''Nothing has changed since the court-martial.''

''You mean to tell me that Harrigan was on the court?''

Scott nodded and could feel the irony of his predicament. ''Might say this is a continuation of the court-martial.''

Fenton exploded a snort of disgust. "Now why would a man carry things that far? Tell me!"

"Couple of reasons. One is Army politics. As a member of the court that made me the scapegoat, the captain doesn't want me along as a reminder of an unfair verdict he'd never admit. Other reason is I've never kowtowed to him or sought his approval like Lieutenant Slocum. In all, he wants to make it rough enough on me so I'll pull out and quit."

"He'd be wise to keep in mind it was the colonel who got you to enlist."

"No officer guards his good name more carefully. He'll stay within official bounds, knows exactly where the line is."

"What if he gives you an order you refuse to carry out?"

"I'll cross that arroyo when I come to it. This campaign is my one chance to get back in the Army, Jake."

"I knew all along what the colonel had in mind for you, but I didn't dare spill the beans. If I had, maybe you'd never've come in."

Scott produced a half smile. "You're a sly old fox, Jake."

"Enough to know I don't like the looks of a campaign where the officer in charge is more concerned with grudges than he is with fightin' Indians."

"Right now all I want to do is get to Holly Warren's as fast as we can."

It seemed an eternity to Scott until the top of the blockhouse materialized through the timber, and next the store and the corral. No smoke. Everything looked untouched. Wagons and buggies still parked about, though fewer than before. That meant some families had left. Scott felt a sudden sweat of relief.

He hailed the store as they rode up. Two armed settlers appeared at the far side of the store and waved. The store door opened and Holly Warren came out on the porch, her face lighting up.

"I take it you're all right here?" Scott asked.

"Haven't seen an Apache since you left," she said. "Some folks started for home this morning."

He dismounted and led his horse to the foot of the steps and said, "There's good news and bad. Geronimo and his band have surrendered. But a medicine man is calling the remaining Chiricahuas together. The Army thinks he's in the southern Black Range or the Mimbres Mountains. These valley raids are part of that gather. Another long Indian war is coming unless he's stopped." Scott had to pause, groping a little. "Holly, to help out, I've enlisted as a civilian scout."

"You mean," she said, "you'll scout till the Indians leave the mountains?"

"No, Holly. For the duration of the campaign. May be weeks—even months."

He watched with pain the wave of disappointment overspreading her face, watched it settle and stay, controlled by her willfulness. She said, her hurting eyes straight upon him, "It just isn't meant to be, is it, Scott?"

"Holly, listen. It doesn't change anything between us. It's also a chance for me to get back in the Army. Colonel Martin thinks so. Besides, we all have to help."

"Oh, yes," she said, her voice taking on a dead, flat tone, "we all have to help. Nobody knows that better than the folks here in the valley."

"I love you. You know that. We'll be married when this is over. What more can I tell you?"

"I'm not sure of anything anymore," she said, and in the dimmest of voices, "I guess it was just something that happened for a little while. Well-meant at the time. Sometimes we expect too much, if we think only of ourselves."

"Holly! Listen to me!"

Scott held his eyes on her as she slowly left the porch and purposely closed the door behind her. He stood unmoving, shaken, until Fenton said softly, "Sorry, Scott. We'd better get back to the command and report. Sorry."

"She thinks I've backed out," Scott said, turning away. "Can't say I blame her, the way it looks. Let's go."

While the afternoon wore away, Scott and Fenton, with Lieutenant Lane and the Chiricahua scouts, picked up fresh sign slanting in northeast from the mountains, joining the day-old horse tracks continuing down the Mimbres.

"Another little war party has heard the call," Fenton said, his jaws working. "This looks like a good-sized band by now. Means the word has gone out to the far rancherías. Ol' Medicine Shirt is packin' 'em in like an arm-wavin' country preacher."

Near dark, the scouts showed excitement and rushed back, pointing and chattering. Fenton listened, then said, "They say the main trail breaks up into smaller trails. I've seen this little dido before. Where they all come together is where Medicine Shirt will be."

They swung back to Captain Harrigan, who listed impatiently. "How do you interpret this, Mr. Fenton?"

"Captain, when a Cheericow band breaks up like this, they have a rendezvous in mind where they'll meet, you can bet on that. There'll be water an' wood there an' likely a cache of food an' clothing. I'd say twenty-five to fifty miles away."

Harrigan regarded Fenton over the tip of his elevated nose. "I am quite aware, Mr. Fenton, that the distances to a rendezvous would vary. What do you propose next, sir?"

"Follow the broadest trail to its end. When it comes in with the others, which it will, that's where Medicine Shirt will be."

"You seem quite positive of that assumption."

"It's an old wrinkle, Captain. They always meet somewhere, though it may be to hell an' yonder."

"What do you estimate is the approximate strength of the band by this time?"

"Thirty or forty, Captain. Some women an' kids."

"We should be able to subdue that many."

"The problem is gettin' at 'em after we spot their ranchería. They'll split up again if we spook 'em."

Harrigan appeared much annoyed. "I find your discussion roundabout and suggestive of what might go wrong. Exactly what do you propose, sir?"

Fenton didn't bat an eye. "For the scouts to push ahead fast. Once we locate Medicine Shirt's ranchería, send word back to bring up the command. Leave the pack train under guard. Hit the ranchería at daybreak."

Harrigan frowned and brushed at some minute particle on the spotless sleeve of his blouse. "I see no other alternative. Very well. We'll bivouac here. Start tracking at first light."

"Mighty fine, Captain."

Walking off, Fenton let out a groan and said aside to Scott, "Reckon I savvy that court-martial better now. This captain goes by the book. What a spruced-up, ramrod-straight son of a buck he's gonna be."

Lane caught up with them. "I've a bottle in my saddle-bag. Would you gentlemen have a drink with me?"

"Lieutenant," said Fenton, "you speak the language of our tribe."

"I can vouch for that," Scott seconded.

They had the drink and afterward picked out a camping place. "Let's build us a big fire," Fenton said. "There's a chill in the air tonight, else I'm gettin' old. Hardtack, bacon, an' coffee will taste like dinner at the Hoffman House."

Scott caught it. "You mean the Timmer House, don't you? The Hoffman House is in New York City."

"I mean the Hoffman House. None other. Had dinner there one time. Fanciest place you ever saw. Waiters with tails on their coats as long as a mountain lion's. Table-cloths that scraped the floor. More forks at a plate than a man would need in a month."

"Remember what was on the menu?"

"If I do say so, I got a good memory. Let's see. Yes, I had Chesapeake Bay oysters on the half shell . . . green turtle *à l'Anglaise* . . . consommé *à la Royale*. . . . fresh Oregon salmon with Sauce Homard, whatever the hell that was . . . potatoes *à la Dauphine* (a fancy name for spuds with some kind of funny-tastin' creamy stuff on 'em) . . . and Westphalia ham, *au Vin de Blanc*. But I tell you, none of that fancy stuff tasted any better than hardtack will tonight soaked in hot bacon grease."

"How in the world can you remember all those dishes, Jake?"

"Same as I do that Edgar Allen fella's poem about the raven. Now, hand me that skillet, Lieutenant."

Soon scores of cottonwood cooking fires sprang up along the banks of the Mimbres. After supper, Scott ambled over to C Troop's bivouac. Here and there a trooper spoke in surprise and shook hands. "Well, if it ain't the lieutenant! How are you, sir?"

"Fine. Glad to see you again, Haines."

"Hey, it's Lieutenant Dunham. He's back!"

"Only as a civilian scout. Colonel Martin talked me into it. Said he needed somebody to tuck you boys in at night and see that you got your tea and toast. . . . Hello, Jenkins. Still putting your corporal chevrons on with hooks and eyes?"

Everybody laughed. "Same old lieutenant. Ain't changed a bit."

"Only been busted once since we left Sill," Jenkins drawled.

"You're doing better. . . . Hello, Parker. The girls still chasing you?"

"More than ever, Lieutenant. More than ever. It plumb aggravates me, it does. No time for solitary drinkin'."

"Tell the lieutenant about the one in Central City the other night that chased you halfway to the post with a butcher knife," a man chimed in.

"Now, boys, you know that was just a case of mistaken identity."

Scott moved on. "Hello, Dawson. Glad to see you out of the guardhouse."

"Thanks, Lieutenant. And I ain't forgettin' the one who used to put me there at Sill."

First Sergeant Ryan said, "Like old times, Lieutenant. We spotted you this morning on the Georgetown road. Hard to believe. It's good to have you with us again."

"For a while, anyway. Damned glad to see you men. Good luck."

An orderly approached. "Mr. Dunham, sir. Captain Harrigan's respects. Report to him immediately."

In the pulsing light of a leaping fire, Captain Harrigan sat stiffly outside his A tent in a chair behind a camp table.

"Evening, Mr. Dunham."

Scott said nothing, wary of what was coming.

"It occurs to me that further clarification of your position as a civilian scout is in order," Harrigan began, crossing his arms. He waited for Scott's response, and when Scott remained silent, he said, "To begin with, I want you to understand that I know what Colonel Martin has in mind for you. Rather, what he hopes for you. Why he enlisted you as a civilian scout."

Scott merely stiffened.

"You seem to be uncharacteristically reticent tonight, Mr. Dunham, unusual for a man who conducted himself so loquaciously as you did flanking questions before the court."

"What else is there for you to say, Captain?"

"Nothing, I suppose, except for me to make myself unequivocally clear. You see, I know that Colonel Martin is angling for your case to be reviewed."

"What's wrong with that?"

"Reinstatement would be tantamount to a reversal of the court's verdict that found you guilty."

"I wasn't guilty and you know it. I was the convenient

scapegoat when three reckless young men, spoiled and contemptuous of any restraint, dashed off on their own."

"That was not the court's finding, sir," Harrigan said, rising from his chair. "Failure to provide an adequate escort at all times. Disobedience of orders, to wit: exceeding the limits of the hunt."

"I believe I can recall the charges and specifications, Captain," Scott said evenly, "without prompting from you."

"I restate them merely to remind you that it is I who will write the field report when this campaign is concluded. And you, sir, will get no blown-up accolades from me."

"What you are saying is, it's a personal animosity you carry. Unchanged since those first days at Fort Sill simply because I, who came up through the ranks, did not defer to you, a West Pointer and officer in the War. Isn't that correct, Captain?"

"Think whatever you wish, Mr. Dunham. Just don't expect me to go along with the colonel's scheme."

"I neither expect nor wish anything from you, Captain. Never have. Let alone friendship or fairness. However, I will point this out to you, something you've overlooked. You need Jake Fenton and you even need me. Why? Because we know this section of the country. You don't. You need us to help make this a successful campaign."

"I have the Chiricahua scouts, Mr. Dunham. It takes an Apache to catch an Apache."

"Arizona Chiricahuas. Hardly comparable around here to the late Victorio's warriors whose favorite haunts were in the Black Range. Fenton and I know this rough country east of the Mimbres River better than the Chiricahuas. Fenton does, particularly, better than I, and from here to the border, even down into Chihuahua. Bringing Medicine Shirt in will mean the promotion you've politicked for so long." He fed mockery into his voice. "The last hostile Apache leader captured or gunned down, Captain Harrigan in command, sir. By the same token, I need that to get a second chance. In short, Captain, we both need Medicine Shirt and he may very well elude us both.''

Before Harrigan could answer, Scott spun on his heel and strode back to camp, seething, his face quivering. He lay awake for a long time, reliving the court-martial and its foreordained verdict. When he did sleep, only a few hours seemed to have passed until Fenton touched him and he blinked at the faint blush of light in the eastern sky.

CHAPTER 9

AT the tiny settlement of San Lorenzo, huddled on the east side of the river, the scouts found both Anglo and Mexican families forted up among the weathered adobes clustered around the small church as if for divine protection. There was no stockade, no semblance of a fort; but Scott remembered that these people, stubborn and valiant, had survived Apache raids long before now.

San Lorenzo's spokesman, a gray-haired Mexican man of some dignity, now excited and greatly relieved, told the scouts, "Yesterday they took horses from one of the outer corrals." He made the sign of the cross. "Mother of God! Only horses they took."

"How many Indians?" Fenton asked him.

"I could not tell, señor, they came so fast and soon gone. Down the river they rode. We shot at them," he added, showing a touch of bravado, as if he must before the military. "But we did not chase after them."

"Good thing you didn't," Fenton said. "That's what they wanted you to do. Likely had a nice little ambush planned for you. I don't think they'll bother you again. They're moving fast. But it would be wise for the downriver families to stay here a few days longer."

Below San Lorenzo the tracks suddenly cut eastward, away into the Mimbres Mountains. For the next three hours the scouts, with Fenton, Scott, and Lane up close, followed the erratic trail through a tangle of canyons and side canyons and over the rocky backbones of ridges. Then abruptly, the tracks bent northward for still higher country. After some time the hoofprints switched around to the southwest, dropping down in the direction of the river miles away.

Fenton threw up a halting hand. "They're doublin' back on us," he said, slightly amused. "I should've known better. But this tells us one thing for sure: they won't gather way up in the Blacks in Victorio's old hangouts."

"About how far do you judge we're behind them?" Lane asked.

"As the crow flies, only eight, ten miles. Not far. In time, hours—some hours. Ol' Medicine Shirt's well mounted at the rate he's goin'."

Lane, with the eagerness of a young officer, asked further, "How do you know this is Medicine Shirt?"

"I don't. Just a hunch. Guess it's the size of the bunch. I figure he's sent some straight ahead to the rendezvous, while others split off like this to confuse us, slow us down, wear us out."

"If the rendezvous isn't in the upper Black Range, where do you figure it is, Mr. Fenton?"

"In the Mimbres Mountains, somewhere."

"That's a great deal of rough country, sir."

"Nothin' ever comes easy in an Indian campaign, Lieutenant. It gets rougher the farther you go, the longer you stay."

They moved on, the hostiles changing directions frequently, these evasions shorter now, always swinging back to the southwest. Sometimes the hostiles chose rocky stretches where the only trace would be where a shod hoof had scraped. Such tactics caused delays while the scouts and the three white men went over the area, sometimes on foot, leading their horses. Late in the afternoon they had lost the trail again below a ridge and could not pick it up as expected. Fenton studied the surroundings for a long while, then rode ahead, while Scott and Lane cut a circle.

About a hundred yards on as Fenton was crossing a sandy wash, he gave the signal to halt.

Scott and Lane rode over and Fenton pointed down and said, "See those tracks? That horse's front feet turn in. He's pigeon-toed. I've noticed it off an' on all day. It's as good as a street sign. Come on."

At dusk the trail changed once more, striking southeast into the Mimbres Mountains. Fenton drew rein. "Lieutenant," he said, speaking to Lane, "better send word back to the captain. Tell him we think the ranchería is between here an' Cooke's Peak, for him to continue on down the river tomorrow in easy stages. We'll send a courier back when we spot something."

Lane scribbled a note in his order book and, after some signs and a few words, handed it to a lean Chiricahua, who threw himself on his horse and heeled rapidly off into the thickening light.

The scouts found water by digging in the bed of a dry creek and made camp. "Enjoy your cookin' fires tonight," Fenton said. "Likely be none tomorrow night." He glanced at Scott. "Know about where you are, Lieutenant?"

Scott closed his eyes for a moment. "Southeast of San Lorenzo. Northwest of Black Mountain."

Fenton grunted a laugh. "I see you haven't forgotten this country south of the Black Range, like we went over in '79 an' '80."

"Think we'll catch up tomorrow, maybe?"

Fenton looked up at the evening sky. "Maybe tomorrow. Maybe next day, the day after. Time's not that important. That's one thing I've learned out here: patience. If ol' Medicine Shirt was headed down into the Floridas or the Hatchets, he'd of been long gone down the river by now. He's up here somewhere."

"You keep saying he's old. How do you know that?"

"Ever hear of a wise man who wasn't old? I'm goin' on what the scouts say. He's seen seventy winters or more. A little man. Kinda shriveled up. Eyes like knives. Big talker. They say he can still ride horseback all day. In his younger days, he traveled the war trail into Mexico. Was wounded. Left him with a limp. After that, he became a shaman. Not unlike a fella I once knew back home who failed at farmin' an' storekeepin'. Failed at just about everything before he took up preachin'. Turned out to be right good at it, too. A mighty shouter an' arm waver.''

A weary hush settled over the bivouac after supper. Lane placed the first night sentries. The other Apaches smoked and gambled. Scott rested. Holly took possession of his mind and what she must think of his broken promise: We'll go to Georgetown and be married. She didn't believe him anymore. Why should she, after giving all of her sweet self and told that he loved her, only to have him leave her. If he just hadn't gone off to his cabin that day, they could have been married in Georgetown and returned the same day. Sometimes a man cut life too fine, pushed too fast, wanted everything in neat order . . . like things . . . when all that was needed was time, just a little time. . . . He could chuck everything and go back; just ride out of here. But, of course, he could not. He had given his word and this was his lone chance for reinstatement. From here on there would be no respite for second thoughts as the campaign advanced; for that he was almost thankful.

The bivouac fell quieter yet, to an occasional rustling. Fenton rose and strolled over to the scouts and slacked down, and shortly Scott caught his low, patient voice mingling with the heavier Apache tones.

Tomorrow, Scott thought. *He's thinking about tomorrow.*

A while later Fenton drifted back and squatted down beside him. "What do the scouts say?" Scott asked.

"They say if Medicine Shirt gets a little jumpy, he's liable to strike out for Mexico anytime."

"You had a long talk with 'em."

"I did. They figured the war was over when Geronimo came in. Now it goes on with Medicine Shirt. They're tired of war. They're afraid there won't be any Chiricahuas left if the government keeps haulin' them off to the hot country, which is what they call Florida. Truth is, this is already the end of the Cheericows. It's sad. They're brave people.''

''Where did you learn their language?''

''I'm not fluent at it, if that's what you mean. I'm no orator. But along with signs, I can carry on a conversation. Picked it up some years back at San Carlos, on the reservation, when I first came out here. Clerked in the agent's store there. Visited and chatted with the Indians. Other tribes there besides the Cheericows: Tontos, White Mountain, Yavapais, Yumas, Mohaves. That was the trouble. They didn't get along. Like cats an' dogs in a barrel. . . . You know, the 'Paches are very sociable people. They like to visit, if they know you an' trust you. I learned to be a listener. You never interrupt an Indian when he's talkin'. It's bad manners. . . . Too, I never cheated them, but I had many chances. . . . The agent was a political appointee who was outspoken in his contempt for all Indians, and yet he claimed to be mighty religious. . . . Later on I found out how religious he was and why he was gone most of the time. He was busy sellin' supplies an' clothing intended for San Carlos to traders in Globe an' Solomonville. That's when I quit an' went to scoutin' for the Army, mainly because I could handle the lingo. . . . Well, think I'll turn in, Lieutenant. Gonna be a long day.''

The scouts were working slower today, more cautiously, since the signs indicated the hostiles were closer than yesterday. Neither, Scott noticed, had the band changed directions such as the day before. Perhaps they thought they had eluded any pursuit. Their tracks, up and down, twisting around and back as the land pitched and fell, continued in a general southeasterly direction, always deeper into rougher country, always toward visible Cooke's Peak, the principal landmark hereabouts, and still many miles away, its jagged summit hooked into the bluest of skies.

At ten o'clock Fenton called a halt and said, "The scouts figure maybe Medicine Shirt will go into camp by late today. He's in no hurry. Acts like he's waitin' for somebody. We'll hold up for a little look-see."

Tying their mounts, Scott and Fenton climbed a piñon-studded peak and flattened out to observe the country, using Fenton's field glasses. For a long time they watched. Nothing moved in the timbered brokenness except omnipresent crows, a red-tailed hawk soaring, hunting, diving, or a *cr-r-rucking* raven, its guttural voice scolding.

"You could hide a whole tribe off there and not see a flicker," Scott said.

"We'll just keep on after ol' pigeon-toe," Fenton said, rising. He merely shook his head at Lane when they came down, mounted, and rode on, a patient intentness about him.

Midday heat squeezed the canyons and boulderstrewn washes. The stumbling racket of a tired horse sounded alarmingly loud. The lead scouts moved with increased caution, for this was prime ambush country, and Scott, likewise, found himself constantly watching the brush-covered high places. Coming to a deep wash twisting down from the heights, Fenton halted and told Lane, "I don't like this, Lieutenant. Let's send a couple of scouts on foot up the right side to see what's ahead of us. We're not far from the top of the next ridge. I'll go along."

"You stay. I'll go," Scott said, and swung down to hand the reins to Fenton.

"I don't ask anybody to go where I won't," Fenton said, balking.

"Main thing is for these scouts to understand a White Eye takes the same chances they do. Isn't that it?"

"It is, but . . ."

"Damn it, Jake. Take these reins." Scott was smiling.

"How's the colonel gonna write me up in dispatches if I don't do something?"

"You wouldn't pull rank on me, would you?"

Lane was already motioning two scouts out of the company, a corporal and a private, and before Fenton could say more, Scott had grabbed his carbine and joined them.

The Apaches started up the steep wall of the wash, their movements quick and catlike. Scott, less agile, heaved after them, determined to keep up. Reaching the top, the scouts, with scarcely a glance for the white man, became stalkers, moving through a tangle of stubby piñons and oaks. Scott, nearby, between them, caught their close drift, a compound of sweat, woodsmoke, and tobacco.

After a time, the timber thinned and Scott saw that the ridge was clear. So was the deep, snaking wash and its broken slopes, on to where the wash made its downward slash from the ridge.

The corporal grinned at Scott, showing white, even teeth, and shook his head a bit disdainfully, his meaning clear: "I told you so, White Eye. Medicine Shirt's not here." He frowned and pointed onward, that meaning also clear: "There. Farther on."

Nodding agreement, Scott stepped to the edge of the ridge and waved the company ahead.

With the sun moving on to afternoon, the tracks dropped down across a meadow, and there a scout, riding in advance, suddenly checked and waved and pointed to the ground.

Closing in with the others, Scott saw a line of hoof marks angling in from the west to the main trail.

"Another little bunch come in to join ol' Medicine Shirt's congregation," Fenton said.

"How many?" Lane asked.

"Eight or ten, which should run the count to fifty or so."

"Approximately how many of those would you estimate are warriors?"

"Twenty or so. I'd figure a third."

"How do you arrive at that figure, sir?"

For an instant Fenton looked annoyed, but only for that briefness. With his usual patience, he said, "One warrior to one woman. As for kids, 'Paches don't have big families. Now, a man can have more than one wife. They's no taboo against it. It depends on how many he can support. I've heard of some men with four wives." He rolled his eyes roguishly. "Happened they were young."

"Four!" Lane exclaimed and grinned. "How would he keep the peace?"

"Just like a white man. Put each one in a separate house or wickiup."

They rode on. The sun reached midafternoon without change on the trail. Not long afterward Fenton stopped beside the tracks and eased down from his horse and nudged something with the toe of his boot.

"Looks like moss," Scott said.

"Moss," Fenton repeated, and threw Scott a waiting look of inquiry, and when Scott said nothing, Fenton said, "I can see you've been gone from 'Pache country for a spell. You've plumb forgot. What this is is more than just moss. It's packin' from a cradleboard to absorb a baby's waste."

Scott nodded, lips pursed.

Fenton, gazing around reflectively, said, "This tells me they passed here less than two hours ago. But you don't rush in when you're this close. Medicine Shirt's the main game. They'll be watchin' their back trail."

Upon that, he slowed the pursuit to a walk, often stopping to look through the field glasses. The tracks led along the foot of a mountain. Scott and Fenton were riding with Lane, while a couple of scouts worked the trail a short distance beyond, when something glinted across on another mountain.

Both Scott and Fenton jerked around.

The glint shone again, now a series of flashes, then ceased.

"What was that?" Lane called. "Sun on a crow's wing?"

"Don't think so," Fenton said, still watching. "Because it flashed four or five times. How'd it look to you, Scott?"

"I think it was a mirror. Those quick flashes. Not just one."

Fenton turned to Lane and slapped the pommel of his saddle. "Lieutenant, that's Medicine Shirt up there. He's reached the rendezvous. Made camp. Has to be. He's tellin' the others to come on, to hurry. . . . Look! He's signalin' again."

"Think he's spotted us?" Lane asked, watching the vibratory flashes.

"No. Else he wouldn't be fool enough to give away his location. Let's pull back, take cover. More of the band will be comin' in before long. Later on, we'll have us an eyeball look-see up there."

"If you're sure that's Medicine Shirt up there, I'll send a courier back to Captain Harrigan."

"I'm as sure as a man can be trailin' Cheericows. This will give the captain all day tomorrow to bring up the outfit." As Lane took out his order book, Fenton, scratching his bearded jaw, said, "Better tell him not to bring up the pack train."

"Why?" Lane asked.

Damn green lieutenants who had to question the obvious!
Scott could see that thought take hold of Fenton; in another moment the scout was saying, with consideration, "A pack train is noisy as hell an' slows the march."

"I'll suggest that," Lane said, beginning to write.

"Make it stronger than that."

Lane glanced up, his young, sunburned face a print of Army propriety. "I'd better not go stronger than that, sir. Captain Harrigan is very touchy."

"So I've heard. Then detail for him that this country is

rougher than a cob, which it is, and the pack train will only slow him down, which it will. The idea is to hit the ranchería at dawn. To do that, the outfit will have to slip in here unobserved and as quiet as a second-story burglar, which a pack train is not. I don't know how else to put it, Lieutenant.''

After the courier left, they turned back into the ponderosa pines below the mountain, moved off the trail into a narrow canyon, unsaddled, and set out sentries and picketed the horses. A scout found a good spring at the base of a cliff. When afternoon shadows lengthened, Fenton nodded at Scott and they made their way back to the trail at the foot of the mountain. Off trail, under cover in a thicket of oaks, they hunkered down to watch.

The afternoon slipped into early evening. Scott was getting restless. Still, Fenton waited. He seemed to be dozing, hat over his face.

Just before dark, Scott heard the *tick* of a shod hoof on rock below them. Fenton pushed back his hat and sat up. Within minutes a mounted Apache became visible on the trail, suggestive of a copper image as he halted his bay horse and scanned the forest. Another horseman appeared, behind him two women and three children astride horses. This man rode up to the first warrior and said something. The lead rider pointed in the direction of the mountain whence Scott had seen the mirror flashes. At that, the two heeled their horses forward and the little group passed, with a tired, barely audible, murmur from the women and children.

Scott rose and stretched, only to feel Fenton's arresting hand on his arm. ''Wait,'' Fenton whispered. He was turned downtrail, head cocked.

Crouching, Scott picked up the oncoming shuffle of hooves from below. In moments figures shaped on the trail, a knot of horsemen. A pause and they came on at a trot, as if eager to catch up with the first bunch. Scott counted four warriors, three women, one stripling boy, and two small children as they passed.

After a brief wait, Fenton said, "Let's follow 'em up there."

"Beats feeling our way up that mountain in the dark."

They left the thicket and followed at a walk, the blending smells of dust and horse sweat still strong. At times they could see the bobbing figures ahead. At times they paused to listen behind them. The light through the lofty ponderosas grew dimmer and the late evening air sent a faint chill through Scott. Under his boots the thick layers of pine needles were as soft as a thick carpet, his steps soundless.

The trail wound around the foot of the mountain, circling until the Apaches halted. Their muted voices carried back, as if discussing the way before they went on. After a while, they turned up the talus slope of a long, narrow ridge. The trail was steep, Scott saw. A horse would stumble and dislodge rocks or start a trickle of gravel that would come sliding down. Scott judged half an hour had passed before the two parties gained the timber-studded top. From there the going was much easier. At this height the fading light still lingered. Now, in the early darkness, Scott sighted the eyes of campfires. A host of voices rose in greeting as the incoming Apaches arrived. Slipping nearer, Scott sniffed the odor of cooking meat that made his mouth juices run.

Fenton put out a detaining hand. "Close enough," he breathed. "Let's don't press our luck."

He did not speak again until they reached the foot of the ridge. "It will take some caution gettin' two troops up there afoot without wakin' up the dead, but we've done it before. The ridge is the easiest approach. One little item bothers me, however. No Cheericow picks a campsite unless there's a back door to it. They'll scatter like a covey of quail if we come stumblin' up the trail."

That night in the cold bivouac, after a supper of hardtack and springwater, Lieutenant Lane sat down beside Scott and hesitantly spoke, "Sir, I'm not one to intrude. But in addition to what Colonel Martin told us briefly at headquarters, that you had formerly served with the regiment, Mr. Fenton tells me that you were shamefully judged at the court-martial."

Scott's chuckle was dry. "That's my opinion. I'm also prejudiced."

"I understand you were blamed for something beyond your control?"

"I was the ranking officer in charge of the escort. As you know by now, in the Army the officer in charge carries the responsibility. There has to be somebody to come back to, to lay it on. That's the way it is."

Lane was silent after that. Then, "I wonder sometimes if I was wise to volunteer for this assignment with the scouts."

"Maybe you haven't given it enough time. For two years I was in charge of the Comanche and Kiowa scouts at Fort Sill."

"Oh, you were!" Lane sounded surprised. "Did you like it?"

"It was rough at first. I hated it, till my feelings toward them began to change. I should say my understanding. That they were human beings, that their entire way of life had been torn up with the slaughter of the buffalo. That we had a common ground man to man. For sure, Lane, it beats being saddled with the duties of post engineer, which inevitably falls on the newest junior officer. Removing tons of manure and post garbage, or building latrines, or as signal officer in charge of erecting telegraph poles and stringing wire. Worse yet, you could be acting assistant quartermaster, or directing the woodcutting detail. Frankly, the adventure of commanding the scouts appealed to me. To experience some of the wild life that's fast disappearing from the West."

"That's exactly how I feel, sir."

"Colonel Martin is high on you, Lane. He commended you. Says you're even learning the language. Don't be discouraged."

"That makes me feel better." His careful propriety returned. "Captain Harrigan doesn't see the scouts as I do. He says I need to shape 'em up, as he terms it. Make 'em more orderly. Sometimes they forget to salute, and their blouses are always unbuttoned."

"They're warriors first, troopers second. But they're paid to be scouts and that's what they do better than troopers. Jake Fenton is the only white man I know who can come close to matching them. Whatever you do, don't humiliate them, particularly in front of other scouts or troopers. They're proud people. They won't take tongue-lashing. You have to show them by example in the field. Then they'll go to hell for you."

"Thank you, sir. I'll remember that." Once again he seemed reluctant and uncertain. "Sir, is it true that Captain Harrigan was on your court?"

"He was."

"That places you in an uncomfortable position, does it not?"

"It does."

"Well, I want you to know that I hope all goes well for you and that someday you will return reinstated to the regiment. It's a pleasure to serve with you." He rose and held out his hand.

"Thank you, Lane," Scott said, warmed, rising to take Lane's hand.

"Good night, sir. I bivouac with the scouts."

"Good night, Lieutenant, and good luck."

CHAPTER 10

THE morning dragged by uneventfully. No more mirror flashes signaled the location of Medicine Shirt's ranchería. No more straggling parties of Chiricahuas passed on the trail to the towering mountain.

Well into the afternoon, the racket of hooves sounded below, and Scott, posted with Fenton and Lane and the scouts above the trail, saw a lone government scout leading the advance. Between the two troops, guidons flying, rode Captain Harrigan and Second Lieutenant Slocum. Behind the last troop of Lieutenant Brad English plodded the head-nodding pack train of mules.

"Be damned if he didn't bring the whole caboodle," Fenton snorted.

"The captain likes to march with all accouterments," Lane said lamely. "In case you wondered, Mr. Fenton, I did recommend that the pack train be left on the Mimbres."

"Let's get 'em off the trail and into the canyon before they alert every Cheericow from here to the border," Fenton flared. "Next thing y'know he'll have the bugler blowin' Retreat this evening." Striding down the trail, making no effort to hide his disgust, he waved the column toward the canyon.

"What damnable country for cavalry," Harrigan said, red of face, as the command filed past and Lane and Fenton, Scott behind them, waited to report. "I trust that you've found a suitable bivouac, Mr. Lane?"

"In a side canyon, sir, as best as conditions warrant. We're too close to the ranchería for fires, but there's sufficient water."

Harrigan stiffened slightly. "I believe, Mr. Lane, that as commanding officer I understand the necessity of no campfires when in the vicinity of the enemy."

"Of course, sir."

"Now, I should like a full verbal report, in addition to what was contained in your flied report of yesterday."

Nodding, Lane summarized the situation concisely, adding the passing of the two small parties of Chiricahuas, and Fenton and Scott following them undetected to the ranchería.

"Very well," Harrigan said in a dismissing tone. "Before evening have a complete written report in the hands of Lieutenant Slocum, Acting Adjutant." He tilted his head back, which Scott remembered as the characteristic stance of the man, and slanted an eye at Fenton. "Mr. Fenton, how do you propose that we attack the ranchería?"

"The way the lieutenant has said, Captain—up the ridge. It's the easiest way, the way Medicine Shirt and the smaller parties took."

"From Mr. Lane's report, that is a considerable distance. Is there a shorter approach?"

"No, Captain. You go around the mountain"—Fenton made a circular gesture—"to the ridge. The trail up the ridge is steep, but it leads straight to the ranchería."

"Did you reconnoiter farther along the base of the ridge?"

"We did not. We's right on the heels of the last bunch of hostiles, because we knew they'd lead us to the camp. Besides, it was gettin' dark."

"In the future, Mr. Fenton, I recommend that you reconnoiter more thoroughly."

"That's always a good idy, Captain, when you can."

"*Always*, Mr. Fenton. *Always*." Head high, Harrigan rode past, and Fenton's only visible reaction was to reach thoughtfully for his plug of tobacco.

In the rocky canyon, while Scott watched his old C Troop set up camp and establish picket lines, a deep sense of isolation from these men he knew so well came upon him. He listened to their grumbling about the hardtack supper without hot coffee or bacon and recognized the true signs: A good trooper always grumbled during a campaign, because grumbling was an outlet. Later, he saw the men of both troops detailed for guard duty assemble for Guard Mount. Meanwhile, he chewed his own hardbread and drank springwater, bivouacked with Fenton near Lane and the scouts.

At sundown an orderly strode up, announced, "Captain Harrigan's respects. All officers and civilian scouts report at once for a staff conference," and left at quick step.

Fenton yawned and stretched himself. Lane, who had finished his written report and delivered it only ten minutes previously, gave an involuntary jerk.

"They always do this the evening before," the scout said languidly, jaws moving on his quid.

It was somewhat like an old melodrama, played over and over, Scott thought as the three of them answered the summons. The captain was seated behind his camp table outside his tent. Slocum close at hand, ready to defer. Lieutenant English tiredly awaiting any new whims. Lane snapped a salute which Harrigan returned with a flip of his hand.

"Gentlemen," he greeted them, "at ease," his gray gaze flicking over the last three arrivals. "There are certain pertinent details yet to be worked out. First, Mr. Fenton, how long will it take us to reach the foot of the ridge, going at a steady rate of march?"

Fenton chewed for a moment or two. "I'd say about an hour."

Irritation flecked the gray eyes. "I do not want *about*, Mr. Fenton. I want the precise time as near as you can determine."

"Same, Captain. An hour."

"So. Now, the ridge. How long will it require to reach the top and be ready to form?"

"Twenty minutes."

"Next, what is the distance from the top of the ridge to the ranchería?"

"Three hundred fifty yards is as close as I can call it, Captain."

"When is first light?"

"Five-thirty."

"Then silent reveille will be at three-thirty. The horse guards will wake up the troopers. No fires. Breakfast on hardtack and water. The command will march at four o'clock, with C Troop in advance. I want us to be in position, ready, some minutes before daybreak."

"Captain," Fenton broke in, raising a hand, "on a night march like this, with only this sickle moon, there's always the chance somebody will wander out of line an' get lost. I figure we'd better march at three forty-five to give us time to gather up any stragglers."

"Very well, Mr. Fenton. Reveille will be at three-fifteen. The march begins at three forty-five. Let's synchronize our watches, gentlemen." He drew a thick, silver-cased watch, eyed it, and said, "I have six thirty-four," and after the officers and Fenton had set theirs accordingly, he said, "That is all, gentlemen. You're dismissed." Rising, he acknowledged their salutes, started to enter the tent, and turning about said further, "Upon reaching the crest of the ridge, C Troop will form a front on the left, L Troop on the right, with the scouts in the center. I myself will lead the advance with the scouts."

Scott and Fenton walked back to their camp and the picketed horses. "We now come to the time," Fenton said, "when the success of an entire campaign hangs on some heavy-footed cavalryman. If he stumbles or makes a racket. If some recruit's carbine goes off. It can be that close. Just one mistake."

One moment there was evening's filtered light bathing

the bivouac. Within seconds the sun vanished behind the canyon's timbered crest and the light was dying fast. As if on signal, Fenton rolled in his blanket and was soon snoring.

Scott followed suit. On a campaign, you took your sleep when you could get it.

The canyon was as black as the mouth of a cave when first Scott sat up, waking to the stirrings of the command, the coughs, the grunted undertones of sleepy troopers, the creak of leather, the stampings as men rose to their feet. He pulled his coat tighter against the chill of the scented mountain air.

They formed vaguely in a column of twos, the sergeants busy here and there, talking them into line. Lane drew up the scouts in front. Harrigan's voice, formal and precise, cut through the medley of rustlings, and the march began.

Off they started in route step, creating a steady shuffling, and then a scuffling and clumping as boots struck rocks and gravel. They were out of the canyon and well on the trail when Scott heard Fenton tell Lane, "Lieutenant, pass word back for the boys to pick up their feet. They sound like a herd of buffalo." Lane did so and the muttered caution was passed along the formless column. After that the sounds merged into a kind of cadence, Scott thought, broken at intervals when a trooper stumbled. The scouts led the way down into a rocky wash and the following troop, Slocum's, unprepared for the sudden drop, floundered and broke ranks, some men falling, so noisy that Fenton told Lane to send back a halt order. Again word was passed and the command closed up and cleared the wash with less confusion.

Now, on the pine-needled floor of the forest, the two troops moved more quietly. They marched for what, to Scott, seemed a long time without delay, the scouts literally feeling their way at times, though he knew hardly thirty minutes had passed. Moments later voices rose behind him and a halt order came, and Slocum was saying,

"Hold up, Lane. Some L troopers have wandered off the trail."

"Come on, Scott," Fenton said. "We'd better get back there."

They eased along the halted column, found the gap between the two troops, and came to a blur of men.

"Lieutenant English," Scott said softly, "it's Dunham and Mr. Fenton. Which way'd they go?"

English's voice, both angry and concerned, replied, "Don't know. It's the last squad. Been lagging all night. Went back to close 'em up and they weren't there. We looked on both sides the trail. Afraid to call out."

"They wouldn't go up the mountain," Fenton said. "Too rough. Probably wandered off to their left. Easier going. They's a dry creek bed that way. They'll come to that, maybe turn back. We'll take a look."

They had covered but a short distance when Fenton bumped into a tree, cursed eloquently, and went on. Every few yards they stopped to listen. All Scott heard was the rustling voice of the wind high up in the pines. Now they groped through tangles of oak brush. After a time Scott felt the crumbling bank of the creek under his boots, below him the grayish smear of the rocky stream bed. He halted at once, and as he did, dimly, he heard voices to his left. "There they are, Jake," he said.

They struck off along the bank of the creek. A little way and Scott called softly, "Hey, boys. Over here."

Boots beat a rapid rush through brush and over rocks toward the scouts. Figures jutted out before them and a winded voice asked, "Where th' hell are we?"

"About a hundred yards off the trail," Scott told them. "Follow us."

The troopers straggling in ignited English's furious voice. "Now, by God, maybe you Dumbjohns will stay closed up. Get in line!"

The column lurched forward again, close to twenty minutes lost, Scott figured. Soon after there was another halt while the scouts felt out the trail across a wash. Again the column stumbled on.

Harrigan sent Slocum to summon Fenton and Scott. "How far are we from the ridge, Mr. Fenton?"

"Not far."

"What does that mean in terms of time?" Harrigan's voice carried a distinct rasp.

"Means we'll have you on top of the ridge, ready to form, by daylight."

"Before daylight, Mr. Fenton! Before daylight!"

Time seemed fixed to Scott, as if they marched forever through the blackness of the ponderosa forest, in silence, broken when a trooper stumbled or a hushed close-up order was heard. It was like that until the high bulk of the ridge loomed dimly above them, outlined in the frail glow of the crescent-shaped moon.

Fenton studied the ridge while the column drew up and halted. He said to Lane, "Lieutenant, pass the word to form single file."

The low-pitched command was passed, after it a shuffling and jostling while the troopers changed from a column of twos.

When all was quiet, Fenton said, "Up we go," and led off, Scott behind him. The trail rose abruptly. At the same time Scott heard the beginning crunch of boots on gravel, of muffled coughs and heavy stumblings, each sound seeming overloud. Fenton walked faster. Now the trail turned and rose even steeper, a turn that Scott remembered.

Not many minutes later, the trail broadened and Scott and Fenton were nearing the crest with Lane and the Apache scouts. It was then it happened, throbbing across the night. A braying, loud and hoarse from below, as piercing in the stillness as a bugler blowing reveille.

Fenton whirled at the noise, snarling, "That goddamned pack train—I knew it!"

Scott said, fast, "We'll have to attack at once, Jake. Else all this for nothing."

Fenton was already rushing back where Harrigan marched at the head of C Troop. Scott, on his heels, heard, "Captain—that mule just gave us away. Better form a front—hit the ranchería fast as we can."

"Don't the hostiles have mules, Mr. Fenton?" Harrigan replied without undue alarm. "Couldn't the mule belong to another band that didn't get in?"

"That close—they'd be in," Fenton snapped. "That mule's in our pack train, Captain. We better get a move on if you want Medicine Shirt for breakfast."

Harrigan didn't stir for an instant. Then he was striding up the trail and ordering Slocum to form the front.

Light was breaking as the troopers lined up and moved forward in quick time, the scouts in the center, Harrigan striding between Fenton and Lane, Colt .45 in hand.

A disturbance, just audible at first, now suddenly growing to distinctness, sounded in the ranchería. Voices. Shouts. Horses running.

"Captain," Fenton said, "they're breakin' camp—gettin' away."

"At the double quick step, Mr. Slocum!" Harrigan ordered and broke into a jogging run. The command rushed forward faster.

There was yet two thirds of the distance to go, Scott figured, seeing low-burning campfires and hurrying figures, shadowy against the firelight. He heard a great shout. After that, he saw the figures no more and a hush seemed to settle over the ranchería.

"Give the order to halt and fire, Mr. Slocum."

Slocum's voice rose. Carbines rattled. The smell of gunpowder came bitter. There was no answering fire.

"Fire again, Mr. Slocum. Then charge the camp."

That volley, and the troopers charged with yells, the scouts joining them with screeching whoops, and swept on toward the encampment. A camp strangely devoid of Apaches, Scott began to see. Only a few loose horses, some brush wickiups, campfires, and hastily abandoned gear met his eyes. Everybody was charging through the place, heads swiveling for nonexistent hostiles.

Hearing the clatter of horses running over rocks, Scott ran to the far end of the ranchería. But the racket died before he got there. Looking down, he saw a trail twisting away, lost in the pines and brush. Nothing moved. Just a film of dust still hanging over the trail. A knowing reached him: Medicine Shirt's back door. This an old camping place, used many times. Jake was right.

Hacking for wind, he flung around at a trooper's shout. A fire burned behind a clump of oaks. An Indian man hung over the fire, suspended by his wrists from an oak limb. Apparently, he had managed to kick the fire apart.

The trooper stared, open-mouthed. Scott, on impulse, ran over and cut the man down and dragged him away from the fire. The Indian lay there, blinking dully, in shock.

"We've got us a captive!" Scott yelled at Fenton and Lane running up. "He was hanging over the fire."

The captive stared at Scott, surprise edging through his dullness. He sat up, rubbing his arms, showing mixed relief and fear, his eyes fixed on the white men.

Harrigan arrived on the run. "What do we have here, Mr. Fenton? I heard no shots."

"A captive, Captain. He was hangin' over the fire. Mr. Dunham cut him down."

"Hanging over the fire? You mean his own people were torturing him?"

"More than torture. I'd say it was an execution. This Cheericow has done somethin' mighty bad for that."

Harrigan swung about, head high, surveying the abandoned camp, his exasperation erupting. "Well, question him, man! Find out something. After all this careful planning and we bag just one damned Indian."

Fenton, a study of forbearance, drawled, "Trouble was, Captain, we tipped our hand," and not mentioning the mule, not needing to, he pulled the stopper from his canteen and held it out to the Apache, who drank thirstily, thankfully, handed the canteen back, and stood up, wiping his dripping mouth with the back of his left hand.

He was tall for an Apache, six feet or more. He had a broad, smooth face of clear bronze and dark, bright eyes and evenly formed features. A straight, proud nose. His mouth, full and expressive, lacked the harshness of many Apache warriors. He smiled frequently, glad to be alive, revealing strong, even teeth. There was, Scott discerned, an earnestness about him. A big man, a handsome young man in his twenties, wearing a dirty calico shirt, belted around the waist, and a white man's dirty gray pantaloons, such as sold at a trader's store, stuffed inside the buckskin uppers of his moccasins, made with the round toe-pieces distinctive of the Chiricahuas.

Fenton ceremoniously gave him a plug of tobacco and motioned for him to sit down. The captive obeyed and Fenton spoke in unhurried Apache and made slow, graceful signs. The Apache seemed to answer in the same conversational way, surprised and gratified to find a white man who spoke his tongue. When he had finished, Fenton turned to Harrigan and said, "He says his name is Antone and he thanks us for saving his life. He says although he's been on the warpath many times, and has stolen many horses and mules in Mexico, he's really peaceful by nature. Says he's never killed a white man."

"I'm hardly fool enough to believe that," Harrigan retorted. "He's afraid of what we might do to him, and nothing I'd like better than to have him shot. Ask him why he was being burned alive. That puzzles me, also fascinates me."

Replying to Fenton's questions, Antone was not above boasting, Scott sensed, watching the play of emotions across the proud face, or affecting hurt or pretending innocence. But who wouldn't pretend if he feared for his life? Scott found his sympathy growing for the personable captive.

"Being a Chiricahua warrior, he's embarrassed to tell this, he says," Fenton interpreted, hiding a grin. "He says women have always caused him trouble. Because he is young and brave, the young girls and widows bring him food and mend his clothes and while gathering mescal in the spring try to get him to go to the bushes with them. That's what happened this time. He says he and a woman who is his cousin were caught in the act in the bushes. Her husband is dead, killed at Antelope's Water by soldiers— that's a water hole between the south end of the Graham Mountains and the Dos Cabezas Mountains."

"Enough irrelevant details, Mr. Fenton," Harrigan broke in. "Why was he being burned alive?"

"Even though the woman was willing," Fenton continued, unruffled, "that is taboo among the Cheericows with a relative. It's also one mark of a witch. So Medicine Shirt and other elders held a kind of trial and decided Antone was a witch, and the way the Cheericows execute witches is burning them alive. They talked about this a long time before they strung 'im up. That's why the camp was up and alert when they heard the mule. Antone hadn't been hangin' long when we attacked."

Antone said something, a tone of urgency in his voice, and Fenton spoke to him and listened, then explained, "He says he is tired of war and afraid his people will die out if the war goes on. He's never followed Geronimo."

"If he's so against war, why was he with Medicine Shirt?" Harrigan demanded. "The man is an evident liar. Anything to save his skin."

Fenton spoke to the Apache again and listened to his reply. "He says he came with the band because of the woman, who is older and wiser and influenced him. He has no family of his own. His parents are dead. His wife, a San Carlos girl, died some years ago." Fenton studied a moment before he went on. "The incest thing is against the Cheericow way, true. But it strikes me that was just a handy excuse for ol' Medicine Shirt. Main reason he wanted Antone out of the way was because he's opposed to carryin' on the war."

"Mr. Fenton," Harrigan said curtly, "I believe we've wasted enough time delving into the social mores of the Chiricahuas as they pertain to the captive, who is obviously a misfit, if not a witch. Question is, what do we do with him?"

"Captain," said Scott, breaking in, "I'd like to ask a question. Does Antone know where Medicine Shirt is headed now?"

Without waiting for Harrigan's permission, Fenton spoke to Antone, who appeared to organize his thoughts before he answered, emphasizing his words with vigorous motions southward. He ended shrugging. "He says Medicine Shirt has talked about a stronghold in Chihuahua," Fenton said, "where no Mexicans or White Eyes could find him, it's so remote. Medicine Shirt is headed there now."

"Why not enlist Antone as a scout and have him lead us there?" Scott suggested.

"There's one drawback," Fenton replied. "Antone has never been there."

"Even so, he can follow a trail, and he should know the springs from here to the border."

"Captain," Fenton asked, as eager as Scott, "what do you say?"

Harrigan stood erect, arms folded, mouth stern, his eyes reflecting that habitual coldness, reserving judgment. Scott thought he was going to refuse.

All at once Harrigan brought his arms to his sides. "We have no alternate choice that I can see, though I don't like it. Enlist him, Mr. Lane, and attach two scouts to see that he doesn't wander. If he makes one false move or tries to lead us into an ambush, shoot him immediately. Proceed."

CHAPTER 11

A delay of two hours ensued before the pack train could be brought up from below. Then, with two government scouts flanking Antone, mounted on an Apache horse, and Lane and Fenton and Scott close by, the command followed Medicine Shirt's beaten trail off the mountain.

By the time the advance reached the Mimbres River, the sun stood at noon. A brief rest and Harrigan hurried the command downriver at a trot on the clearly marked trail, himself in a growling mood. They were soon out in open country, the cottonwood-lined Mimbres on the left, rolling, grassy foothills the color of ripe wheat on the right. Beyond, on the plain, where the Mimbres became treeless, the column rode in clouds of choking dust.

At two o'clock Sergeant Hugh Ryan, in command of the pack train, galloped up and saluted. "Sir," he said, addressing the captain, "the pack train keeps stragglin'. We need more men to help keep the mules closed up."

"Exactly why are they straggling, Sergeant?" Harrigan's voice was brittle.

"Main trouble, sir, is they were taken out of wagon traces. They're inexperienced. Not used to packs and sore-footed from the rocky trail in the mountains."

Turning to his adjutant, Harrigan said, "Mr. Slocum, detail one noncommissioned officer and six privates from each troop to get the pack train moving. Have each man lead two mules.'' He shook his head impatiently and glanced at his watch. ''We'll halt here till they close up.''

Toward sundown the scouts came upon an abandoned horse beside the trail. The gaunt bay gelding stood head down, spraddle-legged, given out, and hardly moved when approached. Several miles on they found another horse, this one down.

''At the rate ol' Medicine Shirt's wearin' out horses, he'll soon have to restock,'' Fenton predicted. ''But as fast as he's goin', we'll sight no Cheericows today, nor will we ketch 'em as long as the pack train slows us down.''

The column bivouacked late that evening on the Mimbres where the river made a bend northwest of Deming, with Black Mountain looming off to the southeast. Darkness had fallen when the pack train arrived.

After supper at a council of officers and head scouts, Captain Harrigan said without preliminary, ''In the morning the scout company will move ahead as rapidly as possible, the command in support, ready to close up if the hostiles are sighted. Since I see no likelihood that the pack train will be in danger of attack in open country, it will follow upon our trail as best it can, to catch up at the end of the day. . . . Reveille will be at three-thirty. We will be ready to march before daylight, and that means the pack train. Lieutenant English, you and Sergeant Ryan will inspect each mule and see that the packs are secure. Yesterday some of the packs had fallen off within the first hundred yards after leaving the bivouac.'' His usual stern expression tightened even more. ''How has Antone behaved, Mr. Lane?''

''Predictably, I believe, sir,'' Lane replied, a bit uncomfortably. ''He's been intent on following the trail, though even our greenest trooper could do so now. I dare say his services will be of more benefit later when we need him to point out the springs and best camping places between here and the border, as Mr. Dunham has suggested.''

Harrigan looked at Fenton. ''Does Antone still insist he

doesn't know where Medicine Shirt's stronghold is in Chihuahua?''

Fenton nodded. "He also says he's never been told where it is, but he claims to know the region south of here on down to Janos.''

"Strange to me, as prominent as Medicine Shirt is, that his stronghold's location would not be common knowledge within the tribe.''

"Except, Captain, Medicine Shirt didn't get prominent among us White Eyes till after Geronimo buried the hatchet. From what Antone tells me, this stronghold is best known to the old Cheericows who used to go there in the old days. The young bucks don't know about it.''

"I don't trust any Apache. Whether Antone favors Medicine Shirt's war or not, he is still an Apache and therefore would not, I think, desire to lead us to the stronghold for fear of hurting his own people. He could be playing for time, meanwhile telling us what we wish to hear, until he can escape. Have him bound tonight, Mr. Lane. If he tries to slip off during the day, tell the scouts to shoot him on the spot. That is all. Dismissed.''

"Captain learns fast,'' Fenton remarked to Scott and Lane as they strolled back. "Either we push ahead with a few days' rations in our saddlebags—press after ol' Medicine Shirt—meet the pack train somewhere down below— that, or ride tra-la-la to the border with the train in tow an' never catch sight of a single Cheericow. Boys, I figure the book campaign is over.''

Next morning as the scouts sighted Deming in the clear distance, a shack town sprung up along the tracks of the Southern Pacific Railway, a group of hard-riding horsemen approached from town.

Lane halted the scouts.

A rifle-toting man in a derby hat, his scowl noticeable even at this distance, dashed up and called out, his tone demanding, "Where's your commanding officer, soldier?

I aim to palaver with him." A long-necked jug swung from his saddle horn.

Lane nodded, not speaking, and sent a scout back, and Captain Harrigan and Slocum arrived within minutes, evidently having anticipated trouble at sight of the riders.

The spokesman, a burly, belligerent individual, gold watch chain looping across the vest of his expansive girth, tobacco stains slanting down the bearded ends of his cranky mouth, announced, "General, I am Adam Whipple, mayor of Deming, and chairman of the Citizens' Defense Committee you see here. We want to know what the hell you soldiers aim to do about them thievin' Apaches?"

"In the first place, Mr. Whipple, I am not a general, instead a captain of the 6th Cavalry, United States Army. Now what particular bunch of Apaches do you refer to, sir, or do you know?" Harrigan seemed more amused than angry.

"I mean the thievin' red devils that swept through our town last evening and took every saddle horse tied in front of the saloons on Main Street and skedaddled before we could get a shot at 'em."

"Probably you refer to Medicine Shirt and his band, of whom we are in pursuit, Mr. Whipple."

"How the hell would we know and why'n the hell ain't you soldier boys closer on their trail? It's a—well, it's a goddamned disgrace, a bunch of greasy Apaches takin' white men's horses." Almost incoherent, swaying as he raged, Whipple found his voice, rushing out his blurred words. "I'm gonna tell you something General. We don't think much of the Army around here. The Army's never caught an Apache and never will."

"Would you care to join forces with us, sir?" Harrigan asked, curtly courteous.

"Join you? That's the Army's job. Damned if we'll do your fightin' for you!"

"It's both the Army's job and the civilians'. Surely you

gentlemen, fortified with the best whiskey in town, won't
refuse to join in this common venture?''

''I said we won't do your fightin' for you. Damned if
we will.''

''Then get out of our way. You're delaying the line of
march.'' Harrigan waved his right arm forward. When
Whipple didn't move aside, Harrigan raised his voice.
''Adjutant Slocum, if these men refuse to clear the way at
once, take them into custody and disarm them and send
them under escort to Fort Bayard for trial on charges of
obstructing military operations. Shoot any man who resists
or attempts to escape en route to the post.''

Whipple's mouth fell. There was an uneasy stirring and
grumbling behind him. Suddenly he reined aside and the
others followed.

Passing on, Scott admitted to himself that Harrigan had
handled the situation quite well, using both bluff and
reason. For that moment Scott had forgotten his bitterness.

Following the trail now angling toward the jagged-looking
Florida Mountains, the scouts worked well ahead of the
command while clouds cast moving shadows over the
land. Far in the distance Scott could see dust trails; but the
scouts drew no closer as the afternoon spent itself. Twice
Harrigan halted the column to rest the horses; taking up the
chase, he held to a relentless trot.

In the Floridas, the trail wound up and around low
ridges and brushy hogbacks that wore down the horses.
With darkness, the tired column bivouacked at a surpris-
ingly good spring.

''At this rate by tomorrow,'' Fenton observed, ''some
troopers will be afoot.''

Harrigan didn't wait for the ritual of supper to call the
scouts together and order Lane to fetch Antone. ''Mr.
Fenton,'' the captain said, ''ask Antone where he thinks
the hostiles' trail will lead us tomorrow and how soon we
can catch up?''

Fenton spoke, employing more signs than words, and

Antone, answering, appeared both sure and unsure. Fenton then translated, "He expects Medicine Shirt to cut southwest from the Floridas, down through what we call the Cedar Mountain range, past Apache Hill, and into the Big Hatchet Mountains near the border. As for catchin' up, he's not certain we will because the hostiles have those fresh horses, which we don't. He points out that we've found no used-up horses along the trail today."

In the amber light of the mesquite fire, Harrigan's face, chin thrust forward, the forehead bulging, showed a grim purpose. "On the contrary"—his voice was clipped—"it occurs to me that our noble Apache friend has undergone a change of mind. Now that we are closing in on his people, he would have us believe that capture is impossible, that we cannot catch up. He is lying, Mr. Fenton, trying to deter us."

Fenton laid his gaze on Antone before he replied. "In all due respect, Captain, I can't agree . . . and for this reason. We can't catch up the way we're marching. We've got to change tactics."

"How, pray tell?"

"Move at night."

"How far are we from the border?"

"Two days' hard march. Once the hostiles reach the Janos Plains, they'll run like scalded cats. If they break up into little bunches like they did on the Mimbres, we're in trouble."

"Yet, Antone still insists he doesn't know where the stronghold is?" Harrigan asked skeptically.

"I believe he's telling the truth."

"Unless he is giving us the runaround."

"I believe he's sincere, Captain."

"On what grounds, Mr. Fenton?"

"Because he led us to this spring. I didn't know it was here, even though I've been through here a couple of times. Neither did the scouts. It's out of their range.

Antone didn't have to lead us here. It's a little off the hostiles' trail, you've no doubt noticed?''

"You say the scouts aren't familiar with this region. Well, Antone is also a Chiricahua. Why does he know it and they don't?''

"After his young wife died, his heart was on the ground, as they say. So he rode over to the Mescalero reservation in the Sacramento Mountains. That's east of us. The Mescaleros—''

"I know where the Sacramentos are, Mr. Fenton,'' came the testy interruption. "Why the Mescaleros?''

"The Mescaleros,'' Fenton went on, as unruffled as if Harrigan hadn't spoken, "used to raid with the Cheericows, mainly with Victorio's Warm Springs Apaches. Some people believe the Warm Springs are the eastern branch of the Cheericows. Now you take ol' Mangas Coloradas, who used to rule the roost up around Santa Rita and plumb down into Chihuahua. Now there was an Indian. One of his daughters was married to Cochise, so—''

Harrigan flung up a silencing arm. "I hardly need a lecture, sir, at this time on the kinship and alliances of the various Apache tribes.''

Calmly, Fenton said, "I say this, Captain, just to point out why Antone rode with the Mescalero raiders and therefore knows this part of the country better than the scouts.''

"All right. So you suggest we march at night to close the gap?''

"I do, Captain. Move out after we've rested a few hours. By morning we should be in the Cedar Mountains. This way we can cross the open country at night between the Floridas and the Cedars without raisin' dust so every Indian in fifty miles knows where we are.''

Harrigan turned. "Mr. Slocum, assign a detail to go back for the pack train and lead it in. There will be no trumpet calls except in an emergency.''

By ten o'clock the command was under way without the pack train, the troopers leading their mounts while the scouts worked out the trail under pallid moonlight. Hours had gone by when they came down out of the Floridas and set out southwest. When daylight broke, they were in the stony foothills of the Cedar Mountains.

The column drew up around a small, natural tank of probably potable water, Scott saw. But as he soon discovered the hostiles had ridden their horses back and forth through it, until it had the consistency of thin gruel. Even so, the thirsty troopers dipped tin cups of the murky stuff and strained it through bandannas. Their parched mounts fared even worse, because even normally there wouldn't have been enough water to go around. This forced the watering details to allow each animal only a short turn at the muddy hole. Meanwhile, Harrigan sent the scouts ahead to look for more sign.

Scott and Fenton were rounding a high ledge of rocks, shielded from view below. Both abruptly jerked reins. Before them lay circles of campfires and a scattering of camp litter: a worn-out moccasin, strips of blanket, a broken bowstring, pieces of firewood, and the butchered carcass of a horse.

Scott dismounted and dug a forefinger into the ashes of the first campfire. "Hasn't been long," he said, looking up at Fenton, blowing on the finger. "Still warm."

"They pulled out last night same as we did," Fenton nodded. "Damned if it's not hard to outsmart a Cheericow. Them with fresher horses to boot."

Harrigan took the report without change of expression, studiously ignoring Scott. "So now what, Mr. Fenton?"

"This much, Captain. If we hadn't marched last night, we'd be farther behind than we are."

"How far behind are we?"

"Four or five hours."

"Translated into miles, that means—?"

"Say, twenty miles. They gained on us with the fresh horses they took at Deming."

Harrigan rested his chin on his left fist, eyes taking on a

distant look. ''Mr. Slocum, we'll breakfast, lay over a bit, and proceed. From here on, it will be short rests and long marches. Day and night.''

Pulling out, Scott looked back and sighted the far dust of the pack train plodding across the plain between the Cedars and the Floridas.

By noon the advance was filing through a saddle-shaped gap in the crest line of a ridge that soon dropped down toward the southwestern flank of the Cedars onto stretches of fine grama grass. Ranching country, Scott noted, pleasing to the eye. Here the hostiles had stopped to butcher a cow. Antelope blurred in the bright distance, their white rump patches bobbing.

The first cavalry mount broke down just as the column, going at a trot in the smoky heat, not a cloud in the sky, entered the lower Apache Hills. The rear guard shot the poor animal and the luckless trooper marched on foot.

Scott flinched at the carbine's report and said to Fenton, ''Like old times. I figure we've covered a hundred miles since we left the ranchería.''

''Or more. It comes down to this, Lieutenant. Push too fast, you wear out your horses. Take it easy, you don't catch hostiles. Be a lift when we get to that spring Antone says is on the other side of these rocky hills.''

They continued on without halting, Scott thinking this was only the beginning of the price of hot pursuit, he and Fenton and Lane on the point of the advance at the moment, following the pocked trail winding around a low ridge of brush and rocks.

Faster than thought, acting on instinct, Scott threw up a halting hand. His mind seemed to flash backward on a scene, to freeze on that. He could be west of Fort Sill, seeing the bronco Comanches rising like phantom horsemen from behind a brushy ridge, charging and firing.

''Jake—Lane—the ridge—look! There's movement there!'' The unnatural voice was his own. Yes, he had spotted movement, unnoticed by the other two while conversing.

Both men glanced up, then Lane swung about, yelling at the scouts, waving them to flank the ridge. They obeyed eagerly, gobbling whoops, low on their horses, welcoming the diversion, because wasn't war also a game to an Apache?

They bore off, right and left, to cut around. Figures bobbed on the ridge, running through the brush, quickly fading from sight.

Scott, carbine out, charged with Fenton and Lane. No shots greeted them. They clattered over the rocks and through the clinging brush, the scouts with them, and reaching the ridgetop Scott saw five riders tearing off below. By the time he had halted his plunging horse and flung up his carbine to fire, the hostiles were out of range.

"Young bucks," Fenton grunted. "Look at 'em go. They have to be on fresh horses. This tells us one thing. We're closer to the main band than I figured. The ambush was to slow us down. Another hundred yards we'd been under their guns." The piercing blue eyes bored into Scott's, curiously, approvingly. "Your eyesight's extra good today, Lieutenant."

"I just happened to be looking that way and maybe the ridge reminded me of something," Scott said, shrugging it off.

After reforming the advance, Lane galloped back to report and the march resumed, the scouts urging their tired mounts faster in anticipation of the spring.

The water looked clean and cool, a pool beneath the outcrop of gray rocks, and the lead scouts rushed up and dismounted. As suddenly they held back. Antone pointed and turned away and the others did the same, not drinking. Antone rode back and spoke to Fenton, his tone manifesting disgust, while holding one hand over his stomach, and Fenton explained, matching the Chiricahua's revulsion. "Ol' Medicine Shirt just pulled another slick one on us.

Killed a coyote—tossed it into the spring, all nicely pre-pared. Wagh!'' Grimacing, with signs, he questioned Antone, who shook his head. Fenton spoke again, still akhing. This time the Chiricahua pointed southwest and replied at length.

Fenton said, ''The nearest water is in the Big Hatchets. That is, if Medicine Shirt's goin' that way, which Antone is pretty certain he is. I calculate that means another twenty-five miles or so.'' He lifted reins. ''Lane, we'd better report on the double so's to lose no more time. Be more troopers on foot before the afternoon's done.''

Lane hesitated. ''What about water in the Big Hatchets? They can ruin that, too, can't they?''

''Not unless they want to waste a heap of time chasin' coyotes. Antone says they's more than one spring where he hopes we'll go.''

Going on, as the afternoon heat took deeper hold, Scott noticed how quiet the marching troopers had become since morning. He heard no joking or singing, and the fellow who played the harmonica now and then, his favorite tune obviously ''The Blue Tail Fly,'' had long been silent.

Out of the sunblasted distance charged a knot of horsemen. Lane drew up. At that, the riders appeared to ride even faster. Up they galloped, a scowling-faced, thick-bearded white man and four Mexicans wearing sombreros tied under their chins, armed like bandits: rifles, knives at their belts, bandoliers crisscrossed over their chests.

''About time you soldier boys showed up,'' the white man bristled, lank jaws hacking up and down. ''Apaches hit my remuda this morning. I'm plumb wore out with Apaches. The do-nothin' Army, too. You gonna run 'em down or not?''

When young Lane didn't reply at once, momentarily taken by surprise, Scott shot back, ''Who are you to come barging up here making demands?''—for once enjoying his neutral role as a civilian hearing the long familiar chant of complaints against the military.

"By God, I'm Hank Spears—that's who—from around Granite Pass," as if Scott should know without asking. "Who in the name of hell are you?"

"Dunham's the name. I'm a civilian scout. This is Mr. Jake Fenton, chief scout, 6th Cavalry, and this is Lieutenant Lane. Behind us are two troops of cavalry in pursuit of a band of Arizona Chiricahuas we just flushed out of the mountains east of the Mimbres. They're headed for Mexico."

Just then the enlisted scouts flowed up from behind, flanking the three advance riders, glaring at the Mexicans, who glared back uneasily and began fingering their rifles. Spears reacted as nervously, jerking his horse back.

"Don't be alarmed," Scott said sarcastically. "These Apaches are enlisted Army scouts."

"Enlisted, are they? Apaches in Army uniforms, drawin' Army pay, gettin' fat on Army grub, ridin' Army horses, all furnished by us taxpayers."

"And worth every cent of it. If not for these scouts, there'd be little chance of catching hostiles," Scott said, and glanced at Lane, feeling that he had said more than enough.

"We understand your concern, Mr. Spears," Lane said courteously. "What is your brand, sir?"

"LX."

"LX," Lane repeated. "If we recover any LX horses, we'll be happy to return them to you on the way back, if you'll be so helpful as to tell us where your ranch is?"

"Straight west of here in the Little Hatchet Mountains."

"Very well, Mr. Spears. Now we must hurry on." Standing in his stirrups, he called out a drawn "Ho-oh!" and motioned forward and trotted down the hostiles' trail.

"I didn't mean to take over the parley, Lieutenant," Scott said as they rode off. "But I'm tired of hearing civilian complaints."

"You expressed my sentiments precisely, Mr. Dunham.

Furthermore, we know where the hostiles got more fresh horses.''

By four o'clock some troopers were leading their leg-weary mounts. The trail, which had been coursing straight south, now switched to the southeast, which placed the rugged Big Hatchets on the right of the marchers.

A halt order was passed along the column, soon followed by another for a council of officers and head scouts.

''Mr. Fenton,'' Harrigan began, ''it appears that the hostiles are heading for the south end of the Big Hatchets. Is there any water between here and there?''

''Afraid not, Captain, on the trail.''

''What does Antone say?''

''The same. I've asked him. But he says there's water at the south end of the mountains. Right now we're on the main war trail to Chihuahua.''

''Summon him here, anyway.''

At Fenton's shout and arm wave, Antone turned his horse and rode leisurely back, smiling at the circle of white men as he came, at ease.

Harrigan, impatiently waiting, told Fenton, ''Ask him where the nearest water is.''

Replying to Fenton, the Chiricahua, still smiling and obliging, pointed southwest toward the upper Big Hatchets, speaking at the same time.

''He says he can find water there,'' Fenton said.

''How soon?''

Antone broke into a broader smile as he answered, and Fenton said, ''He says he can't tell you how far the sun will move before he finds water, but there is water there somewhere and he will find it if he gives his word.''

Harrigan appeared to balance the alternatives, studying the upper Hatchets, studying the lower mountains rising brokenly miles away through late afternoon glare.

Antone smiled again.

''I don't trust any man who smiles too much,'' Harrigan said after a moment, his head high, addressing Fenton.

"In excess, it is like charm, employed as a substitute for intelligence or to cover up guile. A wild-goose search for water in the upper Hatchets would cost us hours off the trail, which we cannot afford this close to our quarry. You say Antone claims there is water at the south end. Well, he had damned well better be right. Mr. Slocum, resume the march at a trot. Dismissed." Before Slocum could rein away, Harrigan spoke suddenly, his tone recalling. "Hold on. First, tell the rear guard not to put any more horses down. Leave them. Possibly some will revive and follow our trail after it cools off tonight. Possibly the pack train will pick up some. Possibly some will smell water somewhere in this burnt-out land and go to it. Horses have a very keen sense of smell, you know."

"Yes, sir," Slocum said.

Scott discovered himself agreeing, surprised, yet not surprised. Harrigan was a true cavalryman.

A time later the column rode to a wide wash. Harrigan halted for ten minutes while the troopers dug for water and found none. Even the scouts, more accustomed to hardships, and now also leading their mounts, were beginning to lag as the command plodded on.

The sun dipped behind the mountains and a faint wisp of coolness touched the marchers. The war trail drew them on, never altering its southeasterly course, as broad and beaten as a country road. *But it has to go into the mountains where there's water,* Scott was thinking.

The miles fell away without change. Early darkness closed down. Still, Antone followed the trail, the Big Hatchets a ragged mass on the right flank.

The trail split. Antone got down in the dingy light to inspect the tracks. He mulled over them and their meaning. Leading his horse, he walked down the main trail and back, and then down the offshoot trail, which turned toward the mountains. He was gone awhile. When he returned, he spoke to Fenton. They were conversing when Slocum rode up fast.

"What's the holdup? The captain wants to know."

"The trail forks," Fenton explained. "One goes toward the mountains. Tracks are fresh on both trails."

"Wait till I report," Slocum said, and tore back. Returning shortly, he said, "Captain Harrigan says follow the main trail."

"Antone says we should take the new trail. I agree."

"Why, Mr. Fenton?"

"It's the shortest way to water."

"What about the fresh tracks on the main trail?"

"They'll swing off the war trail later and join the new trail at a rendezvous in the mountains. It's an old trick, Lieutenant, to confuse us White Eyes, maybe make us divide the command. That way they'd stand a better chance if they jump a smaller force."

Slocum leaned back, head elevated, imitative of his commanding officer. "You understand I'll have to clear this with the captain?"

"Reckon I do. Just tell him what I told you. It's the shortest way to water."

"Do you agree, Mr. Lane?"

"Yes, sir. It's the quickest route to water. We can't go on much farther like this."

Slocum dashed back. A short delay ensued before he returned. "You have the captain's permission to follow the new trail. Proceed, gentlemen," he said in his overbearing way, obviously relishing his conveyance of the order. "And there sure as hell had better be water where the new trail leads." With that, he dashed away.

Fenton glowered after him, muttering, "Believe I could do without one puffed-up, ass-kissin', lord-of-the-manor second lieutenant. If he ever commands a regiment, which I doubt, every man in the outfit would go over the hill the first day."

The scouts took the new trail, some mounted, some walking, the worn horses revived a little by the evening coolness. They seemed to march interminably toward the dark mass of the mountains, and then Antone was leading them into a shallow canyon, and swiftly scouts and horses quickened and tore ahead, and Scott saw the shine of a small stream against the half light, and farther on the bountiful spring that was its source. He joined the surge. For a while there only the slaking sounds of drinking horses, their riders on hands and knees beside them.

When there was a letup, Lane had the scouts build a fire on each bank of the stream, hardly done when the two troops arrived. Headlong, they came, a mob of horses and men, wild, frantic, the men a bit crazed as they gulped and splashed and scooped. They rolled in the stream, they wept, they cheered, and danced in it like clowns, laughing as if touched, dipping and pouring water on their heads.

Antone, on foot, went prowling into the night and disappeared.

Little by little, the frenzy subsided; now and then a trooper would go back to the stream and drink. Others started cooking fires.

Scott and Fenton pulled out of the disorder after watering and tied their horses to cedars and unsaddled and rustled firewood. Soon Antone emerged out of the gloom of the canyon. He gestured and spoke and Fenton said, "Medicine Shirt watered here, then moved on toward the south end of the mountains. There's water there, too. We're not far behind him. This close, Antone thinks we should be on guard at dawn. They may jump us. Means the captain had better hear this."

They found Harrigan standing by a small fire while an orderly erected his tent, Slocum and English and Lane before him. Fenton reported Antone's findings and concluded, "Captain, the fact that Antone led us to water proves he's trustworthy."

"So long as Antone follows the straight path of loyalty, I shall tolerate him," Harrigan said, sounding remote and dismissive. "The instant he deviates, he's a dead Indian. Now, gentlemen, go post double pickets. If there is no dawn attack, we will press the pursuit at once. . . . Mr. Dunham, I should like a word with you.''

When the others had gone, Harrigan said, ''Lieutenant Lane tells me you spotted the makings of an ambush before it could be sprung on the advance.''

''I happened to see movement along the crest of a ridge.''

''Well, to me that is all in the line of duty, Mr. Dunham.'' Harrigan's mocking voice touched a sardonic dryness. ''Just mere routine. No more. No accolades.''

''Of course, Captain,'' Scott said, equally mocking. ''Just mere routine,'' and turned on his heel, back to his cooking fire, his old angry bitterness breaking over him. *The son of a bitch. The high-handed son of a bitch. Just when I was beginning to find a trace of humanity in him because he considered the horses back there today.*

Around Scott the bivouac soon settled down. The desert night brought a penetrating chill. The troopers cooked supper, ate ravenously, lay down, and slept. When Fenton joined him, they drank coffee, cooked bacon, chewed hardtack, and sought their blankets.

Scott's thoughts wandered. At night on a hard campaign such as this, a man's world contracted to the small space he and those around him occupied. There was no more than this canyon and the God-given stream and the winking stars. Nothing beyond this. Holly might never have happened. Blessed Holly. She could be an illusion, no more. Something he had imagined. Perhaps she was thinking the same of him at this very moment on the Mimbres. Groaning softly, he shifted against the gravel, burrowed a place for his hip, pulled the blanket about him, and slept.

The night passed quietly and the day dawned without alarm to the crying and singing of coyotes, a chorus of falsetto voices, and the air cold and hard and clean, troopers coughing and stamping numb feet as they watered horses and built hurried breakfast fires.

While the scouts were assembling, Captain Harrigan

rode up. "Mr. Lane, I am riding with the scouts today. Lead off when you're ready."

Overcoming his surprise, Lane saluted and called "Forr— ard" and led away, motioning Antone to pick up the trail below the stream.

The tracks arced away, skirting the rocky foothills, as if ever reaching out for the sanctuary of Mexico. The sun rose like a great copper eye, burning off the early haze, and at last Scott felt the chill leave his body. The command, watered and rested, moved at a fast trot, Harrigan a resolute figure in the advance.

Well into the morning, Antone stopped at a tank and swept a hand at the circling tracks, moccasin and horse tracks, and pointed to an incoming trail from the north, talking as he did so.

"What's he saying, Mr. Fenton?" Harrigan barked.

"The band that went on down the main trail came in here last night. They all camped here. This was their rendezvous point."

"Camped this close? Good! We are gaining. Water and push on, Mr. Lane!"

But as the morning lapsed there was still no sighting of the hostiles. "Captain," Fenton said during a halt, "they've gone around the Big Hatchets, headed for the Alamo Hueco Mountains on the border."

"So. Keep pushing, Mr. Lane."

Hour by hour, the pursuit continued, with short rests, Harrigan more grimly determined than ever. Gradually, the rugged Alamo Hueco range loomed in detail, stretching southeast to northwest, as islands on the yellow-grassed sea of the Sonoran Desert.

A long time later, the sun now fading to the color of misty iron, Antone and four government scouts, working beyond sight of the advance, suddenly rode out of the foothills and began cutting circles, the old signal for Enemy Sighted, then galloped back to the column.

Antone was visibly excited. He spoke rapidly, also with a puzzlement, Scott thought.

Choosing his words more carefuly than usual, Fenton said, "Antone and the scouts can see what looks like a camp in the foothills. A few wickiups. . . . A horse is tied there."

Harrigan sat up very straight. "A camp? So we've caught up with them."

"It looks like a camp," Fenton said, unconvinced. "But the scouts didn't see any 'Paches about."

"Should we expect them to be out in the open? I'd say they're resting."

"I don't like the looks of this, Captain. They've made an early camp, which strikes me as unusual when being pursued. Main thing is it's too easy to find, an' Cheericows never make anything easy for you."

Harrigan's ascetic features tightened. "Yet you found their camp in the Mimbres Mountains. This is the closest we've been since. I intend to attack at once."

"Captain," Fenton cautioned, "I think you'd better take a good look before you bust in there." Fenton faced him for an answer, standing his ground until Harrigan said, "All right. Let's go take that look-see, as you call it."

. . . . rrigan, Fenton, Antone, Lane, and Scott—until Antone signed for them to tie their mounts to mesquites and approach on foot. They crawled to the top of a little hillock.

"Down there," Fenton said after conversing with Antone. "In that gap."

Harrigan peered through his field glasses. After a while, he said, still looking, "I can see the brush shelters . . . the tethered horse . . . and people moving."

Scott could see almost as much with the naked eye. A few Apaches. Very few. Just that one horse.

"We're going in there!" Harrigan declared. "Mr. Lane, bring up your scouts. Tell Slocum to hurry up the two troops. We'll dismount below the hill here and attack on foot. Be quick!''

By this time Fenton had taken another look. He said, ''Captain, there's one thing that fails to jibe. I see just two bucks. They could be decoys. Where are the women an' children? Remember, they's about fifty in the band.''

The captain flashed him a measuring look. ''Are you saying we should not attack?''

''I still don't like it. But if you're goin' in, send flanking parties around.''

Harrigan raised the glasses again. ''The terrain scarcely favors that. The bucks are still there. Now I see some women at the far end of the camp. That settles it.'' He cased the glasses with a snap. ''We're attacking!''

Chafing at the delay, Harrigan took out the glasses again and studied the camp. Nothing had changed that Scott could see. Under the slanting rays of the sun, the camp seemed to drowse; at intervals a figure stirred.

When scouts and troopers arrived, every fourth man became a horse-holder, unhooking link straps from throat-latches and snapping the strap onto the bit ring of the next horse. Harrigan hurried them. The attack would be frontal, with the scouts in the center, the troopers forming a line of skirmishers.

They trailed around the hillock, formed quickly, and struck out on the double, the scouts at the tip of the advance, Harrigan with them, revolver out. Now they were in the gap, seeing the first wickiups. But there were no Apaches in sight. Not one.

A wrongness warned Scott and kept growing. A quivery feeling.

Fenton was scanning the brushy tops of the defile. Something up there caught his eye, because Scott saw him jerk that way, rifle swinging.

The first shot came before Fenton could fire. A volley burst all at once from both sides of the gap, up high. A scout dropped. Troopers and scouts dived for cover. Scott spun around at a shout of alarm behind him. It was Lane shouting. Harrigan was down, shock massing in his taut face. Lane and Fenton took hold and ducking low dragged him to the foot of the nearest rocky wall.

Scott, firing from behind a boulder at hostiles on the other side of the gap, saw the whole ridgetop lighting up with gun flashes through the blooming powder smoke, the din continuous. As if on signal, it suddenly broke off to sporadic shots. Upon that, Scott could hear a rumbling and crashing and bounding. The Apaches were pushing boulders down the steep slopes of the gap. Troopers yelled and ran dodging. The firing from above commenced again, as heavy as before.

Fenton came tearing over to Scott, chewing furiously on a huge wad of tobacco, breathing great gulps of air. "We're pinned down. C Troop's just behind you. Start workin' back. Take some troopers with you. Let's try'n flank this side. They's no other way."

He was past before Scott could speak.

Keeping low, Scott sprinted along the base of the wall, hearing the whine and sing of bullets ricocheting off rocks, calling to men he knew. When he reached the gap's mouth, Fenton was there with Antone and two scouts. Behind Scott six C troopers ran up blowing, among them Dawson and Haines.

"You tell 'em, Lieutenant," Fenton said, winded.

"We're going up here to turn their flank. When we get on top, spread out. Don't bunch up. Let's go."

Climbing the rocky slope, Scott was suddenly reminded that he had given the order without thinking, as if he were in command. Somehow it still seemed right.

Just below the rim, he waited for the little skirmish line to form, spread them out a bit, and up and over they went, bent forward.

Along the uneven spine of the broken ridge, through the puffs of white powder smoke, Scott glimpsed Apaches firing at the pinned-down men below. At almost the same instant the nearest Apaches discovered the threat on their left flank and raising taunts of *"Aaaaiiah! Aaaaiiah!"* turned to meet it.

Everybody charged with yells, carbines banging. Dawson stumbled awkwardly, went down with a cry, using the stock of his carbine to break his fall.

For long-hanging moments the hostiles were visible, firing and whooping. Of a sudden, the firing tapered off and the Apaches were no longer there; instead, fleet shapes dodging like deer through the brush, pausing to rally on higher ground. The detail continued to fire and advance. Some hundred yards on the hostiles' firing dropped off, ceased abruptly.

When the skirmishers gained the rally point, there wasn't an Apache in sight. The ridgetop was stone still.

"Over here," Fenton called, staring down at a dead Apache behind a rock, naked to the waist. "Reckon he forgot to wear his medicine shirt."

Starting back, Scott realized that the firing on the other side of the gap also had ceased. The ambush was over, the hostiles vanished like smoke. Remembering Dawson, he hastened.

Dawson lay sprawled, breathing hard, his face ashen.

In dread, Scott kneeled beside him and wanted to avert his eyes, seeing that Dawson was shot in the chest. A pinkish froth bubbled on his lips. Scott said, "We'll get you down pronto to the surgeon."

"What can he do? I'm shot through the lungs, sir. I can tell."

"He'll help you. I know he can."

Scott and Haines got him up and with his arms limply about their shoulders carried him along.

The cries and moans of the wounded reached Scott entering the gap. Officers made a cluster around Captain Harrigan, lying half propped against a rock while the contract surgeon examined his wound. Judging by the stain on his shirt, he had taken a bullet below his left ribs.

"Sir," Slocum was arguing, "you can't travel with this. The pack train's just been sighted. Must've marched all night. We can fix you a litter, carry you back to the post."

"There will be no litter, nor going back to the post for me." Harrigan was speaking through gritted teeth. He sat up. "The surgeon will bind me up and I will ride horseback. We must keep after them."

"But, sir—"

"Damn it, Mr. Slocum, don't interrupt me! Hurry the pack train up. Tend to the wounded. Start them back to the post with a detail. We are pushing on with ten days' rations. The pack train will bivouac at the next spring till we return with the Chiricahua prisoners. Proceed!"

CHAPTER 12

DARKNESS caught the pursuers still within the lower reaches of the Alamo Hueco Mountains near the border, and bivouac was made on short water. Next morning, under a lowering sky and the moist feel of a damp wind out of Mexico, they trotted southward on the well-marked trail of the hostiles. The column now reduced in strength about one third: a detail sent back with the wounded, another left to guard the pack train. A bevy of the fittest pack mules jangled along at the rear.

In the distance vultures rode the changing sky. The advance found a floundering horse. Scott put the poor animal out of its misery with his carbine.

"We're gettin' closer," Fenton said. "Just hope the weather holds off, but I wouldn't bet on it."

A halt order was issued and shortly Harrigan called a council of officers and scouts. He still sat his horse, erect, dogged, unflinching, the gray side-whiskers accenting his pale and drawn face. His open blouse revealed a stained binding around his waist. But his voice was as firm as ever. "I have chosen to continue the pursuit regardless of my own personal condition and, I add, without any pretense of bravado. Remember this: The hot-pursuit policy is still in effect"—a weak and sardonic grin filtered across the stern features—"though down here it depends on the mood of the local generalissmo. It is always popular to curse the gringos. Doing so helps cover up local corruption and peonage. In Mexico, style is always more important than results.'' He coughed and wiped his mouth with the yellow bandanna at his throat. Still, his voice was strong. ''Very well. In the event I am incapacitated, Lieutenant English will take command. With that, I remind you that duty is a cavalryman's Bible. Duty—duty!'' He was seized with a fit of coughing and would have fallen from the saddle had not English and Slocum caught him. Together, they eased him to the ground. Someone produced a flask. Tilted to his lips, it brought a tinge of color to his face. He lay back, mouth open, eyes staring.

All at once Antone was speaking to Fenton, pointing away and back to Harrigan. Fenton said, ''Captain, you may not think much of this, but 'Paches know medicines we don't. Antone, here, wants to find cobwebs to stop your bleeding, and wants to make a prickly-pear poultice to put over your wound to draw out the matter and keep it clean.''

Harrigan pushed up on one hand. ''I can do without any primitive cures, Mr. Fenton, thank you, just the same.''

''Captain, since the contract surgeon went back with the wounded, you need help. These 'Pache medicines may be primitive, but they work, I know. I've seen 'em work.''

''Instead, Mr. Fenton, have Antone move faster on the hostiles' trail.'' He coughed again. ''I believe the surgeon left us some carbolic acid, Mr. Slocum. Soak some of that into the wound and rebind it. That should ease the pain. Then assist me to my mount and proceed as instructed.''

Deeper into the morning, the command halted at a wash where a spring ran. Here also the hostiles had watered. Scanning the signs, Fenton commented to Scott, ''Y'know, Lieutenant, the idea of that little ambush ol' Medicine Shirt invited us into is as old as the hills. Fake the camp. Put up a few wickiups. . . . A Cheericow can throw up a brush shelter in ten minutes. . . . Tie a wore-out horse in plain view. Have a few people stroll around. Old as the hills, but it still works on a fire-eatin' horse soldier.'' He shook his head and as they rode off, he kept eyeing the threatening sky.

Still, Harrigan rode near the head of the advance. Glancing back at times, Scott could read the print of the man's pain on his gray, uncompromising face, only his iron will keeping him in the saddle, both hands gripping the pommel, swaying to his mount's hard trot.

Despite his bitterness, Scott felt for him. *He can't go on like this, but I hope he makes it somehow. By God, I hope he does.*

The whipping wind blew stronger and a barrage of thunder crashed and a light rain peppered down. The attentive Slocum flung a rubber poncho about Harrigan's erect shoulders.

Nothing changed for a few minutes. The scouts rode on as before, heads bent against the rain, slashing now, beginning to flail like buckshot. When it happened, Scott wasn't prepared, even though he had expected it: Harrigan's desperate voice torn by the wind. Just one word, "Slocum—"

Slocum reached him first because he was the nearest, Scott and Fenton next, springing from their horses. Slocum looked frantic. "Ease him—ease him—for God's sake." Scott steadied Harrigan while Fenton drew the captain's boot from the stirrup. Gently, they lifted him from the saddle and laid him down and shielded him from the driving rain with their bodies and hats. Harrigan's closed eyes opened when Fenton loosened the yellow bandanna.

"English—get English," he said.

Lieutenant English was already there by this time. "Yes, Captain," he said, bending over him.

"I . . . I pass on the command to you," Harrigan said, teeth clenched. "I can't continue—not enough clarity of mind—"

"You've got to rest, sir."

Harrigan laid a hand over his wound, pressing it tightly. "Absolutely not. Mr. Slocum—make—a litter—"

"But, Captain."

"Tarps in the packs. Use one—string it between two mules—"

Slocum hadn't moved.

"Now—Mr. Slocum!" Harrigan had to fight for breath. "This rain can wash out the trail. Push on after it—long as we can. Maybe . . . we can outrun the rain. Push on, Mr. Slocum—Mr. English!"

There was no letup from the sky. The scouts trailed through a cold, steel-gray void slanting in from the southwest. Behind them, indistinctly, Harrigan swung in his litter, hands gripping the sides of the tarpaulin.

Scott did not know how long they had marched like this when Antone, in the lead, rode back to Fenton and shook his head. He said a few words and capped his talk with a sweeping motion.

Turning to Lieutenant English, Fenton yelled above the roar of the wind, "Trail's washed out. We've lost it."

English nodded his understanding. He sat awhile, considering. "Isn't Janos the nearest town?" he asked, raising his voice, and Fenton nodded. "About how far, Mr. Fenton?"

"We can make it by late afternoon. It's southeast of us."

"Lead off, then. Maybe the Mexican authorities can assist us in some way. Maybe give us an inkling where the stronghold is."

Once again they were breasting the wind-driven world into wolf-gray nothingness, the rain-blackened horses going at a walk now. The afternoon lengthened; little by little Scott became aware that the storm was weakening. The sun, a waxy eye, was slowly burning a hole through the murk. And suddenly the column broke out into rolling country, the air sparkling fresh. In the far distance rose the darkish scatter of Janos.

Almost immediately, Antone pulled back, speaking to Fenton as he passed.

"What's wrong?" English asked Fenton.

"He's afraid the Mexicans will shoot him on sight. Same as the Cheericows shoot Mexicans. The old game. Eye for an eye."

"Mr. Lane," English said without delay, "pull back all your scouts. We don't want any trouble. Mr. Slocum, have each troop bring its guidon forward for prominent display."

Scott looked at English, liking what he saw and heard. Here was a man still a first lieutenant after some seventeen years in the cavalry, a quiet, amiable man turning gray, who had never commanded more than a troop, now in charge of a punitive expedition into Mexico after the last hostile Apache band. If he failed, the political consequences could break him; if successful, he could go virtually unnoticed, depending on the Olympian throne in Washington.

The changes were made in the order of the march and, farther on, English exclaimed suddenly, as if thinking to himself. "There should be Rurales posted here."

"There they are, Lieutenant," said Fenton at the same moment that Scott saw them rising out of a low fold in the desert, a line of horsemen in front of the command and others on each flank. Although the Rurales had a ragtag look, they were lean and hard-looking. Some in shirts and trousers of dirty manta; others in black and gray trousers and leather vests. But all wore big gray sombreros with chin straps, and all carried rifles and sidearms, and all had ammunition belts looped over the shoulder or crossed over the chest or belted around the waist.

English halted his command.

Then out of the mass of big-hatted horsemen, to the accompaniment of trumpeters sounding a mighty fanfare, emerged a magnificently uniformed officer, flanked by many aides. He rode with right hand held high. In turn, English and Slocum and the scout leaders trotted forward. The two commanders reined up about ten yards apart.

In a resonant, accented voice, the Mexican officer said,

"I am Major Viktor Trepov, chief of the Rurales of Northern Chihuahua. Who are you?"

"First Lieutenant English, 6th Cavalry, out of Fort Bayard, New Mexico Territory."

"Please explain your unwarranted invasion of the territory of Mexico."

Trepov, ramrod-straight, astride a handsome gray stallion whose arched neck and concave head spoke of Arabian breeding, wore a gold-embroidered sombrero, a short buckskin jacket trimmed in gold, and tight whipcord breeches of gray down which shone gold braid. A sweeping mustachio made a black curve above his arrogant mouth. The Arabian danced, showing gold spurs on Trepov's polished, sharp-toed black boots and a saddle lavishly mounted with silver. Pearl-handled revolvers sat on his lean hips.

"It is not an invasion, Major," English replied distinctly. "We are in pursuit of a band of Chiricahua Apaches led by Medicine Shirt and lost their trail in the storm. Perhaps you can assist us in locating these hostiles? That is why we have come to Janos. As you know, there is an agreement between our two governments which permits a command from either side to cross the border when in hot pursuit of Apaches."

Trepov's chin rose. "It is my understanding that agreement has been revoked."

"Sir," said English, keeping his voice cordial, "I assure you that is not our understanding. Perhaps you could message your headquarters for further confirmation?"

"My esteemed *patrón*, his excellency, Colonel Terrazas, would have informed me if the convention were still in effect. Therefore, I must ask you to leave at once, or I will be constrained to repel the invasion with force and you will be responsible for the resulting grave consequences between our two nations."

Scott got it. *Face. Face is everything down here. This mercenary knows that, Brad. Work on him.*

"Major," English said, "I assure you that will not be

necessary. And may I interrupt and impose on your generosity to ask if there is a doctor in Janos? We had a fight with the Apaches in the Alamo Hueco Mountains and Captain Harrigan, our commander, was seriously wounded. We sent our surgeon back with our wounded. I am in temporary command."

"A doctor?" Trepov repeated, surprised at the request.

"Yes, Major, a doctor for our commander."

"There is one, yes."

Scott could sense what was building. The *Yanqui* lieutenant must eat humble pie before his request is granted, if it is.

"Therefore," English continued, "I ask you, an officer and a gentleman, to allow us to bivouac here for the night so the doctor may see to our captain."

Trepov glanced at his aides before turning back to English. "Did you say *ask*, Lieutenant?"

A sudden tenseness seemed to envelop both commands.

A muscle throbbed in English's jaw. "I said *ask*. I would even say *implore* to get the captain the medical attention he needs. As an officer and a gentleman, Señor Major, you can understand the need."

Scott felt the hot wind of his anger whirling up through him. *That's it, Brad. Feed the mercenary bastard's vanity. Let him show the hated Yanqui officer pleading for help. Let him show off before his ragtags.*

Again, Trepov glanced at his aides, and, as if pleased, said, "Your request is granted, Lieutenant." He pointed dramatically east. "You may bivouac across the river. The physician will be sent to your captain."

"Thank you, Señor Major. You are generous."

"But there are certain conditions—agreements you would call them in this hot-pursuit policy which no longer exists—conditions which you must observe or I shall attack your camp."

"Please specify them, Major."

Trepov swept his glance back and forth over the troopers. "I see you have Apaches with you." His voice carried accusation.

"They are enlisted Army scouts, loyal to our government. They are valuable to us in tracking the hostiles."

"An Apache is an Apache, no matter what he wears, much to the sorrow of Mexico. They will not be allowed inside Janos."

"I understand, Major. I agree."

"Neither will your *Yanqui* troopers be allowed inside Janos. If they venture there for mescal, they will be shot on sight. We have patrols. No one will be allowed inside Janos except by invitation from me. However, you may retain your arms for the present. You will return to your country after breakfast in the morning. Until then you are, in effect, prisoners of the state of Chihuahua, his excellency, Colonel Terrazas, commanding."

He would have galloped off had not English said urgently, "Señor Major, our mission is of equal importance to both our governments: to capture Medicine Shirt's band and remove them across the border, or exterminate them if they resist. My staff and I would like to confer with you about the possible location of the Apaches' ranchería or stronghold in Chihuahua. You have fought the Apaches for many years. I know you can assist us."

Scott smiled inwardly. *Preen him, Brad. Preen him.*

Trepov held up and slowly favored English an almost indulgent reprieve for being a *Yanqui* intruder. "Duties permitting, I shall consider your request. Also, perhaps, I shall show you something of unusual interest."

On that, he whirled the prancing Arabian, its tail carried high, and dashed away to a flourish of trumpets, his aides sweeping after him in a bobbing wave, the ragtag Rurales forming a column of twos behind them.

"I've heard tell of Trepov," Fenton said thoughtfully. "Claim he was a count back in Europe. Whatever he was back there, he's one of the best Indian fighters in the Mexican Army, one of the few. Seldom goes into the mountains after 'em, but gives 'em hell in the desert. Also executes bandits. You're lookin' at a tough outfit, Lieutenant. Many of his Rurales are convicts. I hope we don't tangle.''

"I gather he wants to put the river between our Apaches and Janos,'' English said. "And what would he have of unusual interest to show us?''

They bivouacked across the river, up somewhat after the storm, and not long afterward a little man in a black suit and straw hat forded the river on a gray mule and rode up to the camp. He carried a much-worn leather bag. Dismounting, he nodded courteously to English, who went out to meet him.

"A pity your *capitán* is wounded. How long ago was this happen?''

"Yesterday, Señor Doctor,'' English said, and showed him to Harrigan's tent. "Thank you for coming.''

The doctor was in there only a few minutes. He came out looking discouraged and paused beyond earshot of anyone in the tent. "The bullet passed through him,'' he said, speaking in his low, courteous voice, "but he bleeds. He is in much pain. I gave him laudanum. I can do no more, which I regret.''

"*Gracias*,'' English said, and moved to pay him.

"No, I cannot accept for a brave man who fights the brute Apaches. I hope you can take him back to his country, God granting. Soon for him.''

Within half an hour a young Rurale sergeant galloped up to the bivouac and motioned for someone to come forward.

"I take it he wants somebody who can speak Spanish,'' English said. "Mr. Fenton, don't you?''

"Enough to get by on. I'll talk to him.''

Afterward, Fenton said, "Major Trepov invites you and your staff to his headquarters at the presidio for a conference. The *sargento* will escort us.'' He gave a sly wink. "You understand that this is a great honor?''

They rode into town along a dusty street of ancient

adobes to the plaza and its cantina and its sagging wooden bandstand and rusty iron benches and the cross-crowned bell tower of the church reaching for the late evening sky, drawing curious glances from doorways as they passed.

Janos, Scott judged, gazing about at its sparse environs, was scarcely more than an outpost town, its population shrunk to a few hundred.

Onward a way from the plaza the sergeant halted before the main entrance of the broken-walled presidio, where two Rurales stood stiffly at attention. Down a long hall, Trepov stood up behind an ornate desk of polished dark wood and nodded a formal greeting. Without his sombrero and not mounted, he looked of far less stature and much older, probably in his fifties, Scott guessed. His close-cut black hair was thinning in front. His dark, mustachioed face was lined. His eyes were his dominant feature: black, quick, intelligent. On the wall behind him in a large gilt frame hung the photograph of a bemedaled, mustachioed man of proud visage. Trepov invited them to be seated and a boy brought glasses and bottles.

"Please serve yourselves, gentlemen," he said, making a gracious gesture. "All my poor Mexico can offer you is mescal."

"Major," English said, "we thank you for sending the doctor. He said there was very little he could do. Our captain's condition is quite serious."

Trepov, as if brushing that matter aside, picked up a sheet of paper and presented it to English. "Señor Lieutenant, here is my written protest of your unjustified invasion of the territory of Mexico. You will present it to your commanding officer when you return to Fort Bayard. I further request that he present it to the President of your United States."

English was silent for a tick of time, caught between retort and diplomatic protocol. "That will be up to my commander, Major," he said respectfully, and folding the paper placed it in a pocket of his blouse. To refuse would insult Trepov.

"You do not agree?" Trepov replied, looking deeply hurt. "You must not understand my position? My district invaded . . ."

The man was also an actor, Scott decided.

"I understand your sensitivity to American troops on Mexican soil, Major," English said, "except I do not agree that this is an invasion. We are looking for Apaches. That is all. We are not occupying land."

"Wah!" Trepov was waving his arms. "I see you do not understand my Mexico . . . the passion, the patriotism, the politics. I trust you realize the extent of my generosity in permitting you to keep your arms and rations in view of this bold intrusion of our soil? It is only through the beneficent policy of my *patrón*, his excellency, Colonel Terrazas, whose likeness you see behind me, that I do so."

"We'll break camp first thing in the morning. But before we do, Señor Major, we earnestly hope that you— because you have fought the Apaches for so many years— can tell us where Medicine Shirt might be heading. He was traveling southwest when we lost his trail."

Trepov seemed to grow inches taller. "If I knew would I not be attacking the Apaches myself? Your United States made a great tactical blunder when it did not message Colonel Terrazas or me that this brute, this Medicine Shirt, was fleeing into Mexico. Thus informed, I would have attacked them when they crossed the border and your worries would be no more."

"You know, Major," said English, breaking into a slow grin, "I believe you have a point there."

Trepov was likewise smiling. He could not have been more gracious as he raised his glass. "*Salud*, gentlemen, and to my *patrón*, his excellency, Colonel Terrazas, who surrounded the brute Victorio at Tres Castillos and finished off his Warm Springs band." As they put down their glasses, English said, "I hope you will allow us extra time in the morning for our departure because of the captain. We shall go directly back to Fort Bayard. Until tomorrow morning, then, Major." He started to leave.

"One moment, please, Señor Lieutenant," Trepov said, a kind of secret amusement coming into his eyes. "I have something to show you."

English regarded him curiously.

"Follow me," Trepov said, and led the way down the hall and outside along a stone pathway, past a gap in the crumbling wall, to a corner of the presidio. There two Rurales stood guard at the wooden gate of a high stone corral. Trepov spoke sharply and the Rurales slid back the bar and dragged the heavy gate open.

Trepov walked in but a few paces before stopping to press a forefinger to his nose. "Apache captives," he said, gesturing, as if he were conducting a tour of a zoo, "taken recently west of here. They had left the Sierra Madre and were making their way back to Arizona. Since we have found it impossible, also thankless, to save the souls of Apache men no matter how earnestly we tried to Christianize them, we executed the few surviving warriors, including the old men. For these heathens a padre comes once a day to offer them instruction in the faith through an interpreter." He sighed audibly. "So far it is hopeless."

Scott recoiled at the overpowering stench of the place while he turned his eyes on the wretched people, some twenty in all: The women, their dark faces pinched with hunger and fatigue, clad in dirty blouses and long skirts of cheap trade cloth, hunkered close to the wall, staring impassively at their captor, or was that controlled hatred? Their shy, big-eyed children, staying close to their mothers, facing away from the gawking visitors, among them a few girls in their early teens. His mounting anger took deeper grip at sight of the hordes of buzzing flies and the piles of horse manure and feces and the litter of corn husks and cobs. There were no pots, no kettles, no wood for cooking. Two children, a boy and a girl, lay against the wall, evidently too ill to sit up.

A Rurale came to the gate lugging a heavy sack. At Trepov's nod, he began tossing ears of corn to the captives. No one moved to pick up the corn, the Apaches just staring, their faces like stone. Then a lean boy ran out and snatched up an ear. A woman called harshly. The boy dropped the corn and ran back, ashamed. The woman put her arm around him.

"They're too proud to take the corn when our men are watching," Trepov said. "But Apaches are realists. They must eat to live. Later, they'll devour it raw."

Scott was smoldering and aghast. *Fed like hogs. But, by God, they won't beg. How I pity them! But how brave they are!*

Another Rurale poured water into the one *olla*.

"Major," said English, his face firming, "may I ask what disposition you plan to make of the captives?"

A question, Scott saw, that Trepov had neither expected nor wished, because he delayed noticeably before he answered. "We do not trade in slaves—that is illegal," he said righteously. "Our genteel families in Casas Grandes and Chihuahua City—the *encomenderos*—will generously take some in as servants for their haciendas. Further instruction will be given them in the holy faith to save their heathen souls."

Almost before he knew it, Scott was asking, "Major, there are young girls among the captives. What will happen to them?"

Trepov shrugged it off. "My *Yanqui* friend, what has always happened to young girls since the beginning of time? Some young men will take a fancy to them and they will take a fancy in turn." He shrugged again.

Like hell, Scott longed to remind him. *They'll be sold as prostitutes. Every captive will be sold, and the money will go to you and maybe a few of your favorite aides. The older women who don't become house servants will work on maguey farms. The children will be separated from their mothers, doomed to servitude of the lowest kind.*

But, in view of the situation, Scott felt he could say no more.

The "tour" was over, he saw now, as the major strolled toward the gate. For some reason Fenton lingered. He was looking at an elderly woman, the one who had called the hungry boy back, her weathered face a death mask of resignation. He went over to her and spoke, his tone friendly and inquiring. In an instant her face changed, vitalized, grateful, wondering. She answered with a torrent of words, her hands moving constantly. Fenton spoke again, softly, inquiringly. When she did not answer, he walked to the gate.

"You speak Apache?" Trepov asked, suspicion sharpening his voice.

"A few words," Fenton said, passing it off.

"What did you say to her?"

"I asked her the name of her band. She says they're part of Geronimo's. Got cut off when Rurales in Sonora chased them into the Sierra Madre. I didn't have the heart to tell her Geronimo's surrendered an' been shipped off."

"Vah! By now you *Yanquis* should know not to waste kindness on a heathen Apache. She would love to drive a knife between your shoulder blades."

They walked back to headquarters where Trepov, his earlier graciousness gone, faced English and said bluntly, "You have until eight o'clock in the morning to break camp and depart north. If you overstay the time limit which I have generously allowed you, I will be forced to attack your command."

"You have my word, Major. We'll be out of here in due time."

Twilight cloaked the empty street as they rode away from the presidio. In the plaza the only light shone from the cantina, hushed at this early hour.

"Lieutenant," Fenton said, addressing English, "I'd

like to ask the *sargento* to get me a bottle of mescal. That all right?''

"Believe we could all use a drink after what we witnessed back there. I'd like one, too. Ask him how much.''

That was arranged, a bottle for each man was purchased, including one for the *sargento,* and they rode on to the river, where their escort left them. They had no more than dismounted when Fenton spoke up. "There's something I'd better report to you right now, Lieutenant. It's sure got my head in a spin.''

"What do you mean?''

"Those captives got cut off all right, but not from Geronimo's band. I said that for the major's ears. They're part of Medicine Shirt's following. They's headed for the stronghold when Trepov jumped 'em.''

"The stronghold? Did she say where it is?''

"Wouldn't say. Afraid we'd tell the Mexicans. She thinks we're friends with the Mexicans.''

"If she only knew! Trepov is aching to work us *Yanqui* invaders over. He'd be quite a hero. Remember when the Mexicans killed Captain Emmet Crawford, probably by design, when he was chasing Geronimo in the Sierra Madre early this year? He was there in uniform under stipulations of the hot-pursuit agreement, same as we are, but it didn't mean a damned thing.''

They were all silent until Scott said reflectively, "She might change her mind if Antone could talk to her.''

"Some decent food and water would be a good persuader,'' Lane said.

"She can't help us as long as she's in that hog pen,'' Fenton drawled.

There was another interval of thoughtful silence, then English, with a sudden gesture, said, "What we're really talking about is getting the captives out of there, isn't it? That would prove she could trust us.''

"Yes,'' said Slocum, "and I'm against it. It would

create an international incident, you can be certain of that, and we'd all be busted—if we survived.''

"Don't think that hasn't occurred to me," English told him. "Yet it's the one chance we have to locate Medicine Shirt. I think we'd better see if Captain Harrigan is able to talk. Will you see about him, Mr. Slocum?''

Slocum strode back in less than a minute. "He's still knocked out from the laudanum. Will be till morning.''

"We can't wait that long. Has to be done tonight.''

"I tell you I'm against this," Slocum said, his voice taking on emphasis. "If captured, we could spend years in some filthy Mexican jail. In my opinion, knowing the captain as *only* I do, he would reject it without hesitation.''

"I don't agree," English said. "I think he'd take the chance.''

"What assurance do you have the woman would tell you where the stronghold is, if you free her?''

Slocum was being his supercilious self, Scott saw.

"We've been over that. We'll go over it again, in detail.''

"Mr. English," Slocum said, his long jaws working, "I refuse to go along with this wild foray.''

"Do you really mean that?''

"I do, sir.''

"I believe you're forgetting that I am in command," English said, a new firmness to his tone. "You will obey orders, Mr. Slocum, or face charges of insubordination. I mean that.''

Slocum flung away, striding fast, head high.

"Well, I'll be damned," English said regretfully, "I never thought I'd see that." He turned to the others. "Let's bring Antone in here and see what we can do.''

CHAPTER 13

THE night was hours old. They could delay no longer. The furtive moon was a mantle for the hurrying figures when it hid behind the clouds, a tallow-faced betrayer when it emerged, bathing the desert with rose-tinted light. The night wind had a nip. They moved single file: Fenton, Scott, Lane, Antone, and three more government scouts. Behind them the troopers stood by saddled mounts, the two litter mules ready, the others packed, some lightly for conveyance of women and children. Only Harrigan's tent, which could be taken down and packed in seconds, was left standing. Now and then a trooper fed the low supper fires to simulate a bivouac.

"If we hear firing, we'll come for you," English had said. "And remember: Avoid bloodshed, if at all possible. This will be incident enough without that. Mr. Slocum has been relieved of duty for refusing to carry out orders. Otherwise, I would leave him in command and go with you."

Fenton slackened step to observe the plaza. Couples still strolled there. Not many, Scott saw. There was music in the cantina and song and laughter and rough voices. Scott could read Jake's mind: He was looking for Rurales. Time became a pressure. Another minute and they'd have to skirt the plaza to avoid being seen by the couples. . . . Now the voices brawled. The music stopped. Across that sudden stillness broke sounds of scuffling, and suddenly two big-hatted Rurales lurched out of the cantina, flailing away at each other. A woman close behind them. One antagonist apparently drew a knife, because the woman screamed and a man cried out. The strollers rushed over there to watch.

In the wake of their movement, Fenton hastened across the plaza and into the street that led to the presidio. There the seven looked back, in their ears the din of many voices. The woman started screaming again. They hurried on.

When the high bulk of the presidio loomed before them, Fenton halted and pressed close against a darkened house. No guard stood outside the headquarters entrance. No light there, either. Fenton moved faster now and presently they came to the crumbling wall of the ancient fortress. Hugging its broken face, he followed along it to a gap. After glancing about, he stepped lightly over the heaped rubble and all at once they were inside the presidio. Dim lights shone across the grounds at the base of the opposite wall. Barracks, Scott figured.

Some fifty yards on Scott made out the stone corral at the corner of the inner wall. They hurried that way. There a sentry was pacing back and forth. Only one. Fenton touched Scott's arm and Scott touched Lane. The three then slipped ahead, the others staying within the deeper darkness of the wall.

Fenton neared the sentry, swaying, staggering. "*Amigo— amigo—*" he called, voice blurred, waving high a bottle of mescal. In close, he offered it straight at the man.

The sentry, startled, instinctively put out a hand to take the bottle. On second thought, he pulled sharply back and grasped his rifle.

Before he could cry out, Scott clamped a hand across the man's mouth and jerked his head backward, while Lane tore free the rifle. Together, they threw him to the ground and gagged him with a bandanna. They tied another around his head and mouth to hold the gag in place and bound his hands and ankles with leather thongs. Foot-steps pounded as the scouts ran up.

At the corral gate, Scott slid back the bar and he and Lane tugged on the heavy wooden barrier. The bottom scraped, its screech keen across the night. They froze for an instant, then lifted higher and swung the gate open and everybody rushed inside the corral.

Scott saw them at once, a dark clump squeezed against the far wall of the stinking corral, huddled for warmth and now likely out of fear. Now, Scott knew, it was up to Antone.

Raising both hands in a sign of trust, Antone walked slowly toward the captives, his low-pitched voice reassuring. He stopped speaking, waiting. There was no response. Weren't they coming? Didn't they want to be free? Antone spoke to them again, his earnestness evident even to Scott, who understood not a word.

Still, Antone waited.

A moment more and Scott saw movement and heard faint rustlings. A child whimpered, instantly hushed. Almost as one the captives rose. There was a flowing toward Antone while he stood waiting in the dingy light. There was a woman's voice. An old woman's high, cracked voice. All at once they were crowding around Antone, reaching for him, eager to touch him, and they were crying.

Scott watched, a choking sensation in his throat.

This moment held and would have gone on longer had not Fenton hissed at Antone, who literally shooed his charges out the gate. Scott and Lane dragged the sentry inside, checked his gag and bonds, shut the gate, and bolted it.

Fenton led off, the captives trailing after, their moccasins raising a faint scuffing, the scouts assisting the weaker ones. Across the way the barracks lights were as sallow eyes, yet fearful. Fenton walked faster.

They were climbing over the mound of rubble when the

moon chose to unveil itself. At almost the same time hooves clattered down the street. Scott sighted two horsemen coming toward the plaza. In a breath, the Apaches melted into the narrow shadows cast by the broken wall. The scouts drew knives and flattened out. A child started to whimper, quickly hushed.

The sombreroed horsemen came on, talking, laughing, bringing the squeal of leather, the tink of spurs, the pungency of dust. Time seemed locked, the horsemen to ride in tantalizing slow motion, never to pass. They were still talking and laughing when they drew even with the gap. There, apparently in anticipation, they suddenly set spurs and galloped by.

No one moved for a full half minute until the Rurales dissolved as dark, bobbing shapes, swallowed by the depths of the plaza. Fenton got up fast, slipping along the long wall of the presidio, Scott with him. At the first connecting street, Fenton turned into it, forced to go around the busy plaza. Here the way was narrow and much darker.

They had covered no more than twenty paces when a man's voice rose alarmingly close. Fenton slowed. The voice, which came from the window of a darkened adobe, was murmuring and amorous, very distinct in the stillness of the narrow street. A woman's just-audible voice joined his, giving in tone, softly muted. The voices faded, fell silent.

Scott smiled in relief. *Hell, they're just making love. They don't see us.* He gave Fenton a little onward push.

From here they could move a short distance without threat. But upon reaching the street's end, Scott saw lights dotting the night nearby in the direction they had to go to avoid the plaza. Fenton stopped. Scott could hear him breathing while he pondered over what to do, the smell of his plug tobacco like a stain on the night air.

Scott whispered, "Trepov's got patrols out. That was a patrol at the presidio. Let's keep to our right to the river. Ford it below. Follow it back up to the bivouac."

"Maybe," Fenton grunted, not convinced. Nonetheless, he angled to the right, roundabout.

"I'll go ahead," Scott said.

He led them on, skirting an occasional adobe, winding around sheds and goat pens and small corrals, working toward the outskirts of the town, the moon sliding in and out of cover. The desert night laid down a distinct chill. A sick child coughed.

Now, there was the river, lying before them, a band of silver in the moonlight. Somewhere along here they could cross, Scott was thinking, and place the river between them and the Rurales. A great fullness of relief surged through him.

He scouted on in advance through scattered mesquite, and was nearly to the river when he stopped, his senses jumping. For once this tense night he could thank the naked moon, because he glimpsed the four riders before he heard them. They were coming two abreast at a trot along the bank of the river from the direction of the bivouac. Keeping low, he ran back to Fenton.

"Patrol's coming. Get 'em back!"

Once again they became as formless shadows, this time lying among the thorny mesquites.

Scott crouched, watching the riders. Fenton and Lane slipped in beside him. While they watched, two horsemen rode on.

"Postin' pickets," Fenton said. "I expected that. Trepov's worried our Apache scouts will slip across the river to raise hell. Anybody got any notions?"

"We've got to get across in time to break camp and have the captives well beyond Janos before daylight," Lane said. "But no gunfire—and no bloodshed, if possible. That's a tall order."

"We'll have to take prisoners," Scott said. "Can't leave 'em here. There'll be patrols along. Besides, we can use their horses."

Fenton shifted around. "I'll get Antone. Imagine tellin'

a Cheericow not to kill Mexican soldiers. To be nice. Just take prisoners.''

''Tell him to detail one man to get the horses,'' Scott cautioned.

The moon, as capricious as ever, decided to parade itself again as the three and the government scouts slipped through the prickly mesquites toward the river.

The two mounted Rurale pickets faced the river while they chatted and watched. One man hooked a leg over the pommel of his saddle and leaned back and turned to his comrade. The light was so bright Scott got a clear view of his face: young and lean, growing a brave mustache. The other man bent his head to roll a cigarette.

The time was now.

Scott sprang to his feet and they all rushed at once. Scott and Lane grabbed the young Rurale, smothering his startled shout, and the scouts the other just as he raised the cigarette to his mouth.

It was over in moments. The bruised pickets gagged with strips across their mouths, hands tied behind them. Antone uttered a quail's call, a plaintive *kway-er,* and the captives scrambled out of the brush.

A certain confusion and delay followed while the weakest women and children were mounted on the horses. The water was cold and rose to the chests of the men, who hoisted the children to their shoulders. Across, they hurried into a dogtrot for the bivouac.

As the chill of dawn burned away, the command was marching north from Janos, Captain Harrigan tossing feverishly on his litter, in and out of his head; the two Rurale prisoners on foot, all the Apache captives on mules except some of the children riding with scouts and troopers, the young ones still munching hardtack given them at the bivouac. Like a matriarch, the old woman rode double with a young girl at the head of the little band.

''She's a medicine woman and I do not like to mention

her Apache name, because that could take away some of her power and she might do bad things to me," the superstitious Antone had told Fenton. "But her Mexican name is Rosa. Call her Rosa."

"What is her power?" Fenton asked.

Antone, in awe, said, "She can see what is not before her eyes. She can see what is going to happen. She knew the captives would be rescued. She prays often to Ussen. Ussen told her to be brave and wait. She did."

During a halt, Lieutenant English sent Fenton to fetch Antone, and when Antone reported, English said, "Tell him to ask the old woman again where Medicine Shirt's stronghold is."

Fenton interpreted and answered, "He says he has an' she won't tell. She feels she would be betraying her people, which is the worst crime a 'Pache can commit. She would be banished an' that is worse than death to them, particularly for her, to be old an' not with her people when she dies."

"We don't have much time," English said, including Scott and Lane. "I expect Trepov to show up in our rear by this afternoon. Mr. Fenton, bring the old woman here so I can talk to her."

She moved unsteadily, a small woman, withered and stooped, her face black-browed and proud, written over with innumerable wrinkles, her thin gray hair like tufts of dry grass. Her nose was straight and broad, her cheekbones high, made prominent by her loss of flesh. Her hands were clawlike, her teeth worn to brown stubs. She swayed a little. But her eyes, the coffee-colored eyes, had vitality and courage.

"Are you still hungry?" English asked, smiling at her.

Fenton, answering for her, said, "She was very hungry at our camp, but not now. She is old an' needs little food, she says. I can tell she's weak, but she won't complain. She thanks us for rescuing her an' the others and for the food. Antone says her Mexican name is Rosa. So I call her Rosa.''

''Tell Rosa that she may ride one of the Mexican horses if she wishes.''

She had no words for the offer, no change of expression.

To Scott, her mind seemed far away, as if she were sad about something.

''Tell her,'' English continued, ''we don't wish her people with Medicine Shirt any harm. Our freeing her and the others should prove that. Remind her that the war is over with the White Eyes. We want to escort her people out of Mexico, where it is always dangerous, to New Mexico, where they will be safe. But explain that we need her to lead us to the stronghold and that we must hurry, because the Mexican soldiers are behind us and may catch up if we don't hurry along. Tell her the Mexicans in Janos know where Medicine Shirt's stronghold is and will attack it soon.''

Listening, Scott moved English's words through his mind. *Why are we so often lying to the Apaches? Trepov doesn't know where the stronghold is, and Brad hasn't told her that Geronimo and his band have been shipped off to Florida. But under the circumstances I guess I would do the same to get them safely out of Mexico. Yet we lie.*

There was a pause, then Fenton said, ''She says she will pray to Ussen about this thing. It is a hard thing.''

''Now?'' English asked, not liking the delay.

''Now.''

She left them and toiled over a swell of desert and disappeared. She was gone so long that English began to show signs of impatience. When she did appear, she dragged herself along with effort. She spoke rapid-fire Apache to Fenton and, finished, stood as if resigned.

Fenton regarded her with a keen sympathy before he spoke, slowly choosing his words with care. ''She says she hasn't long to live. Ussen told her that before the Mexicans captured them, but he let her live to help the others through their captivity, the children, in particular, who got sick an' hungry. Now Ussen has told her again. It is near." He stopped to gather his thoughts and went on. "She longs to see the rest of her people once again before she goes to the Happy Place. She says all the great chief Juh had to offer his people was death. Now he is dead. His people scattered. She does not want that to happen to her band an' Medicine Shirt. She hopes you can take them where they can be safe an' live in the mountains. . . . Because it means life for her people, not death, she will lead us to the stronghold."

English's eyes became bright with elation. His nod for her was more like a salute of respect. "Tell her she is wise, Mr. Fenton, and that we honor her. Ask her if she would like a horse to ride."

Rosa drove more rapid words at Fenton, who said, "She accepts your offer. Let it be a Mexican horse instead of two on a mule. That way she can get there faster. She says for us all to hurry. Her time is near."

"Tell her the horse is hers to keep."

Mounted, she turned without hesitation to the northwest and put the Mexican gelding to a fast trot.

They were now on the Janos Plains, Fenton said.

Scott, thinking of Trepov's pursuit, made some calculations as to distance. It was after midnight before they had reached the bivouac with the captives. Figuring time to break open hard bread boxes for the famished captives and to mount up their charges, and, once under way, allowing for the overloaded mules while also traveling less than the usual cavalry rate of four miles an hour out of regard for the suffering Harrigan, Scott estimated the command had covered about fifteen miles when daylight caught them.

It was close on five o'clock when Scott first noticed the mountain or a clutch of mountains thrusting crookedly out of the plains. He looked in question at Fenton, who said, "That's the Sierra Enmedio, or what white men call Middle Mountain. That's where she's headed, sure as hell. So that's the stronghold.''

"Looks like a stronghold," Scott said.

"Not in the usual sense. It's the remoteness that makes it a refuge. They's a fine big spring on the west side. I understand the old Cheericows would raid in Arizona, then step across the border to the Sierra Enmedio to safety, or go down into the Sierra Madre.''

"You say there's a spring on the west side," English said. "So you've been there?"

"Yes, sir. Once. I was one of the scouts with Captain Tupper when he tracked Loco's Warm Springs band there. But we couldn't hold 'em. Had to back off. They went on south to worse, ran into a Mexican force. Loco lost most of his women an' children. Worst slaughter I ever saw. I can draw you a rough map right here.''

"Do that. This country is all new to me.''

Dismounting, Fenton picked up a sharp rock and set about scratching deep lines in the pebbly soil. "Here's the spring west of the mountains. It's in a kind of basin. In the Tupper fight the scouts moved up at night an' occupied a ridge—about here—several hundred yards east of the spring. That cut Loco off from the mountains, while the troopers took position to the south, which cut Loco off from runnin' to the Sierra Madre. I figure we'd have to do the same. Tupper's strategy was good. We just couldn't hold 'em.''

English gazed long at the mountains, his face a taut study of hard decision. He said, "One little inkling of troops and Medicine Shirt will spook south for the Sierra Madre. What do you men think of making dry camp at the foot of the mountains, no fires? Putting the range between us and the hostiles? Late tonight, getting the scouts on that ridge east of the springs Mr. Fenton described, the rest of us taking a blocking position to the south as Tupper did?'' He looked at Scott and Lane. Since their departing the Janos bivouac, Slocum had ridden back with the troopers.

Both nodded. "We'll have to keep Rosa tightreined," Scott said, and Lane added, "The scouts will see to that."

"Tell her," English prompted, "that she will see her people in the morning." Catching the surprise on the others' faces, he said, "We'll let her and all the captives go in shortly after daylight, but not before we're all in position. She'll be our emissary of peace. Mr. Fenton, you and Antone must impress upon her that we want to return Medicine Shirt's people to New Mexico without a fight."

Fenton looked down and up, frowning. "It won't work, Lieutenant. We're forgettin' the shirts—the medicine shirts. These Cheericows will come out clawin' the moment they know troops are close. No matter what Rosa tells 'em about peace. They don't want peace. They want to be free."

"I don't see another way. I don't want to attack the camp. We have nothing to lose this way. And where the hell's Trepov? Mind you, we'll hear from him before we cross the border."

Around midnight the scouts, on foot, single file, Fenton guiding, left the bivouac and started working along the base of the mountains. Clinging manzanita and chaparral slowed their progress. When they circled the southeastern tip of the range and came out on the basin, Scott saw distant lights and heard a faint singing. Antone loomed up and spoke to Fenton and the scout said, "They're makin' medicine. Good. We can move a little faster. Damned if that ridge don't seem farther away than I remembered it." A moment later he sprang aside, muttering, "Snake! Watch out!"

The night was clearing and the lights of the hostiles' camp became more visible and the dancers' voices more audible as the scouts slipped through brush and cactus toward the ridge, lying long and dark, like a hump on the floor of the broad basin.

Daylight was about an hour in the offing, Scott judged, by the time they crawled to the top of the rocky ridge and lay down. From here the scouts had a height advantage of some forty to fifty feet above the camp, which was about as Fenton had remembered, approximately three hundred yards away, and now silent after the hours of medicine-making. Only a few fires still burned.

Scott shivered a little against the cold desert air. Fenton, between Scott and Lane, bit off a chew of tobacco and rested, just watching as they all were, dreading, wondering how the showdown would turn out. Fenton's voice was barely audible, reminiscent in tone. "A night like this makes a man look back. . . . I helped the buffalo go on the southern plains. Six of us in the outfit. All shared the same—skinners, cook, camp helpers, hunters. I was one of two hunters. . . . Can't say I'm proud, can't say I'm ashamed. The big shaggies had to go, but it was the way they went. That wore on me. I got tired of the slaughter, the stink, the flies, the rot, the little helpless motherless calves doomed to be wolf meat. Why I drifted out here. Now I'm helpin' the Cheericows run out their days, just like I did the buffalo. . . . Boys, we are lookin' at the last of the free Cheericow Nation, the last wild bunch. I don't like it, but it has to be this way. What will it be like after they're gone? It'll be what the white man calls progress or civilization.'' He spat deliberately and settled down into his own private silence.

The purring wind rose off the high-country desert, cold and clean, bearing the scent of mesquite smoke and creosote brush and, Scott thought, of faraway places. He counted the fires in the sleeping Apache camp: only two, burning low. The first hint of dawn pinked the great sky. *Won't be long now.* He began to feel the first tense anticipation, the getting ready, of pending action, which never changed no matter how many times a man had experienced it. He shifted a little, conscious of Fenton and Lane doing the same, carbines ready. The creeping light seemed to loiter on the other side of the mountains behind them. There persisted that impression of arrested time, count by count;

suddenly amber light spilled over the basin, as if illuminating a darkened stage, and from his vantage point on the rocky ridge Scott, in that moment, felt like a spectator.

There was the Chiricahua camp below: wickiups, a few early figures stirring about, horses turned loose to graze. So far no visible awareness of the movements taking place roughly half a mile south on the treeless plain: horses and troopers, the troopers forming a skirmish line. Forthwith, there, a rider became visible and passed through the skirmishers, coming toward the camp, a flurry of movement in the rider's wake.

Scott's attention was riveted. It was Rosa and her little brood. Rosa astride the Mexican horse.

They scurried along at a fast walk. Scott kept flicking his eyes from Rosa to the camp, the hostiles apparently still sleeping from the night's rituals, feeling secure in their traditional sanctuary. The nearer the captives approached, the faster they walked, literally skimming the plain now. They were within about two hundred yards when a hostile gave a huge shout of alarm. In seconds the camp was jumping with shirted warriors.

Scott saw Rosa stand high in the saddle and wave and shout and keep shouting. At the same time she heeled the horse to a gallop and her freed ones rushed after her, their homing voices rising higher and higher.

Scott had a sudden twist of fear. Rosa had led the hated White Eyes here. What would her people do to her? Would they think her a traitor? Scott hadn't taken that into consideration, nor had Jake, nor English, nor Lane.

The tribal reunion of the Apaches milling and embracing didn't last long. Scott lost sight of Rosa in the confusion. In moments the warriors were running here and there, waving everyone to get back.

A bullet splat rock near the three white men and a rifle cracked.

"There's our peace answer," Fenton said.

Lane turned to Fenton. "Tell the scouts to hold their fire

till I give the order. Be damned if we're here to shoot down women and children.''

Fenton did so and Lane pointed southward across the basin. ''English is holding up, too. He's not advancing.''

''There's something going on in the camp,'' Scott said. ''Look.''

There was, he could see, something unusual. A warrior appeared to be haranguing the others. He was gesturing and pointing toward the ridge. He limped.

Scott heard Antone's voice, then Fenton's. ''That's Medicine Shirt. He's stirrin' 'em up.''

Medicine Shirt threw up a handful of dust, whirled, and immediately the warriors spread out and advanced toward the ridge. They came on boldly, disdaining any cover of rocks and brush. Instead of being stripped to the waist, Scott saw, the way Apaches usually fought, these wore what looked like buckskin shirts with long tails.

''Never saw the likes of this before,'' Fenton muttered. ''They've gone plumb crazy.''

''Fanatics,'' Lane said.

The warriors broke into the swinging dogtrot. About seventy-five yards from the ridge, a warrior ran screeching ahead of the others and aimed his rifle at the ridge.

At fifty yards Fenton passed Lane's order to shoot the lead warrior.

Carbines banged. As the warrior stumbled and fell, Scott thought the man had a look of utter astonishment on his painted face. And, oddly, the other warriors were not firing.

''Hold your fire!'' Lane yelled.

The warriors hesitated and froze, eyes pinned on the downed tribesman. Scott could hear their mutterings of disbelief and frustration. Warily, confused, they started to drift back toward the camp.

Lane's voice was shrill. ''Tell Antone to call on them to surrender.''

It all struck Scott as so unreal, then, when an Indian

wearing a feathered hat and a painted medicine shirt of many symbols left the line and shouted up at the ridge.

"He says he's Medicine Shirt and a great man," Fenton relayed. "Today his power has been broken, but he won't surrender till he knows how it was broken."

"Tell him if they don't put down their arms, we'll start firing. They don't have a chance at this range."

"First, he wants to look at our cartridges," Fenton said, after Medicine Shirt had shouted again.

"Why ours?"

"It's got something to do with his power."

"Tell him if he'll look south, he'll see another damned good reason to surrender. English is advancing the skirmish line."

Medicine Shirt looked and replied to Fenton, his speech coming faster than before.

"He says the warriors will lay down their rifles, but he still wants to examine our cartridges."

The scouts descended the ridge and the hostiles, strangely subdued, surrendered their assortment of rifles and carbines, many of current make, a capitulation that continued to baffle Scott, unheard of in Apache warfare, Geronimo's no exception. That raider's power hadn't been broken. He had surrendered voluntarily, weary of pursuit and fighting.

Instead of an air of submission, Medicine Shirt awaited the White Eyes as if he were the victor. Arrogance swelled the cold black eyes and the slit of a mouth. He was wizened and wise and ageless, maybe seventy, maybe ninety, his face as wrinkled as a prune's. A silver pendant hung around his scrawny neck, a silver earring dangled from his left ear. His compressed lips were a rind of disdain. He held his head high, a sculpture of scorn, chin upthrust. He was absolutely unafraid and his flinty eyes flung hate at the slght of the Chiricahuas as government scouts wearing Army blue. His headdress of what Scott took for hawk and owl feathers made him appear much taller than he was. But his most arresting dress was the beautifully tanned buckskin shirt of muted light yellow on which were painted symbols of his power: streaks of lightning, the sun, the moon, the stars, a torrent of hail, a tarantula, a snake, and a sticklike figure which Scott interpreted as an Apache god. All these, no doubt, to protect the wearer from enemy arrows or bullets. Other emblems Scott did not recognize in these few moments of appraisal.

Medicine Shirt's warriors stood behind him, left silent and shaken.

"Be on guard," Fenton warned Lane. "They still have knives."

At the words Medicine Shirt spoke scornfully, and Fenton, in a dry voice, told Lane, "He just reminded me that he don't speak White Eye. Now, he wants to see a cartridge."

"Show him one."

"But before he looks at it, he wants you to know that his power, which comes to him from lightning and wind, is still mighty strong. It didn't work today because the warrior we shot killed a skunk last night near the camp and skinned it. The skunk spoiled his power today. Made the warrior's shirt weak. The skunk did it. He wants you to know that."

Lane covered the ghost of a grin. "Thank him for telling us how it all happened. Tell him I know he is a great *di-yin*. But ask him to explain why we were able to kill that warrior on the ridge when he ambushed us."

Although Medicine Shirt beamed at the praise, his reply was an explosion of speech, mixed with scorn.

"He says that warrior, who was young and foolish, wasn't wearing a medicine shirt. That's why he died. That's true about the shirt, Lieutenant. I remember the warrior was naked to the waist. Same goes for the warriors wounded that day, he says. Those who wore shirts our bullets didn't harm. His power stopped the bullets, he says."

"Show him the cartridge case, Mr. Fenton."

Fenton took one from his belt and made a little ceremony of presenting it, without any patronizing.

The old Chiricahua almost snatched it from Fenton's hand in his eagerness, glaring at it, as if to seize or absorb its power. Puzzled, he turned the brass-cased shell over and over in his veined hands. He touched the bullet end to his mouth, tasting and wetting his lips. He felt of it, he smelled of it, his nostrils flaring, and then, all at once, he nodded and said, "We go now," and turning his back walked away, keeping the cartridge.

"Why, the wily old cuss," Fenton exclaimed. "Bet he savvied every word we said."

CHAPTER 14

At a conference of officers and scouts, it was decided to strike north for the border instead of northeast, where the command had crossed south of the Alamo Hueco Mountains.

"I should think Trepov, if he plans to hinder us, would expect us to return the way we took coming down," English reasoned. "That's the shortest route back to Fort Bayard. About how far is from here straight to the border, Mr. Fenton?"

"I'd say twenty miles."

Apaches, Fenton remarked, could break camp quicker than any white man. Within minutes, Medicine Shirt's people were on the move, some walking, strung out between the two troops. In that wild cavalcade, Scott picked out Rosa on her Mexican gelding. She rode slumped, as if downcast, her earlier erectness and anticipation gone.

Lane was in high spirits as they rode off. "I only wish Captain Harrigan were conscious enough to enjoy this," he told Scott. "We've accomplished our mission."

"I'd feel much easier if we were across the border. It's not like Trepov to let us go without a fight. Think of the face he lost when we took the captives."

"If he wanted to fight, he could've caught up with us by now."

"Jake says Middle Mountain is in Sonora, out of Trepov's jurisdiction. Yet, I don't think he'd let a state line stop him, as aggressive as he is."

As the long column cleared the northern tip of the Sierra Enmedio, the dust of a six-wagon mule train appeared on the right, traveling northwest. At this rate the hooded wagons and the command would intersect. But before that could happen, the train formed a tight defensive corral.

English sent Scott and Fenton to investigate.

A man on a leggy sorrel, flanked by two armed riders, awaited them at the edge of the corral. There was a manner of the hidalgo about him: steeple gray sombrero with a braided cord and red chin string, silver piping on his whipcord jacket, pearl buttons down the seams of his tight leather trousers, flared at the bottom, and shiny brown boots. He rested a rifle across the pommel of his hand-tooled saddle. A handsome, mustached man whose glittering smile was disarming and, Scott perceived, whose eyes were as shrewd and mercurial as any traveling horse trader's.

When Fenton, a bit awkwardly, started a greeting in Spanish, the man stopped him. "I speak the language. I am Don Luis Flores from Casas Grandes, bound for Tucson, where I have many friends and am known as an entrepreneur. My concern, as you see, is not only for Apaches but any armed column. In yours I see both Apaches and American cavalrymen. I am puzzled."

He looked at Fenton for explanation, who turned to Scott. "You tell him, Lieutenant."

"We're with the 6th Cavalry, out of Fort Bayard, New Mexico," Scott said. "The Apaches you see belong to Medicine Shirt's band of Chiricahuas, who surrendered to us this morning after a brief fight. Some escaped from the presidio at Janos. We're escorting them back to Fort Bayard. We also have enlisted Chiricahua scouts with us."

Don Luis Flores looked much relieved. "We traveled most of the night to avoid Apaches." He smiled wryly. "There is another concern. The so-called Rurales of Janos commanded by Viktor Trepov, that *cabrón* of a self-promoted major. Mother of God, they are no more than bandits, almost as bad as the Apaches. I have been robbed by them not once, but twice. Señor, if I may, I should like to accompany your cavalry to the border. My men are all good shots. If there is trouble, we will do our part, I assure you.''

"I'll take your request to our commander. I'm sure he'll welcome more good rifles.''

Scott and Fenton reined away and beyond the wagons, Fenton sniffed, "Entrepreneur, my foot. They're smugglers. They follow a route up through Skeleton Canyon in the Peloncillos down into San Simon Valley. From there they turn to the upper end of the Chiricahuas, pass through Dragoon Gap and across the San Pedro. Don Luis has got *mucho* silver 'dobe dollars aboard. With no customs on what he brings back from Tucson, he stands to make a fat profit.''

Scott shot him a teasing look. "You seem to know a great deal about the smugglers' trail.''

"It's common knowledge in every Tucson saloon,'' Fenton said, straight-faced.

Scott eyed him again, thinking, *Jake, bless him, told you what he wanted you to know*.

Lieutenant English was more than pleased to have extra riflemen, and Scott rode back a way and waved the wagon train forward to swing in behind the last troop.

By midday the advance was approaching the border, following a worn trail. Not far beyond Scott could see the Sierra Espuela, whose southernmost extension marked the approximate line.

Something glittered about where the column would cross. Fenton and Lane sighted it at the same time. Fenton threw up his hand, the familiar signal to halt, and Lane uncased his glasses and was taking a careful look when English joined them. Lane passed the glasses to English and said, "We've been wondering where Trepov is, sir. Well, there he is, drawn up for battle.''

English moved the glasses back and forth, returned

them, and said grimly, "About two hundred Rurales. I believe it is time to parley with his excellency, the major."

They rode slowly out and halted halfway. English lifted his right hand high and held it there. Nothing happened for a while. Nothing until a fanfare of trumpets swelled and a body of horsemen shot forth from the Rurales' line.

Trepov, attired as usual, reined the Arabian to a prancing halt, peremptorily waved a deferring aide aside and roared, "I, Major Viktor Trepov, demand the immediate surrender of the Chiricahua captives you released from the presidio."

"Your request is respectfully refused," English replied, politely but firmly. "The captives are wards of the United States Government and must be returned to Fort Bayard."

Trepov reined a few prancing steps closer. "Lieutenant, you amuse me. Surely you did not think that I would allow you to invade Mexico in violation of international law, then steal my prisoners of war? You have been under the eyes of my scouts since late yesterday. You amuse me even more by thinking you could fool me by crossing here instead of the way you invaded."

"Major, may I remind you that we did not invade Mexico? To invade is to occupy. There is an agreement between our countries. We entered your territory in pursuit of Medicine Shirt, who surrendered to us this morning."

"But you stole my prisoners."

"Because they are part of Medicine Shirt's band and because they knew where he was camped at Sierra Enmedio. Further, Major, I point out that we harmed none of your men: the prison guard and the two pickets, the last two released this morning. We could have killed them easily. All along we have avoided bloodshed."

Trepov blinked at that reminder, and then, blustering, said, "No, Lieutenant. You must release my prisoners."

"I cannot, Major."

Trepov's face hardened. "Therefore, I regretfully inform you that I shall be forced to take them from you."

Whirling the eager Arabian, and with trumpets blaring, he galloped back to his line.

A heavy silence set in, broken when Lane said, "Sir, we can run a flanking movement at them with the scouts. They're eager to fight the Mexicans."

English nodded, considering. "Mr. Fenton, do you think Trepov is bluffing?"

"Not when he's got us outnumbered."

"Logical," English said, with a touch of irony. "I keep going over our mission and its limitations: bring Medicine Shirt back, dead or alive, and avoid shedding Mexican blood, if possible. I hardly see how we can do both. Now, there is the added responsibility of the women and children. Some are afoot. And there's Captain Harrigan on a litter. Like a flotilla at sea, we are tied to the pace of our slowest member."

Behind them Scott caught the restless stirrings of the column: the *tink* of harness rings, the squeak of saddle leather, the hoof stampings, the questioning hum of voices, the dry creak of wagons. He glanced around and saw the wagons drawn up in tandem, and as he watched, a thought, dim at first, sprang rushing to his mind. He let it dwell there, clarifying. Of a sudden he said, "Brad, remember Lieutenant Frank Baldwin?"

"Baldwin?" English said, frowning at the seeming irrelevancy.

"Frank Baldwin of the 5th Infantry. Remember the stunt he pulled on McClellan Creek in north Texas when he charged the Cheyenne village?"

"Charged the village?"

"Remember, he used wagons? Loaded the infantry in and took off running. They went through that camp like runaway locomotives. Remember?"

"Yes . . . but?"

"Why can't we load the walking women and children and Captain Harrigan in wagons and charge Trepov's center? Put some troopers in the wagons? Maybe mask the charge with a diversion?''

English was sitting upright in the saddle. ''We'd have to commandeer the wagons. Our friend might not like that.''

''Don Luis Flores has been robbed twice by Trepov's Rurales. His wagons are empty. He's going to Tucson to bring back goods. I believe he'll go along.''

''By God! Ask him now!''

Scott rode back to the wagons and explained the plan.

''My friend,'' Don Luis said expansively, his teeth glittering, ''I have been looking for a way to get even with that coyote of a self-styled major, who, unknown to Colonel Terrazas, preys upon our citizens instead of protecting them. The wagons are yours and my mules are the fastest in all of Chihuahua.'' He winked suggestively, ''They have to be in my business as an entrepreneur. Just let them run. Give them their heads.''

Scott thanked him and said, ''Now, Don Luis, we invite you to come help us plan the attack.''

''With relish, my friend. With relish.''

After the plan was set, English said abruptly, ''Scott, we've forgotten one thing. Do you realize that C Troop is without a commanding officer, now that Slocum has been relieved of duty? You are now in temporary command.''

Scott was too stunned to speak.

''Well, damn it, will you take it?''

''Why—yes, certainly.'' Further speech was locked inside him. He could find no more words. His emotions rose. In that moment, he understood all that he had lost and missed these past months, and he was left grateful and eager. Excitement filled his chest and raced to his throat. He turned to organizing C Troop.

While the wagons were being loaded, Medicine Shirt rode up and began haranguing Fenton and making threatening motions toward the Rurales. ''He wants us to know that he's on our side,'' Fenton told English. ''There's one condition, however. He wants all the weapons given back to his warriors.''

"Condition, hell!" English growled. "Remind him he's still our prisoner.''

That set off another harangue and more agitated histrionics. "Since you won't give him back his rifles and carbines," Fenton said, "he feels he must show you how Cheericows fight. How they dodge bullets and wrestle with the enemy."

"For God's sake, Fenton, we're trying to get organized. Get rid of that old Indian!"

There wasn't time to stop him. Teeth bared, grimacing, snorting, grunting, Medicine Shirt was already dodging from side to side, now whirling, now dodging again, now slashing with a butcher knife, now grappling with an imaginary enemy and plunging the knife. That, and he gazed at the White Eyes for approval and shouted at Fenton, who translated sheepishly, "Now, he's goin' to bring in his power to help us whip the Rurales."

The wizened old man removed his medicine shirt and waved it east, south, west, and north. That, and he sang a song of quavering notes, sang to the east, the south, the west, the north.

"He ain't finished yet," Fenton told the chafing English.

From a buckskin pouch at his belt, Medicine Shirt took pollen, which Fenton, like a prompter cueing actors, explained came from tule cattails, and sprinkled it toward the Four Great Directions, as he had waved and sung to them, and now, in apparent finality, he took more pollen and faced Fenton and, rigidly formal, so like a benediction, marked a crescent on the scout's forehead. Scott was next, then Lane. When English held back, in exasperation, Fenton said, "It's all right, Lieutenant. He wants to protect us with his power." As if to get it over with, English allowed the touching and marking and the old shaman, enormously pleased and proud, showed a worn-tooth grin and pumped English's hand four times, the magic number.

"Go fight now," Medicine Shirt said, stepping back, pointing toward the Rurales. "You are safe now. You have my power." He mounted and rode off majestically to join his people.

"Just don't anybody kill a skunk," Lane said, rolling his eyes.

It was time.

The mounted troopers and Don Luis's riflemen formed a broad front; to their rear the six wagons drew up side by side, two teams to each, the fractious mules under tight rein, the white hoods of the wagons swaying wormlike in the wind. Behind them came C Troop's horse-holders and the mounted Apaches and the pack mules.

At English's hand signal Lane and the Chiricahua scouts cut out wide at a brisk trot to simulate a flanking maneuver. When the trot quickened to a dusty gallop, English shouted "Forward—ho!" and swung his arm and the troopers and riflemen moved out trotting and the wagons creaked into motion.

Scott, riding in the center of the wagons' formation, saw the scouts swing wider yet, as if to sweep in behind Trepov's waiting line. As the wagons rolled, the distance between the two lines suddenly shrank. Three hundred yards. Two fifty. Scott saw English, watching, gauging, turn his head from the scouts to the Rurales. *Now*, Scott thought. *Now*.

English barked a command and a trumpeter sounded the brassy rat-a-tat-tat of Charge and the front line of troopers and riflemen pulled out of the way and the Mexican drivers lashed the mules running into the gap and the C troopers in the wagons with the huddled women and children yanked off the wagon sheets and commenced firing over the heads of the charging, wild-eyed mules.

It happened fast. The terrified mules tearing at a dead run, ears laid back, walleyed, fleeing to escape the uproar of their cursing drivers and the yelling troopers and the deafening banging of the carbines and the wagons rumbling, trace chains shaking a wild medley.

Before Scott, all at once, he saw the smoke of gunfire, the Rurales just now recovering from their surprise. And an insight flashed across his mind: *Trepov was bluffing at the parley. But it's too late now. We've called your bluff, you mercenary bastard, you slave-dealing cabrón of a tin major. We're going through.*

A lead mule broke stride, humping, staggering; for breathless seconds the rush of the three remaining mules carried the wounded one on, only to break down in a tangle of harness and chains. As the wagon slued to a stop, troopers jumped out firing, forming a cordon around the women and children. Gathered, they ran toward the border, the troopers keeping up a lively fire.

The other wagons rolled on. Over on the right flank, Scott heard carbine fire: Lane and the scouts. No simulation there.

Suddenly the wagons were through, the Rurales breaking, milling, scattering. It was over.

They camped that afternoon at a spring on the eastern face of the stony Peloncillos, well beyond the border. In celebration, Don Luis Flores broke out bottles of brandy and passed them around. Captain Harrigan, revived somewhat by the excitement of battle and the smugglers' generosity, was made as comfortable as possible in his tent. Horses went on picket lines and the troopers and Apaches built cooking fires. Soon coffee and bacon smells scented the desert air.

Seeing the flap open on Harrigan's tent, Scott stopped and scratched on the canvas for admittance.

"Come in."

Harrigan, flat on his back, eyes half closed, glaced up as Scott entered.

"You're looking better," Scott said, hoping to cheer him. The tent reeked of carbolic acid.

"Another man's liquor is always a lift." Harrigan said, with a weak smile. He looked worn and exhausted, his face flushed, his eyes feverish. His breathing was audibly ragged.

"Well, sir, your mission was successful. The last hostile Apache band has surrendered, its leader captured. Trepov's bandit-Rurales routed. We didn't lose a man in the charge. Though three were wounded."

Harrigan made an abrupt, staying motion. His tone brushed aside any additional details. "Lieutenant English gave me a full verbal report." He coughed and with a bandanna wiped a froth of blood from his lips. He turned his head and looked straight at Scott, an unusual thoughtfulness relaxing the stern mouth. "I've always been regarded as a hardass . . . Uncompromising. . . . Always went by the letter of orders and regulations . . . 'stead of the spirit." He bed to pause for breath. "My nature. . . . But I know men. I knew English could command. . . . First chance he had to show his real worth as an officer."

"Yes, sir."

"He's a kind of hardass himself. Even relieved Slocum, which few would have done. . . . Slocum—my favorite young officer. There I failed in judgment. . . . Mistook agreement for character. Now his career is finished. . . . Too bad." He coughed again, a racking cough.

"Would you like a drink of water, Captain?"

"Instead, hand me that smuggler's bottle."

Scott took the bottle from beside the cot and held it to Harrigan's lips. Harrigan took a short swallow and sank back, murmuring, "I think I'm going to die, Mr. Dunham." Suddenly, a stark knowing stood behind the gray eyes. "I sense it, I feel it, I know it. Am I, Mr. Dunham?"

"No—no, you're not! You're going to make it, Captain."

The knowing passed slowly, in its place the old mockery. "You always were adept at flanking the question, Mr. Dunham. You still are."

Scott had to grin. "Which I still have to deny, sir. We'll

make Deming tomorrow. Maybe farther. You'll soon be at Fort Bayard in good hands.''

"It's a long way." Harrigan closed his eyes, his breathing labored. "Believe I'll nap a little now."

"Yes, sir. That's a good idea and we'll be close by. You're going to make it, Captain."

Scott was going out when Harrigan's crisp voice halted him. "Mr. Dunham."

Scott turned and the captain, as official as ever, said, "Lieutenant English said you didn't do too badly. There must be some hardass in you, too."

Scott didn't know what to say.

"Dismissed, Mr. Dunham."

That evening Scott heard a chorus of wailing start up in the Chiricahua camp. The wailing grew to a howl and as it continued, coyotes joined in from their haunts on the ridges.

The scouts ceased their chatting and gambling and fell solemn. Antone drifted slowly across to the camp and was gone a long while. His well-made face was sad when he returned. He spoke to Fenton, then sat with the scouts.

"Rosa just died," Fenton said. "As Ussen said she would. Ussen never lies, Antone reminded me. The Cheericows don't have a new dress for her to wear, they are too poor. But in the morning they will paint her face an' comb her hair an' cover her wrists with bracelets an' string beads at her neck an' make her ready for the journey to the Happy Place.''

The wailing went on all night, as did the high-pitched singing of the coyotes, which sounded much alike, as if the coyotes grieved in sympathy.

At sunrise a wailing procession left the camp, Rosa's body on a litter of yucca stalks. A warrior led her Mexican gelding. In the stony foothills, the mourners buried Rosa among the rocks, facing the rising sun, wrapped in the camp's best blanket. While all wailed the death song,

Medicine Shirt sprinkled pollen over the grave and scattered some toward the four sacred directions. Provisions, such as piñon nuts, mesquite beans, acorns, and yucca and prickly-pear fruits, were placed near the grave for Rosa's spirit journey. The warrior, because he had no gun, stabbed the Mexican gelding and left it by the grave to carry Rosa away.

Being a captive, Rosa had no possessions beyond what she had on her body and the Mexican gelding. Had she owned a wickiup or other clothing, or blankets or cooking utensils or jewelry, these would have been destroyed.

All this Antone related to Fenton, who told Scott and the others.

CHAPTER 15

THE command reached Fort Bayard late in the afternoon of the second day after the fight at the border. Some miles behind it trailed the pack train left in the Alamo Hueco Mountains.

The Chiricahuas, Scott learned to his dislike, were immediately herded into camp under guard near the stables. Yet, what else? Weren't they captives? They were, once again within the ironclad supervision of the Army. By now he thought of them only as human beings with whom he had shared privations and danger.

Scott and Fenton, at Lane's invitation, went to the bachelor officers' quarters and refreshed themselves, including baths, drinks, and dinner. They passed up poker at the Officers' Club for sleep under a roof.

Scott's restlessness redoubled with the coming of morning, his mind torn between riding at once to the Mimbres store or seeing Colonel Martin. His enlistment as a government scout was over. *For the duration of the campaign:* That kept pouncing through his head. He was free to go. Still, he ought to pay his respects to the colonel.

Shortly after Boots and Saddles sounded for mounted drill an orderly found him. "Colonel Martin's respects, Mr. Dunham. He asks you to report to headquarters."

George Martin was beaming. A warm handshake and a close scrutiny of Scott's face, which said he approved of what he saw, and then he said, "I can't tell you how pleased and proud we are, Scott. An incredible campaign Into Mexico and back with Medicine Shirt's band in tow It will be talked about for years. General Miles messaged his congratulations just half an hour ago from Fort Bowie. The Apache wars are over, Scott. Thank God for certain this time. The citizens of southern Arizona and New Mexico are indebted to every last man of you, troopers and Indian scouts. Your return also puts to rest the wild rumors of disaster circulating in the frontier press before and since the detail with the wounded got in. One report had you all but wiped out in the Alamo Hueco ambush. Another, that there'd been a big battle with Rurales at Janos and the command defeated.''

"There was a fight with Rurales at the border when we broke their line and charged across."

Martin nodded that he knew. He bowed his head and a change came over his ruddy face, a somberness. "There's a price for all this, Scott. There always is. I regret to inform you that Captain Harrigan died at six o' clock this morning."

"No!" Scott's high feelings faded at once. Regret filled him. His shock was sudden and surprising, even though they had all known the captain wouldn't survive.

"Yet, despite his condition," Martin said, "last evening with the assistance of Lieutenant English, Captain Harrigan insisted on making a full report to me of the campaign. Kept two clerks busy. It was almost as if he had rehearsed what he was going to say."

"I am truly sorry to hear it," Scott said earnestly. "I had come to respect him as a man and a soldier. He was absolutely courageous, unswerving in purpose, and unsparing of himself. He refused to come back with the detail of wounded. Maybe he'd still be alive if he had."

"I'm glad you feel that way after what happened at Fort Sill."

"Field service strips away a man's facade and shows what's inside." At once Scott felt the need to talk as a release. "Captain was very low when we reached Deming. Worn out, of course. There we commandeered a wagon for him, and he rode easier after that. Seemed the closer we got to Bayard, the higher his spirits—and the faster he hurried us. He could move a column, you know. He knew his time was running out, but he was determined to get here—and, by God, he made it."

"There's another matter, one I am intensely reluctant to face, but must consider. Lieutenant Slocum will face court-martial."

Scott could only shake his head, feeling no gladness, no vindictiveness.

Martin made a visible effort to shake off the gloom they each shared. He turned to his desk and picked up a sheet of paper filled with written lines, glanced at it, and stood there, showing Scott a smile, a kind of secretive smile. He said, "As we both are well aware, Captain Harrigan was not one to slack his duty. In his long report, he included certain commendations which give me great pleasure." Martin cleared his throat for emphasis. "Among them are special commendations for one Scott Dunham, enlisted government scout. To wit: 'For alertly discovering an ambush in the Apache Hills before the hostile Chiricahuas could surprise the advance. . . . For leading a flanking movement with Chief Scout Jake Fenton that forced the hostiles to break off an ambush in the Alamo Hueco Mountains. . . . For aiding firsthand in the release of the Chiricahua women and children held captive under deplorable conditions in the presidio at Janos; said captives turning out to hold the key to the location of Medicine Shirt's stronghold in the Sierra Enmedio northwest of Janos and leading the command there. . . . For beyond the call of his duty as a civilian scout in organizing C Troop for the wagon charge that broke the Rurales' line on the New Mexico-Chihuahua border.' " Martin paused, pride glowing in his face. "There are more details. This is the gist."

Scott stood as if rooted, upon him a crashing sense of

utter unreality, of astonishment, of final reprieve. He had to look down to hide the mist clouding his eyes.

"He's made up for everything, Scott. Did it like a man."

"He did—and more."

Martin moved within a step of Scott, his genial features alight, his tone fatherly. "Don't you see what this means? Your reinstatement is virtually assured. Your rank restored. Your good name as an officer. You'll be back with your old outfit. Everything you've lost will be yours again. I've already started moving on this. I . . ." He hesitated in midspeech. "What's the matter? Don't you see that?"

"Yes, sir. I see it—everything I've longed for—and I am grateful. But . . ."

"What is it, Scott?"

"What happens to the Chiricahua captives? Where will they be taken from here?"

Martin drew a long breath and facing Scott turned upon him a look of inevitability. "I regret to say that in General Miles's message this morning he said the captives will be sent to Florida like the rest."

"Not Indian Territory?"

"Washington has decreed otherwise."

Scott stepped back a pace. "It's inhumane, sir."

"This is not the doing of General Miles. He recommended Indian Territory, among the Comanches and Kiowas near Fort Sill."

"—and again he has been overruled," Scott interjected, shaking his head. "Sir, I have seen these Chiricahua women and children in a stone-corral prison at Janos. Their only food ears of corn thrown to them the way hogs are fed. The girls doomed to be sold as prostitutes, the others to become slaves in homes of the well-to-do, or to slave on maguey farms or in the mines. We're just as unfeeling on this side—or worse—because we have the power to do better."

Suddenly they were shouting at each other.

"Scott, listen to me! You have to realize this is beyond the Army's control! It's out of our hands!"

"The hell it is!" Scott jerked. "General Miles could do more. Isn't he Sheridan's favorite?" His rapid breathing trailed off as he struggled for control. "Does this order for removal also include the enlisted government scouts?"

"It does. All Chiricahuas."

"Who by all fairness should not be because they're not hostiles," Scott said bitterly, thinking of Antone. "They're enlisted men and we've all fought side by side."

"My dear Scott," Martin said gently, "we're all caught up in the inevitable forces of change far beyond our control. I beg you to look at this realistically."

"I am, sir. We're sending them off to die in Florida. It's a form of execution for these mountain and desert people." He kept shaking his head, as if already seeing the consequences. "If the clammy climate doesn't do them in soon enough, the poor Army rations and homesickness will. I wish now they were all free somewhere in the Sierra Madre, where no one could find them."

"Scott, you are being oversentimental."

"On the other hand, I am, as you asked, being realistic. Florida means the death of a tribe, in fact, the death of a nation. It's genocide. I believe I said that once before in this very room. . . . I can't trade on this, sir. I'd lose all respect for myself."

"Exactly what do you mean?"

"I'm asking you to withdraw the request to review my dishonorable discharge."

Martin became profoundly hurt. "Scott, you can't mean that when it's this close to approval. You can't . . . ."

"I do, sir."

Martin lifted his hands in a gesture of understanding. "Think about this overnight, Scott. Sleep on it. It's been a long, hard campaign. You're tired."

"I've already decided."

"Is this final?"

"Yes, sir, it is."

They faced each other stiffly, each delaying the final, irrevocable words, dreading them, hating this moment. Martin's usually calm face underwent a subtle change. His eyes softened, saddened. "Scott," he said, "you've been like a son to Genevieve and me. You and Emeline were family, like our own. I ask you to reconsider this for your own good, for your own future."

Scott couldn't speak. His throat was too full. Quickly, awkwardly, he embraced George Martin hard and, choking, averting his face, went straight from the room, head bowed.

For a long time he rode with little conscious awareness of where he was, taking the turnoff at Central City, heading into the rolling foothills, riding past Santa Rita, and, now, turning northeast into the greater bulge of hills that sheltered Georgetown. After a while, realizing that he was pushing his mount too hard, he reined in the tough mountain sorrel from a fast trot to a walk. He had the vagueness of moving through a great void, his mind anchored back at Fort Bayard, balancing what, to all purposes, he had given up with where he stood now. Second thoughts, regrets, the Martins? Certainly, he had them. He had hurt the Martins, and yet he knew they understood, because they loved him and he loved them. There would be that bridge between them always; it gave him a warm sense of consolation.

At rowdy Georgetown he watered and rested his horse. Then, glancing at the advancing sun, he mounted and took the rocky road to the Mimbres River. Once past the stamp mill, he hurried the leggy gelding again. Here, in this favored valley, the past gradually paled and he responded to his surroundings: the leaves of the giant cottonwoods turning golden in the sun, dancing, quivering, shaking like sequins; the singing river and its chorus of many voices.

The river trail curved around the foot of a steep bluff and there before him stood the adobe ranch house where he and Holly had taken shelter from the storm and found each other. He rode slowly by, reliving those moments. In the scrutiny of afternoon sunlight, the house, still unoccupied, seemed so much smaller than he remembered. Somehow the sight depressed him, left him uncertain. Well, enough of this daydreaming and brooding. He touched flanks, and rode faster.

The trail wound endlessly on, in mottled shadow, in brassy sunlight, the distance to the store seeming much farther than before. By now the gelding was lathered with sweat; feeling guilty again, Scott watered and uncinched and rested ten minutes before hurrying on.

Long, long after, it seemed, much longer than the journey should have taken, he caught his first glimpse of the blockhouse through the river timber, and then everything fell into place: the adobe store, the stone corral, the apple orchard red with bounty; beyond, the other adobe where Juan and his family lived, and the pole corral there. He saw no one and was suddenly concerned. Her old Shuttler wagon wasn't parked in front of the store, and he feared that she had gone for supplies.

He tied up at the hitching rack and stepped to the door of the store and knocked and called her name. There was no answer. He called again without answer, certain now that she was gone. He went around the corner of the house. To his surprise, there was the wagon near the stone corral and the two mules poking their heads over the corral gate, a questioning in their long faces. His pulse jumped. But, seeing the back door of the adobe open, he called again and had no answer. He moved past the corral toward the blockhouse, turned anxiously, and looked in the direction of the orchard.

At that moment he saw Holly and his heart gave a great bound. She was coming on the path from the orchard, with a small basket of apples.

It was another moment before she saw him. Her step

lagged. She stopped short, staring, as if not comprehending who he was.

"Holly, it's me!"

She put down the basket, still staring, the oddest expression on her face. He could see her trembling.

"Holly!" He started running.

Her face suddenly crumpled and she ran to him and he caught her up in his arms and swung her around, and then he kissed her again and again and held her to him again.

When he could look at her, he saw that her eyes were red from weeping. Before he could reassure her, she ran her fingers over his face, saying, "We heard many of you had been killed—maybe all of you—wiped out by Apaches. I didn't know. Nobody knew. I've tried to stay busy, but I couldn't." She started crying, tried to hold back, but could not.

He drew her against him, caressing her, stroking her hair, murmuring, "There was an ambush, true. And there was a fight with the Rurales. But most of us got back. I just came from Bayard. Wild rumors reached there as well. We brought Medicine Shirt's band in. The war's over, Holly. The last Apache war."

"Over," she repeated slowly, and as a child might ask, shyly, fearful of its meaning, but needing to know. "Now you'll be going back to the Army?"

"I backed out, withdrew my request for a review. There's much more to tell you."

"Don't explain. You don't have to."

"Plenty of time for that, but I want you to know why. I will tell you." He looked down at her, seeing the fine black eyes, the little sun wrinkles at the corners, her mouth, which he had once thought so firm, full and giving now, and the chestnut-brown hair, playing softly and errantly across her forehead. Her face so open and lovely, the self-suppression gone forever. "Think you could go to Georgetown now?" he asked.

"You'll have to drive the wagon."

"I intend to. And afterward there'll be no drifting from here. I love you. I love this valley. It pulled me back, it led me to you." He held her again. "Be dark when we get there."

"I wouldn't go if I didn't love you. And don't we always travel at night in Apache country?"

About the Author

Fred Grove has received the Western Writers of America Spur Award four times: for his novels THE GREAT HORSE RACE and COMANCHE CAPTIVES (which won the Oklahoma Writing Award and the Levi Strauss Golden Award as well) and for his short stories. He lives in Silver City, New Mexico.

GREAT TALES from the OLD WEST

OWEN ROUNTREE

Available at your bookstore or use this coupon.

___CORD: HUNT THE MAN DOWN	31019	2.25
___THE BLACK HILLS DUEL	30758	1.95
___CORD	29589	1.95
___CORD: THE NEVADA WAR	29590	1.95
___GUNMAN WINTER	29591	2.25

 BALLANTINE MAIL SALES
Dept. TA, 201 E. 50th St., New York, N.Y. 10022

Please send me the BALLANTINE or DEL REY BOOKS I have
checked above. I am enclosing $_____ (add 50¢ per copy to
cover postage and handling). Send check or money order — no
cash or C.O.D.'s please. Prices and numbers are subject to change
without notice.

Name_____

Address_____

City_____State_____Zip Code_____

07   Allow at least 4 weeks for delivery.   TA-77